Flowerheart

Flowerheart

CATHERINE BAKEWELL

HARPER TEEN
An *Imprint of HarperCollinsPublishers*

Content Warnings:

Absent parent

Anxiety and depression

Body horror

Emesis

Fantasy substance abuse

Medical issues

Non-consensual enchantment

HarperTeen is an imprint of HarperCollins Publishers.

ISBN 978-0-06-321459-0

Typography by Catherine Lee

Interior art illustrations by Yejin Park

23 24 25 26 27 LBC 5 4 3 2 1

First Edition

To my family:

I flourish because of you.

G ladioli for courage. White carnations for luck. Helle-
bores for peace.

Though I'd filled the sitting room with flowers and
wrapped myself in their sweet perfume, I could not forget
the Council's warning.

Miss Clara Danielle Lucas, representatives of the Most Esteemed
Council of Magicians will pay you a visit today at ten o'clock.

My heart beat in rhythm with the clock, ticking ever
closer to the hour.

I threw the windows open wide and let in the delicious
summer air. The magic within me hummed delightedly as
I stood in a sunbeam. And then, after a moment of calm, it
whispered, *The Council has no use for a witch like you.*

My hands clenched in the fabric of my sky-blue dress. I
hated the taunts of my magic, but this time, I feared it was
right. I could not help but think of other witches my age,

picking out white gowns and trying on elbow-length gloves for the induction ceremony and the ball. Finally beginning the careers to which they'd devoted their lives.

And I thought of Xavier Morwyn. My dearest friend from my childhood had been certified a year ahead of schedule. He was running a shop alongside his parents. He helped people; he made miracles. He'd become all that the two of us had dreamed we could be.

I wondered if he ever thought of me. Or if he knew what a disappointment I had become.

The kitchen door creaked open, and Papa pushed his way through, holding tight to a tray of three teapots and an assortment of mismatched cups. His blue eyes glimmered with hope—a fire within him that never seemed to go out, no matter how many times I'd failed.

"Don't you fret," he said. He set the tray on our low, weathered table and navigated through a maze of chairs—every one that we owned, since we didn't know how many Councilmembers to expect—until he reached me, clapping his hands against the puffs of fabric at my shoulders.

"You're the most talented young witch I know," he continued. "I'm certain they'll recognize that."

On most days, his confidence in me was sweet and refreshing—but today, it was as cloying as a bowl's worth of sugar in my tea.

"The Council isn't known to make house calls for good

news, Papa," I murmured. Magic pulled my muscles tight and quickened my heart and whispered relentlessly, *Failure, failure, failure.*

It drew out my memories, lit a spark to fuel the burning shame in my chest. The time I'd set Madam Carvalho's curtains on fire. The fit of laughter that had caused lilies of the valley to grow up through Master Pierre's floorboards. My magic had taken the power of my own anxiety and twisted it until it broke all of Madam Ben Ammar's potion bottles.

Behind Papa, something rattled and clinked, like a strange musical instrument. One of the teapots had begun to wobble to and fro, threatening to spill its contents. I glowered and marched over to set my hand hard against the pale pink lid. Sometimes my magic frightened me—other times, it simply annoyed me.

Please, I begged it, *please behave yourself.*

There was a soft knock on our front door.

My plait whipped against my throat as I whirled back towards Papa, wide-eyed. "Will you stay here for the meeting?"

His freckled brow furrowed. "But dear, I'm not magical—"

"Please." The word was small, like I was just a child.

He nodded, stepping towards me to squeeze my hand.

As I faced the door, my magic dug its claws into my heart. With all my might, I concentrated on being brave. An ounce of fear would be all my magic needed to wreak havoc on our little cottage, right in front of the Council. Buckle the buttercup-yellow door. Send clouds of pollen from the flowers into the air. Shatter our windows.

I could not let that happen.

With a deep breath, I reached for the doorknob—but the door was already creaking open.

Where my front lawn ought to have been was a dimly lit chamber with marble floors and ceilings. A foot away from me stood a witch all dressed in black, as was traditional, with the golden sun pin that marked her as a Councilmember. Her cold blue eyes made my shoulders tense. I remembered that stare so well—and the lectures that always followed.

"Miss Lucas," said Madam Albright, my very first teacher.

I grimaced and bowed my head to her. "It's good to see you again, Your Greatness."

She sniffed and wiped the front of her black silk gown like I'd sullied it somehow. Papa hurriedly offered her our "best"—only—armchair.

Next, a wizard stepped through the doorway, sweeping a silk top hat off his head.

"Miss Lucas," said the wizard, "I'm Master O'Brian."

I curtsied. Magic hammered against my breastbone. "Welcome, Your Greatness."

I let him step through, and at once, Papa set about shaking the wizard's hand and finding him a seat.

Another wizard filed into the room, and then a witch, and then another, until there were eight of them, dressed in their austere black gowns and suits. As I bent in curtsy after curtsy and welcomed each magician, Papa scurried into the kitchen to find a stool.

I looked back at the group of magicians—a small murder of crows, the lot of them—and my mind stirred. *What sort of judgment have they come to bring me?*

All I could do was hold tight to the doorknob and to old lessons on how to calm my magic. *Focus on your breath,* my teachers had said.

I inhaled deeply and drew the door closed—

A shiny black shoe stuck itself into the crack of the door.

"Sorry," came the voice of a young man—a voice I knew.

With a frown, I pulled back the front door.

My thoughts scattered about like leaves in the wind.

Xavier Morwyn.

As a child, I had always found him comely, but now, to my great chagrin, I found that he had grown to be *very* handsome. He was taller than before; we used to look one another in the eye, challenging each other to stare the longest without blinking. Now his hat nearly brushed the lintel. His once neatly trimmed hair now hung past the stiff white collar of his shirt. He was paler than I remembered, too, and there were dark circles around his brown eyes, like he hadn't slept in many, many nights.

He slowly removed the top hat from his dark hair, pressing it to his heart.

"Hello," he said softly.

If we had been children, we would have embraced each other, laughing and chattering away and picking up right where we'd left off.

Perhaps we still might have done so now if he had ever bothered to write me back. If he hadn't ignored me for five long years.

And now, of all days to visit, he'd chosen this one.

"What are *you* doing here?" I asked.

A blush painted his pale cheeks and spread to his ears. "Oh, er, they called a meeting of all the Councilmembers in the district." He pointed to the golden sun pinned to his black cravat.

Envy pricked my heart. We were nearly the same age. There was nothing truly different between us; *I* should have been practicing magic. Instead, he was here with his peers to bear witness to my failures.

I offered him a stiff curtsy. "Welcome, Your Greatness."

He winced and opened his mouth to say something, but seemed to think better of it. Instead, he bowed and stepped over the stoop, hanging up his hat with the others. I shut the door behind him and, turning back, found that he was still standing in the entryway.

"Papa will help you find a seat," I said. In the back of my

mind, the whispering of my magic started up again, growing in intensity every time my gaze flitted to Xavier's.

His eyes were so beautiful. I'd forgotten.

"Miss Lucas?"

His voice was warm and gentle as spring air, marred only by the coldness of his address. I'd always been Clara; in our earliest letters he'd even called me "my Clara."

Xavier meekly pointed at my hair. "You've got some . . . some flowers."

My hands flew to my frizzy, bright orange plait, where large pink camellias had indeed started to grow.

Almost every night, Papa used to read to me from an old book that had belonged to my mother—*Waverly's Botany Defined*. The book had no story; it was just illustrations of plants with their names, their origins, how to grow them, and what they meant. After years of repetition, the cadence of the flowers' meanings was etched into my mind.

Pink camellias, I could hear him say in his honey-bright voice. *For lasting affection.*

I let out the calmest laugh I could manage while I grasped for any excuse that could spare me some dignity. "Oh! Oh, yes, I grew them on purpose. I thought they'd look nice."

Xavier pressed his lips together and dropped his gaze to the floor. "They do, Miss Lucas. Look nice. The flowers. I—"

"Master Morwyn?"

Xavier leapt at the title, one I'd only ever heard his father be called. It was odd, I thought, that his parents hadn't come with him, when they too were members of the district.

Across the little room, Master O'Brian frowned at us. "Do you two know each other?"

Xavier frantically shook his head. The wound in my heart ached and deepened. "Yes, we were, erm, friends, when we were younger, sir, but we haven't spoken in a great many years. It shan't be an issue, I assure you."

I wished to shout that it was *Xavier's* fault we hadn't spoken in so long and that it certainly *was* an issue, but the magic burning under my skin and the muttering Councilmembers reminded me of more pressing matters.

Xavier tipped his head to me once more in a little bow and ducked into the sitting room. Before the Council could see me, I ripped the camellias out of my hair and dropped them to the floor.

Papa was quick to greet Xavier with a cry of delight and a pat on the back so firm it made the young wizard flinch. They argued for a moment about whether Papa could give his seat to Xavier, and then if they should offer it to me instead, but ultimately, Xavier leaned against the far wall, as though he was as much an outsider in this group of great magicians as I was.

I offered tea to every Councilmember. Each shook their head, except for Xavier, who accepted a large, misshapen mug with a meek "Thank you."

"Your hospitality is much appreciated, Miss Lucas," said

Master O'Brian as I set the tray on the table once more. "Though, I think it would be better for all of us if we were to begin with our business."

"Have you decided to certify Clara?" Papa asked brightly.

Heat flared in my cheeks, and for a moment, I regretted asking him to sit in on such a serious meeting.

"No, sir," said Madam Albright. "In fact, the Council is greatly concerned that Miss Lucas is unable to be certified altogether."

A chill sliced through me. "Madam—Madam Ben Ammar seemed to disagree," I said. My favorite teacher had been forced to give me up, but at least she hadn't marked me a failure—she wrote to me even after we parted and expressed her confidence in me. "W-where is she? I'd imagine she'd want to attend such an important meeting—"

"Madam Ben Ammar is currently leading an investigation in the name of public safety." Master O'Brian held up a hand. "She has made her opinion known to the council in the meantime. But the fact remains, Miss Lucas, that we've never seen a magician like you before. A witch whose magic doesn't obey her."

"It obeys me sometimes," I offered, wringing the fabric of my pale blue skirts in my fists. "I've made a few potions. For colds, and sore throats, and for arthritis—"

"Your temper set my kitchen on fire," said Madam Albright.

My cheeks warmed. "That was years ago."

Master O'Brian sighed. "We have a rather extensive record of your magic's . . . eccentricities. It's clear this is a persistent problem."

Every gaze in the room was upon me, pointed and scalding as hot pokers. Worse still was that when I looked to Xavier, the boy who should have encouraged me, there was pity in his eyes.

"We've decided to present you with some options," continued Master O'Brian.

A dark silence passed over the sunlit room.

"Options . . . for teachers, you mean?" Papa asked.

Master O'Brian was quiet.

The cold in me spread.

You're going to get what you deserve, whispered my magic. *You're no better than your mother.*

"Please, sir, go on," I said, overly loud in an effort to drown out my magic and push aside any inkling of *her.*

Master O'Brian glanced at his fellows before saying, "The first option is a binding enchantment—"

"No."

I lifted my head, gaping at Xavier's interruption.

"It would only lessen her magic," Master O'Brian told him.

"Yes, but not without cost," Xavier insisted. His gaze met mine, his brown eyes wide with desperation. My heart skipped, and I hated it for doing so. "It would make spellcasting very painful." He looked to Master O'Brian imploringly. "Please, Your Greatness; it's reserved for criminals. Miss Lucas has done nothing to deserve such a spell."

I imagined my magic being smaller, obedient, contained; and me, overcome with pain if I were to brew even a little potion. I couldn't do much healing that way—and the thought of the Council placing a spell like that on me, one meant for criminals, made my stomach turn.

"And . . . what was the other option, Your Greatness?" I asked.

A silver-haired wizard was the one to answer. "We could neutralize your magic."

At the back of the room, Xavier had grown very pale, like he might be ill.

My heart knocked against my breast. "Neutralize?" I repeated.

Master O'Brian nodded. "Remove, Miss Lucas."

Remove. I pressed a hand against the magic buzzing within my ribcage, imagining them ripping it out of me, tearing out my very heart.

"You—you can't," I breathed.

"It may be for the best," said Master O'Brian.

Madam Albright nodded furiously. "We fear your magic could harm someone. And then there's the matter of your mother. If she were to try to use your power for her own ends . . ."

"Her mother left before Clara could even remember her!" Papa insisted.

Mother. That word. Bright and destructive as lightning. My magic coiled tight, and there was a loud *pop*. The pale pink teapot exploded, scattering bits of porcelain and nearly, *nearly* splashing Madam Albright with hot tea. With a scream, she staggered out of her chair, glaring at the spill and then at me.

I rushed to the table, mopping up the tea with my apron. "Forgive me," I said, "I didn't ask it to—"

"This is precisely the sort of behavior we fear!" snapped Madam Albright. She frowned at Master O'Brian. "She's nearly of age, for heavens' sake, and she has no control!"

"A broken teapot is not the same as poisons and illicit potions," said Papa.

My hands trembled as I delicately placed the ceramic shards back onto the wooden tray. Hatred boiled within me. *Mother.* A ring. Some books. A lifetime of rumors. A box on our stoop the day I'd turned sixteen—a box that I'd thrown away as soon as I'd found it.

The wretched magic she'd passed down to me.

Focus on your breath. The recitation in my head was beginning to sound more like a plea.

"Althea," said Master O'Brian in a calm voice, "we cannot compare young Miss Lucas to a criminal, not even her own mother." He held out a steadying hand towards Papa. "We don't suggest these solutions to punish Clara. We fear her magic could hurt someone. Or worse."

I'd never let that happen. Perhaps I was weak for being unable to control this magic of mine, but I would *never* allow it to cause true harm to someone.

"There must be another way," I said. "I—I'll find a way to train it." I took a shuddering, steadying breath. "Please give me some more time. If—if everything had gone right, I would be preparing to become a witch on Midsummer. Maybe something can change before then."

Xavier only watched me. I wanted to beg him to speak, to *help* me, to tell me if he'd thought of me at all these past five years.

The witches and wizards around me exchanged glances. Some murmured to each other in tones too low for me to hear. They thought me wicked, uncontrollable. No better than the mother I never knew.

The Council needed to know that I wasn't like her.

"Being a healer is all I've ever wanted," I told them. "When I was little, I saw the Morwyns save a man's life." I remembered it so clearly, how we'd hidden behind the sofa in the sitting room and watched as his parents performed a miracle. The man, barely able to breathe; his lips, turning blue; his wife, weeping. Xavier had held my hand so tight.

"Madam and Master Morwyn used their magic together," I recalled. "With their potions, with their enchantments, they saved him from the brink of death. The joy that filled that room after . . . I knew I wanted to do something that important. That powerful. All I want is to help people."

I shut my eyes, drowning out the world, the Council, the thought that my magic would retaliate if I took one wrong breath.

The silence in the room was grim.

"I'm sorry, Miss Lucas," said Master O'Brian. "We need your decision."

Bile rose in my throat. It was a choice between two poisons. Between a life with no magic at all, and a life where this wild gift of mine would hurt me with every spell I cast.

I thought of my mother, who'd defied the Council, who'd fled from them, who'd carved a reckless path for herself. I was not like her. I intended to help people. To heal them.

No matter the cost.

With a shaky breath, I nodded. "The binding spell," I said.

Papa grabbed my arm. "Clara, no!"

"I am entirely opposed to this," Xavier shouted over the murmurs of the Council.

"You'd see me powerless, then, Master Morwyn?" I shot him a glare and squeezed my hands to keep my scalding magic at bay. "If it's pain or a life without magic, I choose pain."

"It's not your decision to make, Morwyn," said the silver-haired wizard. He jerked his head towards me. "She thinks she can endure it."

14

Doubt bloomed within me the more they spoke of the binding spell.

Xavier stepped forwards again, setting aside the mug of tea and pressing his hand to his heart as he faced Master O'Brian. "Sir, surely there's another option—"

"I would be slow to speak, Master Morwyn. You've been rather cavalier in your contributions to the Council thus far," said Madam Albright snippily. Xavier flinched.

Master O'Brian clapped a hand on Xavier's shoulder, as if *he* were the one receiving bad news. "We will respect Miss Lucas's decision." Turning back to me, he smiled. "So you truly wish to be a healer, no matter the consequences. I think that's very brave, young lady."

I gave him a perfunctory curtsy. Within me, my magic was screaming.

"How soon will the binding spell be performed?" Papa asked.

"It's quite powerful. I'll need more Councilmembers. But we should be ready by tomorrow evening."

My heart lurched. *"Tomorrow?"*

"Yes." Master O'Brian fetched his hat from the coatrack and placed it back on his head. "In the meantime, I'll do my best to find you a teacher who can complete your training once your magic has been bound."

I imagined it stewing within me, angry and biting and loathing me for having diminished it. Every pain a spell

15

would cause me would be its own act of vengeance. I prayed it would be worth it.

If I'd had my wits about me, I would have thanked Master O'Brian for putting more effort still into trying to find me a teacher. I'd have wished him farewell and curtsied. But I stood there, numb.

Master O'Brian led the queue of wizards back to the front door. He drew it open, and once more, the marble Council chambers lay beyond. The witches and wizards filed out, some deigning to wish us farewell.

And after the rest of the magicians had left, Xavier lingered in the entryway, worrying the brim of his hat with his pale fingers. He was looking at me. Being near to him felt like it had when I'd visited my old schoolhouse yesterday. There was a fondness, yes, but grief, too, and the imposing sense that I no longer belonged there.

"I'm sorry about all of this," Xavier said, his voice so very gentle. He cast a glance back to the doorway leading to the Council chambers. "I—I must go. But I would like to see you again, Miss Lucas. Under some better circumstances."

"Come along, Master Morwyn!" called Madam Albright.

Xavier jumped at the sound of his title, and then reached out a hand for mine. I cautiously gave it to him, anger and confusion and sorrow and delight warring within me.

He gave my hand the faintest kiss. He had done that as a boy, copying the prim etiquette of his wizard father.

"Goodbye, Clara," he said, and before I could register it, before I could ask him why he opposed the Council's spell, why he'd stopped writing me—why he was acting as though he never cared for me at all—he slipped through the entryway, shutting the door behind him.

2

When I threw the door open again, the Council chamber was gone. There was only the colorful garden that Papa tended and the oak tree I'd climbed as a child. It was as if the Council, their meeting—*Xavier*—had been nothing but a dream.

But it was no dream, and soon my magic would be tightly, painfully bound.

I ran outside, sheltering myself beneath the oak's branches. I squeezed my eyes shut, held my palms out to the sunlight, and breathed in the perfume of summer: flowers and dew and earth.

Some people believed that magic came from the sun, spilling into the ground and bringing life. It was why our magic wove together so beautifully with nature. When I was like this, basking in a summer morning, it felt like I was back where I belonged.

Perhaps if I tried hard enough, I'd come up with some sort of plan to convince the Council to keep my magic intact for one more week, one more day, one more *moment*. . . .

Far away, softer than an echo, sounded the faintest clap of thunder. I shivered. That was me. My magic, worming into the world around me without my permission. "Behave yourself," I whispered to it. But the clouds continued to loom in the distance.

"Clara!"

Papa marched down the hill and plopped into the dirt beside me. His forehead was deeply furrowed. "What happened in there—well, how are you feeling about it? What are you going to do?"

I let out a bitter laugh and pressed my knees close to my chest. "There's nothing I *can* do, Papa. The Council has made up their minds."

"I think you're giving up too soon."

"No." I rested my chin on my arms and watched the sun sparkling on the dew-slicked grass. "I've tried for five years. I've fought so hard to tame it on my own. Maybe it's better this way."

The sounds of teachers shouting at me, of breaking glass, of my own sobs, filled my head.

"Something's wrong with me," I murmured, more to myself than to him. "With my heart, perhaps. If—if I was a really *good* witch, then I'd be able to—"

"No, blossom, no." He shifted closer to me, draping an arm around my shoulders. His other hand, callused from years of gardening, covered mine. "You are a good person, you hear me? Nobody bad would have worked so hard to become a healer."

I wiped my sleeve against my teary eyes. "It shouldn't have been a struggle at all," I said. "Magic reflects what's in our hearts. Every teacher's said so. It's this force inside of you that harnesses your emotions. So my emotions must be horrible."

Papa was painfully quiet. The silence echoed my own words back to me so I could hear how silly they sounded.

"I think it's more that your magic can hardly keep up with you," said Papa eventually. "You're ready to save the world, but your power . . . well, it just needs a little more time."

The brightness of my love for him was clouded by the dark reality of my situation. "I don't *have* time." When I closed my eyes, I could see those Councilmembers surrounding me like birds of prey, claws at the ready to snatch away my magic.

Papa's hope for me was constant and sweet. But it was also naive.

I turned from him, folding my arms tight against my middle, where magic thrummed impatiently. The dark storm clouds that had loomed in the distance now hovered over our cottage. "You don't know what it's like. You haven't seen me in my apprenticeships. You don't know what my magic does." I could almost hear Madam Ben Ammar's scream that day when my hands had gone up in flames. How even she, calm and brilliant, had been frightened by what my magic could do.

"I just . . . I just think you should fight. Fight to keep your magic the way it is."

"Fight the *Council*?" I fiercely shook my head. "Papa, I don't know what you see when you look at me, but when the Council looks, they see *her*." My voice broke on the last word. The fire in my heart grew. My mouth tasted like ash.

She was everything I hated. Wild, thoughtless, impulsive. Just like my magic. The magic she had prayed that I would possess, too.

"My magic is all I have," I said between staggered breaths. "The power to help someone. And still, it's not even mine— it's hers. She gave it to me." Tears rolled down my cheeks. "I was foolish to think I could be different from her."

Papa carefully drew me close, my head resting against his heart.

"I hate her," I said—to the air, to the sun, to my magic, to myself.

"Clara. Listen to me."

The more I thought of her, the more my magic seemed to be a real, white-hot flame emanating from my body. My chest tightened; my shoulders quaked; heat rolled through me—

Papa gasped and pulled back from me. Over his heart,

where my cheek had just been, the yellow fabric of his shirt was scorched, curling and black. And from his skin, small pink blossoms poked forth.

I screamed.

Papa clasped a hand to the flowers on his heart, shuddering. His face turned the color of bone as more pink blooms poked out from the gaps between his fingers.

"What's happening?" I asked, my voice quivering and weak.

I touched a trembling hand to his cheek and he yelped, flinching away. A bright pink burn was left behind.

My head whirled like a seed spinning from a tree. Thunder crashed, and suddenly, buckets of rain fell from the sky, soaking our cottage as well as the village of Williamston below. I became drenched as I scrabbled to my feet and stumbled back from Papa, afraid to look away, but equally terrified to see my magic ravaging him.

He coughed, an awful, rattling sound. He covered his mouth with his hand, and when he drew it back, five pink petals lay in his palm.

His eyes were wide and bloodshot. For the first time, he was looking at me with the same fear as the Council had.

"Clara." My name was faint and hoarse. The flowers on his breast were blooming.

Azaleas, that old book had said. *A sign for care—and for stubbornness. Poisonous if ingested.*

Papa glanced at his chest and seemed to realize it the moment I did.

"Get help," he breathed.

I laid Papa on the sofa and darted to my bedroom.

I couldn't help him, even if I knew how; not after my touch alone had hurt him. I needed a magician who was skilled enough to save him.

Beside my bed was the case of flowers and spare supplies I'd brought back from my time with my most recent teacher, Master Young. I unlatched the lid and threw it back, digging through little glass phials and stems of lavender and lilac.

A green maple leaf was tucked neatly at the bottom, a charm used for sending messages—although it would take too long to reach anybody, especially given my wild magic. And I couldn't waste a moment.

There was another option. The Morwyns lived close by. If Xavier could not help me, then his parents would.

I set aside the maple leaf and dove under my bed to pull out the small jewelry box that contained my life's savings. Every coin I'd scrounged up from selling scraps of fabric or doing chores about town. Every tip from a generous patron, from my time assisting various witches and wizards. The pearl earrings Papa had given me for my sixteenth birthday. The gold band my mother had thrown at Papa before disappearing in a cloud of smoke fifteen years ago.

I dashed into the hallway. Just beside the front door, Papa's boots and mine lay cast aside. I tugged on my dusty gardening gloves along with Papa's overcoat and the bowler he wore when we traveled. It would be little protection from the rain, but judging by the growling thunder and the turmoil in my heart, the storm—and my magic—would not let up any time soon. As I stuffed the coins and jewelry into the coat's pockets, I dared to glance at my father.

He had grown quiet, eyes shut and chest heaving. Sleep would help. But there was no telling what the azaleas' poison could do, given time.

I swept into the sitting room and hovered over him, cautiously touching the cracked leather of my glove against his index finger. His eyelids fluttered open.

"I'm getting the Morwyns," I whispered. "I'll be back before you wake."

"I love you," he said, the words jumbled and slow.

My teeth pressed hard into my lip as I tried to tamp down the tears and the magic writhing in my chest. "I love you, too."

When I strode out the door, I did not look behind me. If I told myself I could be seeing Papa for the last time, I'd start to believe it. And as I'd learned in my time as an apprentice, once my heart took hold of an idea, my magic might very well act upon it, whether I wanted it to or not.

My boots strained against the mud as I sprinted down the road out of town. I climbed hill after hill, and at the top of the final one was the strange and beautiful house I knew so well.

Morwyn Manor had a cobbled-together look: a mix of a watchtower and a palace and a cottage, a combination of several different eras of architecture. On one side, a turret seemed to have been taken from an old fortress and made to adhere to the mansion. On the other end of the house was a chimney covered in ivy that crawled all the way up to the roof. At the top of the roof stood a weathervane with a blazing sun, a sign for "magician" that anyone could identify even from afar.

When I was a child, my time at the Morwyns' mansion had been spent rolling down hills, weaving crowns of daisies, and playing hide-and-seek in its wild, twisting halls. Every Saturday, Papa let me ride in our wagon filled with flowers on his way to the market, dropping me off at the Morwyns' while he worked. I'd bounce eagerly in the back of the wagon, jabbering to Papa about the games I would play with Xavier and his little sisters, Leonor, Dalia, and Inés.

Now an altogether different, altogether more frightening sort of anticipation filled me. Every step was a second in which Papa was suffering. Today I was at the Morwyns looking for a savior, not a playmate.

I climbed the slick path snaking up the hillside until I

passed under a swinging sign reading *Morwyn*. Standing on the porch, I leaned against a square, faded-white column to catch my breath. My sides ached. My head spun. My boots had rubbed my heels raw where my stockings were worn thin.

My legs wobbled like a fawn's as I approached the emerald-green door. Above it hung a little golden bell that rang as customers came and went. Garlands of white heather streamed from the lintel—a charm against robbers.

On either side of the door were square, white-trimmed windows, aglow from the light inside despite the sign that hung in one declaring the shop *Closed*. The interior was warped by the glass; I could make out the outlines of shelves and a counter and perhaps a chair or two, but no people. Still, the lamps were lit. Someone was home. Someone could help my father stay alive. I imagined Dalia, Leonor, and Inés racing to call their parents and then their brother.

I tugged on the handle, but the door was locked. I beat my fist against it. My magic was already whispering eagerly in my ear that my efforts were hopeless. Instead of yielding to its teasing, I took out my anger on the door, hitting it harder.

"Madam Morwyn?" I shouted. "Master Morwyn?"

Why did you even come here? asked my magic. *You're too late!*

I kicked the door, scuffing the bright green paint. "Xavier?"

Perhaps he was upstairs. My cynical magic insisted that he

was ignoring me—*Just like he ignored your letters*.

"All right," I mumbled to my magic, "if you're going to be so chatty, you may as well help."

I stepped close to the door and inhaled deeply, concentrating on the way my power boiled inside my middle, on the burning in my cheeks, on my outraged thoughts, on the way my elbow quivered as I held the handle. I imagined opening the door fluidly, as if it had been unlocked all along. On my exhale, I whispered, "Open," and then pushed.

There was a loud *crack*, and the door flew off its hinges, ringing the shop's bell with fervor as it slammed to the floor. I yelped, hopping away from it with my hands over my mouth.

Frantic footsteps pounded close by.

I stepped into the shop, tracking mud over the fallen door, and craned my neck towards the sound. At the far end of the room, at the bottom of a spiral staircase, Xavier appeared, still in his prim, Council-appropriate suit, but with mismatched socks and a butter knife he wielded like a dagger. His dark eyes, ringed purple with fatigue, darted from the door to me.

"Miss Lucas?" he asked. The hand holding the knife fell to his side. "*You* broke down my door?"

An explanation was on the tip of my tongue, but I thought better of it—my father was forefront in my mind. The fear in his eyes. The flowers bursting from his heart.

"I need help. From you or your parents or anyone; I just

27

need a magician." I crossed the room, turning out my pockets and holding out the ring, the earrings, the coins. "I'll pay—"

His hand lightly touched the back of my glove, slick with rain. With his other hand, he tucked away the knife into his pocket as subtly as he was able. "Miss Lucas, please—I, I don't understand. What's happened?"

I took a long breath and kept my gaze averted. The confusion and worry in his eyes only made my own panic grow. "It's my father. He collapsed. He . . . he has azaleas blooming from his heart."

His already pale face turned lily-white. "Was it your magic?"

The monstrous thing squirmed inside my chest at the mention.

Tears muddied my vision as I nodded. This was precisely what the Council had feared.

"That doesn't matter now," I said, the tremor in my voice breaking any illusion of resolve. "Please, he's in danger." Once more, I held out my dripping, gloved hands filled with payment. "This is all I have. Heal him, please, you *must*—"

"Of course I will," he said, his voice stern but soft, like he was calming a child. "Let me get my case."

I dropped the money into his cupped hands. With long strides, he entered the room I'd blasted the door off of, which served as a storefront and a kitchen all in one. The pouch and jewels clattered against the countertop where he set them down. My heart lurched at the sound, at losing all I had ever saved, and to someone who I'd thought was my friend—but I would make any sacrifice if it meant saving my father. I wrapped my arms around myself to keep from trembling from the cold and from fear.

Xavier kept his back turned to me as he plucked bottles and jars from cabinets. He stuffed a large green jar into his potion case and then snapped it shut.

"Follow me," he said. "I'll make the portal."

He approached the kitchen's pantry, which would serve us in lieu of his broken front door.

In a language I didn't understand, his voice gentle as a lullaby, he sang over the door, pressing his forehead against the wood. A few times in my life, my teachers had created portals for me to visit Papa in Williamston. But never before had I heard the portal spell sung. Listening to his song, my heart pounded. As I stood there by his side, I felt like his friend again for just a minute—despite the horrid purpose of this visit.

When he pulled back the door, the air was heavy with a sickening, flowery perfume.

3

I stepped through into the comfort of my own living room—the table with our broken tea set from this morning, my old cross-stitch on the wall, and Papa on the sofa where I'd left him, his chest rising slowly, still sprouting flowers.

With wide eyes, Xavier halted in front of my father. "Curse me twice," he muttered. "There really are azaleas."

I stood a pace away, folding my hands tight to keep them from trembling.

Kneeling, Xavier unlatched and drew back the lid of his case. He looked to Papa and touched a gentle hand to his cheek. "Mr. Lucas?"

Papa's eyes opened. His forehead wrinkled with confusion. "Did . . . did I forget your delivery?"

"No, sir. Your daughter called on me."

Papa grinned, his head lolling against the arm of the sofa.

"She's a gem, she is. You should be her teacher."

Xavier averted his gaze. "A little delirious, I see." His fingers hovered over the flowers blooming from Papa's chest. He tenderly tugged at one of the dark green stems, but stopped at the sound of Papa's sharp, frightened gasp. I flinched, and Xavier leaned back, his lips pursed. "It's possible they're latched in deep." He glanced back to me, a notch in his brow. "If we're lucky, there aren't any more growing internally."

My blood chilled. "He—he coughed up some petals. Do you think these flowers are connected to the ones inside him?"

The very idea made bile rise in my throat. My magic, infesting his heart as well as his lungs with flowers like parasites . . .

"Perhaps." He withdrew a stethoscope from his potion case and then lightly tapped Papa's shoulder. "If you would, sir, I'd like to listen to your heart."

Your fault, your fault, your fault, chimed my magic. I forced my palm against my chest like it could smother the sound.

Xavier pressed the metal of the stethoscope over Papa's heart and ribs.

"Your heartbeat is irregular. And I do hear something in your airway." Xavier reached inside his case, where each bottle and jar had been tucked away perfectly like little soldiers in formation. He selected a long phial filled with a thick, dark green liquid. "Miss Lucas, I'll need a large bowl or a bin."

31

"Why?"

He jostled the little potion bottle. "I want to see if an expectorant will help in expelling the flowers."

I sped out of the room and into the kitchen, swiping a mixing bowl from the shelf over the washbasin.

When I returned, I found Papa clutching his chest, moaning in pain. My throat pinched shut and I squeezed his hand through the thick fabric of my gloves.

Is this truly my *fault?* Had my magic acted on its own, and I was just too weak to stop it? Or was there something within me, something unknowable and awful, that would drive my magic to hurt him?

With the mixing bowl in his grasp, Xavier turned back to my father. "This will be a rather unpleasant experience, sir."

Papa released my hand and rested the bowl against his lap. His head was bowed, like he was ashamed of himself. "You don't have to see this, Clara."

I pulled a chair close to his sofa and kept my hand braced against his arm. "I've been an apprentice several times over. I've seen my share of foul things."

He sighed and then nodded to Xavier, who passed Papa the little green bottle.

Within moments of drinking, Papa was coughing into the bowl, expelling bright pink petals as well as leaves, whole stems, and long, spidery roots, wet with saliva. As his body lurched, trying with all its might to cast out the magic, I clung tight to his arm, biting hard on my lip to hold in tears.

Eventually, my father collapsed against the arm of the sofa, chest convulsing. His cheeks were waxy, and his pale ginger hair was slick with sweat. Though he was exhausted, his breathing was clearer and no longer so labored.

After a quick inspection with his stethoscope, Xavier confirmed that the flowers had been cleared. But his face was still troubled.

"What happened there on your cheek, Mr. Lucas?" he asked, pointing.

Papa touched the raw spot where my hand had been. He looked to me before mumbling, "I'm not sure, myself."

My stomach tied itself in knots. Of course he'd try to defend me, even when I had hurt him.

The lamp on the table beside us started to rattle as I grew unsettled again. "It was me," I said. I stared at my tan gardening gloves. "I just touched his cheek, and it burned him, somehow."

Xavier procured a small silver pot from his case and applied a buttery mixture to the burn. "That could scar," he noted softly. "Magical wounds are hardly predictable." He wiped his pale hands on a handkerchief and then lightly felt Papa's pulse. Xavier's frown made my own heart leap.

"What is it?"

His brown eyes flitted to me. "Miss Lucas . . . did you say anything hostile towards your father before he fell ill? Did you have an argument?"

I bristled. This was how people spoke about curses. Dark,

cruel spells. A young woman who had begun rapidly aging. A boy with thorns growing from his fingertips. They said my mother had done that sort of magic. But I never would.

"No," I said.

"You weren't cross with him at all? You didn't . . ." He cleared his throat and glanced at his socked feet. "What did you say in your curse?"

I clenched my fists, anger burning in my middle. "I did *not* curse him!"

There was a piercing, ringing *ping*, and the lamp on the table exploded, littering the floor with shards of glass.

I leapt from my chair, away from the sofa. Papa turned to look back at me, his face white.

Even after causing him such pain, my magic still wasn't satisfied. It *craved* destruction.

"I'm sorry," I said from behind my hands.

Meanwhile, Xavier took a calming breath, stood to his full, alarmingly tall height and extended a hand towards the mess of the broken lamp on the floor. He swirled his finger in a circle, as if trying to make the rim of a goblet sing. The shards wobbled against the floorboards and zoomed upwards, fusing themselves perfectly around the flame they'd been encasing moments ago.

When Xavier turned back to us, his cheeks were bright red, the rings around his eyes were darker, and sweat glimmered on his temples. I'd seen such simple repair spells before, but I had never seen them make a wizard so weary.

"Mr. Lucas," he said, smoothing the front of his vest, "may I speak with your daughter in private?"

Papa tipped his head to me. "It's her you should be asking."

"I'll talk with him," I said. "Stay here and rest. Can you do that? Can you keep still for a few minutes?" I flitted to his side to fiddle with the thin blanket thrown over him.

Papa let out a wry laugh before nestling himself among the worn cushions and shutting his eyes. "Yes, yes. Go on, don't fret over me."

An impossible request.

Still, I strode to the kitchen door and held it open for Xavier. He swept up his potion case before following me dutifully into the next room. I shut the door behind us, but stayed pressed up against it, my eyes on him. It ached, how the years had flown by, and we were suddenly two different people.

We had been apart for so long, and now he'd visited my home twice in one day. It was like a cruel joke.

Xavier set his case atop the table and leaned against the kitchen counter. He chewed on his lip. The old clock on the wall ticked noisily, like it was impatiently tapping its foot at us.

He opened his mouth to speak, but at that same moment I blurted out, "Do you think he's going to be all right?"

Xavier grimaced. "I—I don't know. Curses are extremely difficult to—"

"I. Did not. Curse him." I stepped forwards, gripping the back of the nearest chair to keep my temper and my magic in check. "I've studied magic for five years, and I know as well as you do that a curse must be spoken with intention. I didn't say anything like that, and on my life, I would *never* intend anything wicked upon my father."

"I believe you," he said. "You didn't *intend* to hurt him. But your magic is still afflicting him."

My stomach dropped "Still? But the flowers—you said there weren't any left!"

"They poisoned his blood. He will continue to be light-headed and nauseated and he will possibly experience other symptoms of azalea poisoning. And the flowers may yet return."

Poison. It brought my mother to mind. It made me hate my power all the more, because it was so like *hers.* "Can't you administer an antidote?" I asked, my voice broken and raw.

"If it were *merely* poison, I could treat him. However, this is magic—*your* magic specifically. It is only by your words that you'll be able to fully heal him."

I crumpled into the nearest chair. "He can only be healed by *my* power?"

"Yes. I believe if you cast a blessing over your father, with the full strength of your magic, you'd free him from whatever hold it has on him."

A blessing—a spell only powerful, controlled magicians could perform. The kind that could save someone's life; the kind that made healers collapse in exhaustion. A spell for the desperate.

"I—I'm not capable of something like that," I said. "My magic doesn't listen to me, and more than that, come tomorrow, it won't *be* at its fullest strength anymore." I slumped back in my chair, pulling my curls from my eyes. "And it's done what we all feared it would do! What if the Council just takes it away?"

"I'm going to ask that they give you more time," said Xavier. "It's in our creed to do no harm. If they took your magic, they'd be signing away your father's life."

A sob broke from my lips. I clapped both hands over my mouth, my shoulders quaking with the effort. My magic wobbled a teacup on the kitchen countertop.

Xavier rounded the table, sliding a white handkerchief onto the table before me. I gratefully accepted the little cloth, embroidered with an M, and dried my eyes.

He sat across from me, silent and calm as I caught my breath. His straight posture, his neat, black uniform, his serious expression—he was truly the perfect image of a wizard. It was strange, almost dreamlike, to see this person from my childhood now placed in the role of an adult. It suited him.

"Your father can be helped," he said, soft and soothing.

"If the Council gives you time, you can teach your magic to yield to you. Then, you can cast a blessing or any other spell you'd like."

Flames of magic seared the back of my throat. He didn't understand. "You heard the Council; I'm hopeless, I—"

I paused.

I remembered peering into the Morwyns' kitchen with Xavier at my side. Watching his mother and father touch their hands to a patient's heart, and the room filling with golden light. An old, powerful ritual. The Morwyn family was well-known and celebrated in the magical community. For generations, they'd performed complicated magic and healed thousands of people.

"Your parents perform blessings," I murmured.

Recognition and worry flickered in his eyes. "Yes, they do."

"My other teachers didn't."

"It's very difficult magic."

I leaned across the table towards him, my heart beating faster as my plan made more and more sense to me. "Perhaps they could take me on! They could teach me how to cast a blessing!"

"They—they're out of the country, Miss Lucas—"

"Then you!"

Xavier blinked rapidly. "Me?"

"They taught you about blessings, didn't they?"

"Well, yes, but—"

"Teach me," I said, slapping my gloved hand against the table. "You aren't like my other teachers. You know me. You aren't afraid of my power."

He opened and shut his mouth like a fish on land. "I have a prior engagement," he said.

I glowered at the flimsy excuse. "A prior engagement?! My father is dying!"

His ears turned red. "I have a very important potion due to the Council on Midsummer—"

"Is it more important than my father's life?"

In the stunned silence, my voice echoed through the kitchen like we were in a concert hall. I drew back, my arms tight around myself. The shock of my words, my anger, my magic, rang through me.

"You're the only hope I have," I said. "You don't have to help me as a favor. I'll pay you. I'll give you anything. I'll work for free, all day long. I'll clean your house, darn your socks; whatever you like." I pressed my hand to my face, blotting out the world. Xavier and I had once wished on clovers for our magic to come. And when our powers arrived, mine and then his, we ran about and whooped and hollered and declared we would work together as partners. *Morwyn and Lucas.* We'd had beautiful, wild dreams of using our powers to save lives.

Now my magic had nearly killed my father.

I wanted nothing more to do with it.

"I'd even give you my magic if I could," I whispered.

"Don't say things you don't mean." His voice was cold and sharp as ice. When I lifted my head, his eyes were the same.

"I mean every word," I said. "You've seen my power. It's good for nothing." It hurt me to say it, my magic burning my throat to punish me for the insult. "I'd trade it away in a heartbeat."

The severity had vanished from his face. When he met my eyes again, I felt like we were children again. Equal.

"If it were possible," he murmured, "if you could give your power to another person—*would* you?"

A chill danced up my back. Magic was a gift that appeared to so few. To trade away such a gift was foolish, was *heart-breaking*. . . . But for Papa, I could bear such things. "If you taught me to bless my father, then yes, I would."

He touched his fingertips to his mouth. His thumb, I noticed, had a black band inked around it.

"You made a vow to someone," I noted.

It was a practice used between magicians when striking certain bargains. Some of my teachers bore black rings on their fingers; promises to coworkers, to the Council. Master and Madam Morwyn had them in place of wedding bands. When we were younger, Xavier and I used to make pretend vows. We'd clasp hands like we had seen magicians do, and promise to be friends forever, or to always share our secrets with each other. We'd mark our fingers with little bands of ink.

But we weren't children anymore.

"What was it for?" I asked.

He hid his hands beneath the tabletop. "It was for the Council. And it's a vow I propose to you. If you truly meant it, if you truly wanted to, you could give your power to me."

I shivered. To make a true vow, as two grown magicians— it felt strange. Our childhood game, made more serious than I could have ever fathomed.

I didn't understand why he would want my volatile power. But if this was the payment he'd take in exchange for his help, I would not question his reasons.

"You'll teach me to bless Papa," I said, "and then once he's well, I'll pay you—with my magic?"

"Precisely."

I could imagine Papa pleading with me not to give up my gift, my future. But a future without my father was bleak and empty. And a future *with* my magic would be fraught with trouble. Besides, after what my magic had done, the Council would surely forgo offering me the "mercy" of the binding spell and take my power away from me altogether.

"I agree to it," I said. I reached a hand towards him.

"You'll need to take your glove off, Miss Lucas. For the vow."

I drew my hand to my chest. My throat tightened. "When my skin touched Papa's, it burned him. What if it does the same to you?"

41

He shook his head. "I'm sure you mean me no harm."

"I didn't mean to harm Papa, either," I muttered.

He grimaced. "Then we will say the vow quickly."

I squeezed the stiff gloves into fists.

"Don't fret," he said. "I've got some extra salve in my potion case, if you were to really hurt me. And if you do, I won't blame you for it."

Finger by finger, I pulled off my right gardening glove. I slipped my hand into his hold as gently as possible, like it would soften the blow, but the moment our skin touched, he gasped.

I leapt back. "I told you!"

He shook his hand like it'd been held over a stove. "It's so curious," he murmured. "Your magic doesn't obey your own heart."

"Curious?" I spat. "It's maddening."

Xavier reached for my hand again, our eyes aligning. There was the faintest stripe of pink along his palm where I'd touched him. "I'll help you. We'll get your magic sorted out. And after your father's been healed, your power will burden you no longer."

My magic curled up inside me. It hated being called a burden.

That's what you are, I told it. Over the years, it had only become more fitful. Spells had been difficult the first few months of having my power; then they'd grown wild, unruly, and too strong. Now my magic was dangerous, pure and simple. Perhaps when wielded by someone else, it would be more manageable.

Still, jealousy and disappointment ate at me like parasites. Xavier was only a month older than I was. And though we'd gotten the same magical education, he'd graduated a whole year early. Been inducted to the Council almost instantly. Succeeded in every way I failed.

I could only hope he would succeed in helping me bless Papa.

Taking a gulp of air, I clasped Xavier's hand, looking him in the eyes, and he didn't flinch back this time. My heart soared into my throat as magic zipped through my veins, pooling in my palm. Light exploded all around us, golden motes floating around our hands and drifting by our cheeks like fairies.

And the light danced in his eyes. They were beautiful and warm, not flint-black but really a deep brown, and fringed with long lashes. Yet there were dark shadows beneath his eyes.

Xavier's hand trembled, but his gaze didn't waver as he spoke. "I vow to you, Clara Lucas, that I will teach you all I can, until the day you are able to free your father from the magic binding him."

His words were soft, secret, but ricocheted somehow off the pale yellow kitchen walls and echoed through my mind.

The pulse in his palm fluttered against my hand. The flecks of golden light thrummed in time with his heart.

Words spilled from me as if I'd practiced: "I vow to you, Xavier Morwyn, that upon the day I bless my father and free him of the magic binding him, I will give to you all of my magic. Willingly. Readily."

He held my hand tighter. "Let neither of us speak of this vow to another soul."

To have our hands clasped like this reminded me of our childhood. The secrets we'd kept for the other. The things we'd admitted with teary eyes beneath blanket forts. Such promises had felt so serious then.

Magic pulsed along my arms, aching like a pulled muscle. Then a bolt of electricity sang up my arm. I gasped and pulled back my hand. It stung as if I'd stuck it into a fire; and then, as quickly as they appeared, the lights and pain vanished.

My skin was not red and throbbing as I'd expected it to be—it was the same, if not for a thin black band inked around my ring finger.

Xavier flexed his hand, which now bore a matching black band. The skin of his fingers and palm were raw and pink.

"Your hand! Oh, Xavier, I'm so sorry—"

"It's not your fault." He turned to his potion case, which opened with a soft *click*. Procuring the little jar of salve from his bag, he nodded his head at it. The cork flew out on its own. After he applied the cream to his hand, he bound the wound in gauze.

"Does it hurt?" I asked. In part, I wanted to know if Papa was suffering terribly from my hand on his cheek.

"It stings," he admitted, and left it at that. Before closing his case, he placed a golden calling card and a square bottle into my still-gloved left hand.

"This is a sedative," he explained. "Your father will continue to be quite frail. A spoonful will put him to sleep. And he won't feel pain." He pointed to the card. "If something unforeseen happens, burn that and I'll come to help."

I looked at the card, which simply said *His Greatness Xavier Morwyn, Wizard*. I felt a pang of envy. I was just as smart and talented as he was. I should have been called "Madam Lucas."

Now I would never be.

I curled my hand around the little potion. "All right."

"I'll call on the Council shortly. I'll explain the situation, get them to postpone the binding spell. And they'll be able to provide additional aid for the both of you."

I did not relish the thought of the Council visiting me a second time—but I needed help. I'd accept it in any form.

Xavier turned back to his case, sweeping it off the table.

"How will I afford to pay a Councilmember?" I peeped. "I gave you all the money I have."

"Not to worry. You're my apprentice now. They will tend to your father if I ask them to." He lighted his hand on the doorknob for one moment before looking back at me. "One last thing. I know we only live an hour apart, but perhaps it would be wise to keep your father far from your magic. Do you understand?"

I hesitated. He wanted my magic—he wanted *me*—away from my father.

"You want me to live with you?" I asked.

"It *is* customary for an apprentice to move house."

I couldn't help but scoff. Customary? For one's former best friend to act in the place of an older and wiser mentor? For a witch to accidentally curse her own father? For two young people to make a bargain like *this*?

Xavier turned back to the door. "Will that be a problem, Miss Lucas?"

"No," I said—though the thought of leaving my father behind in such a state made my heart sink. I squeezed the end of my braid with my ungloved fingers. "I'll do whatever's best for him."

Xavier nodded. "We'll start tomorrow morning, then."

As he turned the doorknob, I piped up with one more question.

"Might I see him on the weekends, do you think?" I asked. "Would that be safe?"

His fingers danced against the scalloped metal of the door's handle. "I'll need your help on Saturdays."

"You didn't need an apprentice at all until five minutes ago."

He let out a sharp, one-beat laugh—the sincerest part of himself I'd seen since our childhood. "Very well. Saturdays and Sundays, you may see him."

Xavier inhaled deeply and pressed his forehead against the kitchen door. He whispered to it and then began to sing his song again. It was soothing, hypnotizing—my eyelids started to fall. I blinked, and the door clicked shut. When I opened it again, I found my sitting room, plain as ever.

Papa, wan and thin, sat up from his little makeshift bed. "I heard lots of ranting and then the kitchen started to glow," he said. "What happened? What sort of magic was that?"

I thought of the black band that now marked my finger and quickly tucked my hand into my pocket. I couldn't let him see any evidence of this bargain. That, in exchange for his life, I'd traded away the magic he called my treasure.

"Xavier asked me to be his apprentice," I said, "and I start tomorrow."

4

Despite Papa's protests, I spent the night on the floor beside his sofa. I lay awake watching his chest rise and fall, worried more blossoms would grow. Sometimes he would reach for me over the edge of the sofa, attempting to pet my hair or give my shoulder a squeeze—but I inched away from him and instead turned to the spellbooks I'd piled on the floor beside me.

The oldest ones contained information on blessings. *Da Ponte's Guide to Healing Incantations* claimed, *This type of spell is the most difficult of all. Simply practicing the recitation of a blessing will not suffice. One must be a master of their magic in the utmost.*

A master. Despite my years of training, my long nights of studying, the tears I'd shed over failed potions—I wasn't one. I might never be.

The words swam together, taunting me as much as my magic. And then, somehow, the pages that were once bathed in white moonlight turned pale gold with the dawn.

Someone knocked on the door.

Dizzy and exhausted, I wobbled to my feet, whirling for a moment to check on my father. Seven azaleas still bloomed from his chest. And even in sleep, he clenched his fists and held his breath, his brow beaded with sweat.

I slid to the door on stockinged feet and opened it to find a witch's shop, decorated with pale pink flowers and plush carpets. Two people stood in the doorway, and at the sight of the woman, my heart soared.

Madam Ben Ammar was breathtaking, with deep brown skin, eyes the color of ebony, and long black curls that spiraled around her head and down her back. And she was as kind as she was lovely. When we had last parted, she had cried. She'd said that she didn't think I was a bad student. That she was confident that another teacher might be able to help me where she could not. She was the only teacher who hadn't blamed me for my magic's outbursts. What would she think of me three years later, still a failure?

I gripped the door tighter to keep from embracing her. If Papa was *still* under the adverse effects of my touch, I could not allow my magic to get too close to her, either.

Her eyes were soft and full of pity. "Hello, dear," she said.

I smiled up at her. "I can't believe you're here—they said you were working on some investigation!"

She nodded, her long black skirt swishing as she crossed

the stoop. "Yes, but when Master Morwyn sent a note to the Council about your situation, I snatched up your case as quick as I could."

Relief washed through me. If I had to deal with more Councilmembers, I was thankful there would be one who actually liked me.

The witch gestured to the person tailing her—young and thin, with large, round glasses, golden-brown skin, and scarlet hair tumbling down to their shoulders. "Clara, Robin is my apprentice. They will be tending to your father while you are away with Master Morwyn."

Robin stuck out a hand with a dimpled smile. "A pleasure to meet you, Miss Lucas. Madam Ben Ammar speaks very highly of you."

A lie, my magic whispered. "Thank you, Robin." My whole body trembled as they robustly shook my gloved hand up and down.

The three of us approached where Papa lay. I bent close to him, careful not to let even the end of my plait touch him.

"Are you awake, Papa?" I asked.

He pried his eyes open, his hand fast against his chest. "Yes, dear, I'm—" At the sight of the two others, he started, scrabbling to sit up.

Madam Ben Ammar bowed her head in greeting. "No need to fret, Mr. Lucas," she said. "We're here to help."

He opened his mouth to reply but was again interrupted by his own coughing. He grimaced and made a retching sound into his hand. When he drew it back, two pink petals rested on his palm.

Fear gripped my heart. "I don't understand," I said. "Master Morwyn gave him an expectorant, and I haven't touched him again, haven't said anything curse-like. . . ."

Madam Ben Ammar bit down on her full lower lip. "Your magic is volatile, pet. It follows no rules, not even your own. I suspect it's done your father no good being so close to it."

I stepped farther away from Papa. He sighed and balled up his fists in the ivy-green blanket. "It's not your fault. It's as she said—your magic isn't *you*. I suppose it just decided it didn't like me."

"It's foolish, then, if it dislikes you of all people."

"Mr. Lucas." The sweet sound of Madam Ben Ammar's voice helped draw me from the storm of worries continuing to brew within me. "Robin here is in their final year of apprenticeship and will therefore be tending to you at all times. They may ask some silly questions and take superfluous notes, but it's all part of the apprenticeship process. I think the world of them, and I know they'll take great care of you."

Robin was much more delicate in shaking Papa's hand.

Madam Ben Ammar turned to me, her face soft and comforting despite her commanding height and sharp features. "Now then, go get your things and we'll be off to Master Morwyn's."

From my room, I took my humble potion case and

carpetbag, the same ones I'd taken with me to my first apprenticeship. I'd left home five times for my training over the years. This time, the farewell ached even more.

The first time I had left for an apprenticeship, I'd laughed, I'd smiled; I'd told Papa to stop turning into a puddle over me. Now I was the puddle, tears streaking my cheeks even though I'd only be an hour away.

Staring down at him, I wanted to kiss him goodbye, or say something lovely—but the thought of magic twisting my own words frightened me. Furthermore, the secret of the pact I'd made with Xavier sat heavy and hard in my middle.

I'd always told my father everything in my life: at age twelve, when I'd been madly in love with Ada Framingham. In primary school, when I'd slapped a girl for calling us poor. When I had cried in Xavier's arms over my long-gone mother. To keep a secret from Papa, especially one so important, made me feel unclean.

But Papa smiled up at me, his face bright as sunshine in spite of his bloodshot eyes and heavy breathing. "You'll do wonderfully," he said. "And I'll see you on Saturday."

"I love you," I whispered, hoping that I could stave off any more wicked magic if I spoke softly.

"Clara," said Madam Ben Ammar, "Master Morwyn told me he'd given you his card. Could I have it, so I can take us to him?"

I withdrew his golden card from my pocket and gave it to

the witch. She took a few steps from me to an empty space near the window. Extending her arm, a delicate jet of flame bloomed from her fingers. The smoldering card fluttered to the floor.

Golden smoke billowed from the floorboards. When it began to clear and the whispering of the fire ceased, Xavier's door—scuffed but reattached after I'd broken it down yesterday—stood in our living room.

I turned to Papa one last time. He waved farewell. And I ducked through the doorway before he could see my face crumple with more tears.

In my rush yesterday, I hadn't noticed that the inside of Xavier's shop was just as lovely as I remembered it from my childhood.

It was fragrant with the smell of cloves, bergamot, and cinnamon. Drying flowers hung from hooks on nearly every wall, some bleached by the sunshine filtering into the storefront. At the back of the shop stood a wooden workbench, piled high with bottles and cauldrons and mortars and pestles. The honey-colored cabinets behind the table had windows that displayed row after row of potions and powders of every color. Somehow, the shop seemed just as big as it had when I was a little girl. And it certainly wasn't as fearsome or dour as the outside of the house made it seem.

Xavier stood in the potion-making area at the back of the

shop, among the petals and stems and little jars of salve on the countertop. A cloud of steam rose from the cauldron behind him. Upon hearing us enter, he lifted the white apron from around his neck, slung it over the counter, and approached us in one fluid motion, like a dancer.

In less than a day, he'd changed yet again. Gone was the unkempt boy making dangerous promises last night. A prim, professional wizard stood before us.

He'd cast off his traditional black coat, and the sleeves of his pure-white shirt were rolled to his elbows. He still wore the black vest and trousers of a certified wizard, as well as a black cravat fixed in place with the same gold sun pin that Madam Ben Ammar wore as a brooch.

"You've got shoes today," I remarked. They were black, too, and so finely polished that I would have believed him if he'd told me they'd been carved from marble.

He bowed his head in greeting. "You'll notice I also have a door."

I grimaced, glancing at the toes of my own shoes, caked in dirt. "I'm sorry about that. Hopefully you'll be able to keep my magic in check."

"Yes, we all hope so," said Madam Ben Ammar. The ice in her voice alarmed me, but when I peeked at her, I found that her look of consternation was not directed at me but at Xavier.

His cordial look faded as she neared him. Moments ago,

he'd appeared mature for his age—but before her imposing height, he was just a boy.

"Would—would you like to sit down for some tea?" he offered, pointing a gloved hand to a little salon to the right of him.

"No," she replied. "Master Morwyn, I was surprised to see that you had so magnanimously taken on Miss Lucas. That you, of all people, chose to oversee a case of such responsibility. Do you think that you can handle magic that an experienced magician cannot?"

My mouth hung agape. Even in my silliest mistakes, she had been kind and forgiving to me. Now, Xavier looked as though he stood before Death herself.

"I do not pretend that I'll be able to tame her magic by myself, and I would never claim to be more skilled than you in any aspect, Your Greatness," he murmured.

"Then what *are* you playing at? What do you have to gain from her?"

Her accusation left me as shaken as he appeared to be. He *did* mean to gain from training me, but why he wanted my magic, I still couldn't understand. I found myself drifting behind Madam Ben Ammar—to shield myself from him or from her own wrath, I wasn't sure.

"You and I made the same vows," he said to her. "It's our purpose as magicians to take care of others. If it's in my power to help Miss Lucas and her father, I want to do so."

"I honor that purpose with all of my might, young man. Can you say the same?"

I gasped and then bit down hard on my lip to keep quiet. Xavier shut his eyes and sighed softly instead of a proper reply.

"Now, then," she said, "I'd like a final word with Miss Lucas, alone. If you'll excuse us for one moment."

He opened his mouth to speak, but in a whirl, Madam Ben Ammar opened the door once more and shepherded me through, this time onto Xavier's porch. She closed the door behind her and laid a hand against my shoulder.

"Clara," she said, "in light of your father's condition, the Council is delaying any action regarding your magic. They're going to wait and see if you can perform this blessing." She smiled—but only barely. "It's my hope that performing such complicated magic will help restore the Council's faith in your capabilities. They may decide to leave your power untouched."

She sighed. My body tensed.

"However," she said, "I want you to be prepared, should you be . . . unable to bless him."

My breath caught tight in my chest. Magic thrashed against my ribs and hissed at me, *He's going to die; he's going to die!*

I shook my head to rattle the thoughts out of my brain. "I—I can't. I can't think like that."

The faintest idea of a world where the Council called me

a criminal and left me powerless, where I had no one, where my father lay dead because of my magic . . .

"All right," she cooed. She lowered her head, her gaze meeting mine. "I promise I'll do everything I can to help you and your father. And I want you to know that I will be here for you. No matter what."

Thinking of my little family and of the wild magic I'd inherited—it picked away at the wound that had broken open in my heart ever since I'd hurt Papa.

"This . . . this dangerous magic. Is it like hers?" I whispered. "Imogen's?"

"I only know your mother by reputation. But . . . her magic is powerful, yes." A line formed between her eyebrows. "Clara, I know you didn't mean ill against your father. The Council understands you have extenuating circumstances. We want to help you." She touched the puff of pale blue fabric on my sleeve. "You aren't like her. We know you're faithful to our cause."

I chewed the inside of my lip and kept my eyes trained on the deep brown wood of the Morwyns' porch. Yes, I was faithful to the laws of the Council of Magicians, but what did that matter? My magic would have its way, regardless of what I wished.

Madam Ben Ammar wrung her hands. "Have—have you heard from your mother? Has she attempted to contact you at all since last we spoke?"

"No." *Thankfully*. Just thinking of her caused my magic to prickle in my chest.

"You'd tell me if she did?"

I frowned. "Yes, of course, madam. Why? Does this have to do with your investigation? Has she done something?"

Madam Ben Ammar tipped back on her heels, glancing into the window beside Xavier's front door. She leaned close to me.

"A new potion is circulating, much the same as her poisons did five years ago." She bowed her head, her eyes meeting mine. "If Imogen tries to talk to you, or if you hear anything of this potion—Euphoria, they call it—I want you to call on me at once."

She reached into the pocket of her black gown and held out a light blue card. "Keep your eyes open and be cautious. People who've taken Euphoria are quite easy to spot. The potion makes them delirious with artificial happiness. And we've found victims who have started growing dandelions on their skin."

Nausea rolled through me like a wave.

"Imogen's coven continues to evade the Council," she continued, "no matter how careful we are in our investigations. We fear that they may be spying on us." Her eyes flashed. "The Council also wants to keep the public from knowing too much about this potion just yet. We don't want to raise demand for it. So you'll keep any talk of it between the two of us, won't you?"

Another secret to keep from Papa. "All right," I told her, gazing down at the card, a little rectangular piece of sky. "Do you think she *would* contact me?"

Madam Ben Ammar lifted a shoulder. "She's unpredictable. But you are about to come of age. In truth, I—" Her voice broke, and she cleared her throat, smoothing the wrinkle-free front of her black gown. "I fear that she would seek you out as an apprentice."

The very idea was absurd, verging on offensive. I shoved the card into the pocket of my skirt as if to silence the doubt now blooming in my mind. Even if she *did* want me, I'd refuse. I'd *fight*. "I want nothing to do with her."

She squeezed my free hand through my thick gardening gloves. "Good girl. And truly—if you need anything, simply call on me."

Madam Ben Ammar opened the door for me and let me through. Xavier had retreated to his spot beside the counter, his foot tapping and his arms folded. I supposed he had grown out of eavesdropping.

"Miss Lucas will be sure to report to the Council if she sees anything . . . out of place," said the witch as she stood in the doorway. "She will be watching you closely."

"I will?" I peeped. Was I to be some sort of spy for her? Was Xavier even *worthy* of such suspicion?

But he just bowed to her. "Understood."

She smiled to me, said, "Goodbye, Clara," and snapped the door shut behind her.

We turned to one another with wide eyes.

"What did you do to offend her?" I asked.

His hair flopped over his eyes as he lifted my bags. "A great many things, I'm sure. Now, then, let's reacquaint you with the house."

With a tilt of his head, he gestured to the kitchen, warm and bathed in morning light. "The kitchen and shop area, as you'll recall. You'll help me sort and label the potion ingredients there. As for food, you're welcome to anything in the pantry—"

Despite the storm clouds in my mind, a fanciful memory made me clasp my hands together in excitement. "Does the magic cupboard still work?"

He laughed. "It does. Shall we check it?"

I nodded and he set my bags back down. Following in his footsteps, he led me to a cupboard next to the washbasin. It was pale white, not honey-colored like the rest of the kitchen's storage.

"It seemed so high up when we were young," I murmured. Now Xavier didn't have to reach very far at all as he twisted the knob of the little white door.

The cupboard was empty, except for two small chocolate bonbons, wrapped neatly in white paper. I gasped delightedly.

"I suppose it knew I'd be having company."

When we were children, all five of us together, we'd beg

his mother to open the magic cupboard for us. There were always treasures hidden inside, little sweets or toys or even books the size of a child's palm.

"Who built the cupboard again?" I asked as I unwrapped my bonbon. "Your grandfather?"

"My grandmother." When he smiled, his eyes crinkled at the corners. "Every Morwyn who has magic adds something to the house. Father enchanted the bookshelves upstairs, Great-Grandfather made the staircase, Great-Great-Grandmother made the ceiling in the tower room . . . on and on for six hundred years. And Grandmother wanted something that would delight the children who'd live here." He dropped the second chocolate into my gloved hand. "Here, you can have mine."

He breezed past me, sweeping up my baggage again. I gaped at how quickly he'd brushed aside the memories, but was startled into moving by his call. "Come along!"

I scampered behind him and kept my chocolate in my cheek like a chipmunk. "What did *you* add to the house?" I asked his back.

"Nothing yet. I've not had the time."

That sounded like nonsense to me. Xavier used to babble excitedly about how, when his turn came, he'd make a room that spun until you got dizzy, or a floor that let you jump three feet in the air. For him to be so uninterested now was entirely uncharacteristic.

"If it were up to me," I said, "I'd make a room with an orchard. And you could pick fresh berries every day for tarts."

He snickered. "What if the door opened into a different bakery every day? So you could get berry tarts all you wanted."

I could almost picture us as children, grabbing up as many pastries as we could carry. "For free, of course?"

"Of course."

Down the hall from the potion shop was a large dining room. Six matching chairs surrounded an old mahogany table.

"I have supper at around seven," he said, "but you don't need to eat with me, if you don't want to."

Papa and I didn't have a dining room; we just sat at the little table in the kitchen. Or, more typically, we ate the food while we were still preparing it. Neither of us was patient when hungry, and we got such a thrill from trying new recipes and sharing them with one another that we hardly ever made a dish pretty enough to put on a plate. The memories left a sad, sour taste in my mouth. I nibbled on the second chocolate to try to disguise the ugly feeling.

Next, Xavier led me up the stone spiral steps, lit dimly by sparse windows and sconces. More memories rushed back, this time of the surprise that this staircase held.

"Which sconce is the secret lever?"

"Up near the top," he said. "By the tower, remember?"

"Right," I murmured. "Can we—?"

"Not right now. We have a great deal of work to do, Miss Lucas," said Xavier, stepping out onto the second floor.

There were six doors along the corridor, and the olive-green walls were dotted with multiple paintings in differently shaped frames.

In the nearest, a young man stood tall behind a sofa, where his three sisters sat. His black hair was short and neatly combed. His eyes were clear and free of fatigue. He wore a defiant smirk, his chin held high.

"When was this done?" I asked.

"About two years ago, I think."

I hummed a thoughtful note and tipped my head at the painting. How was it that his painted eyes seemed more vibrant than they were in real life?

"You've changed so much," I said.

"Adolescence is a marvel." His voice was flat. He pointed the bags towards a set of double doors made of deep brown wood. "Here, I'll show you the library."

I longed to linger in the hall, to reminisce, to ask him more questions. With the breakneck pace of this tour, I was inclined to think that he was *avoiding* all talk of our past. Or at least, any conversation with me. I took one last glance at the portrait before dashing after him into the library.

Bookshelves lined the walls, with a rolling ladder propped against one of the shelves. In the middle of the room, two desks faced one another. Three armchairs and a sofa circled one corner of the library. The whole place felt empty.

"How long has your family been gone?" I asked.

"Three months."

My heart lurched. "And they left without you?"

He crossed his arms and smoothed a fold in the rug with his toe. "Well, I'm standing in front of you, so evidently—"

I groaned. "I meant *why*. Why are you here when they're abroad?"

Xavier straightened a pen lying on the desk before him. "I have work to do here."

My brow furrowed. "What could be so important that you'd separate yourself from your family?"

"My work is extremely important. What I'm doing can change lives. Save lives."

My work. Not *our* work.

I selected a scarlet book from one of the shelves and delicately pushed aside page after page. This book, as well as most of the others, had been written by Morwyns of old, containing their personal wisdom on casting magic. Potions to cure warts or remove cataracts. Spells for peace. Protection charms.

"Do you hear from them, at least?" I asked. "I've not seen them since we were children."

"They write me frequently. They're doing very well, and they're much happier in Álbila. Mother thought it was too dreary here, anyway." He joined me by the bookshelf and absently shifted a book from one row to another. "Leonor has gotten much better at guitar. Dalia finds the Albilan boys very exciting. Inés has taken up painting."

They write me *frequently.*

There was that small, bitter grievance within me again, like a pain that only came when it rained. "Do you write to *them*?" I asked.

He pursed his lips. "As often as I can. I'll be sure to tell them that you're here now. They'll be thrilled." He gave the spines of the books on the shelves a little pat. "Anyhow, these books bear a great deal of knowledge on old magic; blessings and curses and the like. You can come here to study whenever you want. You'll learn more from the books than from me, I'm certain."

I shut the book and held it by my ear with a smirk. "Well, the books don't seem to be as adept at conversation as you are."

He dropped his gaze to the floor. "I suppose human company is preferable." He about-faced and marched out into the hall. "I'll show you your room."

I placed the book on a nearby table and followed him. Just as I crossed through the doorway of the library, I heard a fluttering sound behind me, like a bird taking flight. I whipped my head back to see. The crimson book I'd placed aside had lifted itself up, zipping through the air like a cardinal, and lightly placed itself back on its perch on the shelf. I smiled, remembering. Xavier and I used to play in this library, seeing whose book could fly back to its shelf the fastest.

"Miss Lucas?" Xavier called. He was waiting for me in the stairwell.

"Why do you call me Miss Lucas?" I asked as we ascended. "Do you insist I call you 'Master Morwyn' or 'Your Greatness'?"

"Well, I—it's proper. We aren't children anymore."

"'It's proper,'" I echoed. "It's just the two of us here!"

It was beginning to feel like he'd completely forgotten that little boy he'd once been. Skipping rocks, racing down dusty roads, giving me tight hugs when I grew jealous that he had a mother. *That* was Xavier. This person was the all-important and respected wizard, His Greatness *Master Morwyn*.

Up one more flight of winding stairs, we reached a small landing with a single pale door, the chipped paint exposing bits of wood. He twisted the pewter handle and held the door open for me.

I faintly remembered this room. It was round, with stone walls painted white. There was a birch table with a chair and a mirror. A bed was draped in a quilt dappled in pink, orange, and yellow diamonds. Beside it stood a nightstand with a stub of a candle left in the candlestick, and hanging over the bed was a bundle of dried flowers. There was one round window over the length of the bed, and another on the opposite curve of the wall. A little embroidery hoop was affixed near the window, embroidered with drooping flowers and messy script declaring *Welcome* to the lodger. Above, the domed ceiling was pale blue, covered in real, wispy clouds that drifted past and then evanesced into nothing.

"I'm sorry to put you in the guest room," he said in a small voice as he set down my valise and carpetbag. "My family's rooms are technically available, but—"

"It's beautiful," I said.

It was nothing like my room in Williamston, cluttered full of memories and books and always smelling of vanilla and sugar from the kitchen across the hall. But it was charming, and seeing the desperate, timid look in his eyes, I made sure to show him the most genuine smile I could muster.

I craned my neck, peering out the window. Lime-green hills spread across the horizon like ocean waves.

I gasped as a memory struck me. "We used to play pirates here!"

Xavier's brows rose. "I remember. You were always the captain."

Not anymore. I opened my carpetbag and removed the apron I'd folded into a tight roll. "Now you're at the helm," I said. "We should start our lessons. No good in wasting time chattering."

"How did your father fare last night?" he asked.

I pressed the apron hard against my chest to combat the groaning, tugging feeling of my magic. *Your fault, your fault, your fault.*

"He isn't doing well, I'm afraid," I said. "Madam Ben

Ammar has her apprentice taking care of him, but . . ." I let the rest of my thoughts dissipate into thin air. "I hate to think of it. That even being *near* my magic could poison him, somehow." My stomach fell. "What if—what if it hurts you, too?"

"You've lived with your father all your life and hadn't hurt him so far. And I believe you'll be ready to bless him in a few weeks." Xavier shrugged, as if this was all perfectly normal and manageable. "I should be perfectly safe for so short a time," he said. His confidence verged on naivete. Dread and fear coiled in my stomach and made my lip tremble even more.

Just like yesterday, a handkerchief entered my line of sight. Xavier offered it with a weak, apologetic smile. "Now, here. Cry as much as you like."

I snatched up the handkerchief, my cheeks burning. "I—I thought expressing emotions exacerbated one's magic."

"It releases it, yes. But if you don't express your power somehow, it'll build up and become even more dangerous. So crying, it's—it's good, you see."

In all my years of training, I'd never heard such an idea. Papa had once said if someone wrote down everything I said in one day, they'd fill a library twice over. But now I was speechless.

"I, er . . . I missed you," he said.

My head jerked up.

His cheeks had turned red, the same as when we were children and his mother fussed with his hair in front of me.

Seeing him blush, and knowing that I was the cause, made my stomach flutter.

Even so, the words stung.

"You *missed* me? But you never wrote," I said. "I thought you hated me."

Xavier lowered his head, as if he were suddenly fascinated by the swirling grain of the wooden floorboards. "I'm sorry."

It wasn't enough.

But it was something. It was a start. A door had been locked fast between us, and now, after so long, he'd started to unlatch it.

"I wish I could have seen you at your initiate ceremony," I said softly. I imagined him, painfully handsome in a suit and tails, with a white bow tie, golden sparks and flowers filling the air around him as he received raucous applause.

Xavier scuffed the floorboards with his shoe. "You didn't miss very much. Just a lot of magicians giving speeches."

I laughed, nervous and light. "You still look away when you lie."

His eyes met mine. My pulse leapt.

"Well," he said, "I'm sorry you weren't there, too."

Reality was a harsh blow. I wasn't a noteworthy magician like him. I hadn't been certified as a magician a year early and then made a member of the Council at so young an age. I was a mess whose magic was killing her father.

My shoulders tensed. Blood thrummed in my ears and my

69

magic echoed my thoughts, *killing her father, killing her father.* As I lost my grip on hope, on the brightness of this moment, the room seemed to grow darker, too. A cloud passed over the sun outside, and the enchanted ceiling above us dimmed at the same time.

Xavier took a glance at the magical ceiling above and cleared his throat. "Well, I—I ought to leave you alone." He retreated to the doorway, gesturing to the wall behind him. "You, er, asked about the lever. It's the sconce over here. For the, er. For the slide. If you want." His eyes darted from me to my suitcases to the handkerchief in my grasp. Then—

"I'll let you get settled," he said.

I clutched the handkerchief tight. "I thought you said we had work to do."

"Soon enough. You can, erm, unpack. Or tidy up. Or whatever it is you need to do." His shoulders hunched, like he was shrinking in on himself, trying to turn invisible. He kept his gaze firmly to the floor and took another step back. "Goodbye," he said, and hastily shut the door between us.

I stared at the painted-white door and listened to the rapid *thump* of his footsteps down the stairwell. Closing my eyes, I imagined the boy I had once known. My closest friend. And just for a moment, he had been that boy again; silly and awkward and shy, listening to my worries. But he was also cold and distant, far too . . . severe. As if he hadn't answered my letters simply because he'd stopped caring for me.

Perhaps he'd *never* liked me at all. Perhaps he'd only taken me on as an apprentice because he pitied me. Or because he was desperate for my power.

When I was alone, my magic was particularly loud. It wasted no time in hurling insults at me. It flashed images in my mind: the petals falling from Papa's lips. The tears in his eyes. The blistered, pink skin on his cheek in the shape of my fingerprints.

Each thought was worse than the last.

Wilting onto the floor, I tried and failed to drown out the whispers. The images grew more violent, more vivid. The reality that my father could be dying at my hands. The weight of it all broke me. My lungs strained from holding in sobs, and the harder I tried, the worse I ached, and the louder my magic screamed. It was all too much, and with one breath, I lost all resolve, and then I couldn't *stop* weeping. Every time a tear fell, plants bloomed up from between the floorboards. Before long, I was kneeling in a carpet of flowers.

Artemisia—*I miss you.*

Marigolds—*I grieve for you.*

Purple hyacinths—*I'm so sorry.*

5

For a first lesson, my previous teachers often liked to dazzle me with their magic. Madam Ben Ammar had promised me I'd be able to summon fire like she could. Madam Albright had showed me the spell she used to find anything lost. Master Young had made his house tidy itself up all on its own.

When I finally calmed myself and made my way down to the Morwyns' shop, Xavier handed me a broom.

I frowned at it. "How is this meant to help me bless my father?"

"I'm afraid we have the workday to overcome before we can begin your lessons. After we close up shop, I'll teach you about controlling your magic. Once you can do that, you'll be able to bless him."

He made it sound so simple. A trifle. He turned to the washbasin, his sleeves rolled up as he scrubbed at phials and beakers. I bristled at his indifference.

"Why must we play shopkeeper when my father is suffering?"

His shoulders lifted and fell with a sigh. "Because it's a Monday, and customers will be coming. There are other people who *also* need our help. I can't just shut down my shop. I'm sorry."

I scowled. He was right, though I'd never tell him so. "If you mean to help me control my magic, aren't you going to teach me some sort of cleaning spell?"

"I don't use them. It's better for me to reserve my strength for our lessons this evening."

"Reserve?"

He nodded. "Most of my power is spent making potions."

None of my teachers had mentioned conserving their magic. It was a bottomless well, they'd said, fueled by emotion and words and the beat of one's own heart. It was a gift from the sun itself, strengthening us and tying us directly to the earth and the plants that we used in our potions. It wasn't like gold, meant to be stored up and spent wisely.

"You can't run out of magic."

His gaze lowered to the floor. "No. But these days, I have a particular knack for growing tired."

I frowned. It certainly seemed so. The bags under his eyes. The pallor of his skin. By the minute, I was realizing how fortunate he was to have a helping hand around the house.

"Why, though?" I prompted.

He rolled his eyes. "Must it be a trial to ask you to sweep for me?"

With a huff, I breezed past him into the back potion-making area. I swept up dust and powders of many colors and carried them to the dustbin. Clearly, the man had better things to do than clean his own house.

"Earlier, you said bursting into tears was good for one's magic," I mentioned, rolling back the rug in the entryway to sweep there, too. "Do you cry to subdue your magic as well, or does that also exhaust your power?"

He turned from me, reshuffling the hoard of bottles cluttering up his workbench with great determination. "Yes, I *cry*, Miss Lucas—"

"And if you're angry?" I asked. "Do you rant and rave and shout?"

"Yes. Any emotion fuels one's power. If a magician does not honor a feeling, their magic can get too strong. The stronger the magic, the harder it is to control."

I frowned. "My other teachers said that was why we had to keep our emotions in check. To keep from feeling too much or else our magic would be out of control."

"Well, most people are of that mind. Like my father." His expression was hidden behind the curtain of his black hair. "My mother is of a different school of thought. There are some who believe that embracing emotion, not withholding it, is what leads to controlling one's magic."

"What if that magic is already too difficult to control?" *What if,* I thought, keeping my worry locked up in my heart, *what if my emotions are nothing but trouble?*

He finally turned to me, the faintest ghost of a hopeful smile dawning on his face. "I believe anything can be tempered with enough time and dedication."

The bell over the shop door rang. I stood at attention, still clutching the broom. I thought, *This must be how actors and musicians feel waiting for the curtain to rise.* My stomach fluttered. Magic tickled my throat.

A tall man with dark hair and a beard stepped across the stoop. He wore a smock covered in sawdust. "Good morning," he said meekly.

I curtsied. "How can we help you, sir?"

"My wife is ill," said the customer. "Her stomach troubles her—she can barely move." He reached into his pocket and removed five copper coins. "Is there something I can get for five? I'll pay more with interest, if need be. It's urgent."

Xavier eyed the money and nodded, approaching his shelves. He ran a finger along the array of bottles, but then his shoulders drooped.

"I'm afraid those particular potions have been in high demand," he said. He rubbed his temple. "I apologize, I usually have more tinctures stocked—"

"It's all right," said the customer, his shoulders sagging.

"There's another wizard a few hours from here, isn't there?"

"We'll help you, sir," I told the man. "You shouldn't have to travel so far."

I glanced back to Xavier, who was fidgeting with his silk cravat.

"Yes." When Xavier looked up, there was a mischievous glint in his eyes. "If you'll give us only a few minutes, sir, Miss Lucas will prepare the potion for you."

My face grew cold. I darted over to his side. "I will?" I whispered furiously.

Xavier nodded. "I'll show you how to make it. You'll do just fine, I'm sure."

Glancing at the customer, I remembered with great dread Xavier's comments about magic and strength and excessive emotion. Would my downpour of grief an hour ago be enough to keep my magic at bay? "Master Morwyn," I said under my breath, "does your lesson involve me sobbing in front of a stranger?"

Calm as ever, he turned to the customer. "If it wouldn't trouble you, sir, would you mind waiting for us on the porch? We'll call you inside once the potion has been made."

The man shuffled out the door, his brow lined. The bell over the door jingled as he shut it.

I spun towards Xavier, my stomach doing a somersault. "I can't do this!"

He scoffed as he set two bowls on the workbench. "You've surely made potions with your other teachers."

"They let me chop ingredients and mix them together— they almost never let me cast spells! And I've only *sold* a potion I'd made a few times—"

One of the bowls wobbled and then flung itself off the tabletop. Xavier clicked his tongue disapprovingly—at the bowl. He stooped down and replaced it, his hands firm.

"It's perfectly normal to be nervous," he said to me. "I know it's a new way of training. But the more you deny your feelings, the more restless your magic will be. You must become comfortable with your power if you intend to control it."

Every failure could determine Papa's future. The other bowl quivered, and Xavier stilled it with a hand. "What are you afraid of?" he asked.

I swallowed. In my mind, I could see Papa's eyes blown wide with horror as the flowers bloomed from his heart. I could see a woman who looked far too much like me, with angry, red hair, and the ability, magical and not, to break and bend hearts. "Plenty of things."

The bowl trembled again. Xavier shook his head. "Be as specific as you can."

I stared at my hands, quivering against the deep brown of the stone countertop. The hands that had burned my father. "I don't know. There's just . . . so much."

He uncorked a round bottle filled with light pink liquid and set it in front of me. "You're being too hard on yourself," he said softly.

"What am I supposed to be doing?" I squeaked, imagining Papa's eyes. His scream. His dying heart. All because of a power I never asked for, inherited from a person I couldn't even remember. "What if my magic hurts you?"

"I'll be fine," he said. "But I want you to harness the energy of the fear you're feeling. I want you to pour that power into the bowl. Use that restlessness within you, and with all your might, think of peace."

I choked out a laugh—but even that frightened me, since the tiniest emotion or action seemed enough to release my magic. "How can I? What if my magic hurts that man's wife?"

He placed the bottle in my gloved hand. I met his gaze again. I was so fraught with emotion that my whole body was quaking . . . but he didn't seem to find me silly or pitiable. He was serious, but gentle-eyed. Like he was listening intently to my every word. The way he *used* to listen to me. "My magic gives me trouble, too. I don't expect you to be an expert." He nodded to me. His voice was smooth and calm. "Let the fear roll through you like a tide. Then let it pass."

I shut my eyes and pictured that wave, the color of night and roaring at me like a lion. It twisted in my gut, then crashed into itself. The water I envisioned swirled in my middle like a whirlpool.

"Your feelings give your magic strength. Use their power; don't force them down," said Xavier. "To release that power, you need intention and something to channel that intention into. Your fear, your sadness—take that energy and hold it." He lifted my hand, sending a chill up my back. I breathed deeply and focused on the maelstrom within me. "Ideally, the potion we're making should help an uneasy stomach. Speak of peace, balance, and comfort to it, and you can make it so."

"Peace," I said. Nothing happened. "Peace."

"Picture it in your mind. And breathe."

My lungs filled again. My mind turned, as it always did, to my father. I remembered childhood summers spent on the porch, curled safely in Papa's lap, listening to crickets and watching the stars. Winters by the fireplace, drinking chocolate and reading stories together. Spring nights, with sweet-smelling lavender hanging on my lintel, his lullabies wafting through the room, and his fingers brushing baby hairs from my brow. It had always been just the two of us— but that felt like so much more than enough.

"Peace," I whispered. The storm in me cooled. I poured out some of the liquid and felt a rush of energy leave me as well, loosening my shoulders and my chest.

He pressed a square bottle, some other ingredient, into my hand. "Continue."

"Peace, tranquility, balance." I let the energy pour from me like the fluid from the bottles, one after another. My words slurred together, slowly morphing into my father's lullaby. I sang the words until the verse was done and let my voice echo in the room and fade into silence.

Cradled in my hands was a bowl full of lilac-colored liquid. It shook like it was caught in an earthquake; like the potion was trying to burst from the bowl. Then the brew swelled and grew like a tidal wave of its own, rising up, overflowing and flooding over the counter in an impossible amount.

"Curse me four times over," I grumbled.

"Mop!" cried Xavier, holding out a hand. On cue, one zipped out of the supply closet and into his hand. He passed it to me with a grimace. "And—do not swear, if you can help it. I don't want your magic getting any ideas."

He was right. Speaking *Curse me!* into the world was tempting fate. I bit down hard on my tongue and mopped up the thick lilac mixture.

As I cleaned the floor, Xavier paused beside the bowl that had overflowed. He frowned at it— *What else had I done wrong?*

"I wonder," he murmured.

He filled a teaspoon with the potion . . . and then tasted it.

I gasped. "Xavier!"

"I want to see if it works."

"What if it hurts you?"

He shrugged. "I feel perfectly fine."

My heart rose. "You mean—you mean I made the potion all right? I just created too much of it?"

"Perhaps, I—" Xavier cut himself off, his brow furrowing.

He approached the counter, plucking a raspberry from the small bowl we kept for use in potions. With a look of deep concentration, he popped the berry into his mouth.

"What are you doing now?"

He hummed thoughtfully. "I seem to have lost my sense of taste."

"*What?*"

Xavier waved a hand. "I'm certain it's only temporary. But it's a curious effect, nonetheless. Something that merits more study—"

"Now?" I gestured around me at the sticky countertops and the violet puddle at my feet and towards the customer still waiting on us outside.

"Right. I'll make a new potion as quick as I can."

While I mopped up the remains of my failed potion, Xavier brewed a new, better one.

Mint extract. Chamomile and vervain tea. Oil of ginger and roses. He poured drops of each into little cups and inspected them to be certain that they were all the same amount. *Equality of ingredients is necessary for balanced potions,* Madam Carvalho had once taught me.

The lovely smell helped distract from the anxious nausea caused by my magic.

At least *his* potion would do as intended.

Within minutes, he finished the medicine, bottling it and taking it to the customer outside.

Leaving me alone.

I could feel my magic squirming around inside me like a snake. I held my hand to my forehead.

Fool, my magic whispered. *You can't even make a nausea potion without destroying the shop and hurting your teacher. How on earth can you hope to save your father?*

"Stop it," I growled.

You only bring destruction.

Leaning my head against the damp countertop, I covered my head in my arms. I tried to remember what Papa used to tell me. That I was strong. That I wasn't my magic. That my magic was a blessing. That he and my mother had prayed I'd grow to be a witch.

You have magic like her, said the voice. *And you're weak like her. Cruel like her.*

I wanted to cry or shout but was too afraid. Would I make lightning strike the house? Would Xavier start to grow thorns? Would I flood the kitchen with flowers?

Again, the door opened to the sound of a jingling bell. Xavier gasped, his gaze on the floor as I looked up.

Dozens and dozens of pink peonies had popped up between the floorboards. *Peonies: a sign of shame,* said *Waverly's.*

I dropped to the floor and tore up the blooms.

"Stop! Stop!" Xavier cried as I crumpled flowers and ripped their stems in half.

I paused, my chest heaving, my cheeks clammy with tears.

He knelt before me, delicately plucking a flower. "Peonies are useful in all sorts of healing and protective potions. We could use these for ingredients."

"Then you should thank me. I've given you enough to last you a lifetime." I rubbed my sleeve hard against my eyes. "I'm sorry about the potion. And your sense of taste. And *this*. I can't even *stand still* in your shop without my magic destroying something. How . . . how am I supposed to learn to bless my father?"

"We'll find a way." He continued to gather flowers, and for the first time I noticed how his hands shook. How loud his breathing was. How his skin had grown white as chalk.

I was so wrapped up in my own failure I hadn't noticed that he was in pain. "Don't trouble yourself with these," I said, tugging on some flowers tucked between the floorboards. "You're exhausted."

"No, no, I'm fine. My magic can make me a little winded, nothing more."

My stomach clenched. "Are you certain you're all right?"

His eyes wrinkled at the corners when he smiled. "Never better."

He might be a talented wizard, but he was a dismal liar.

6

With every spell he cast, Xavier seemed more and more weary. And he was casting many spells. Perhaps even more than he usually would, thanks to my mistakes. After the incident with the anti-nausea potion, he'd decided to follow in the footsteps of my prior teachers, allowing me to combine the ingredients but never to imbue my power into the mixture.

At five o'clock, Xavier shut the door behind our final customer—one of dozens that day—and turned the sign from *Open* to *Closed*. He dropped into the chair beside the little kitchen table and massaged his eyes.

I cautiously approached his table, setting a steaming cup of tea before him.

"I figured it's the least I could do, after today," I said, my voice small and defeated. "And if you can taste it, well, I'll feel just a little better about myself."

He thanked me and took a careful sip. When his shoulders loosened and a tired smile crossed his face, relief passed over me like a cool breeze.

"Lavender," he said. The smallest spark of humor lit up his eyes. "See? No irreversible damage."

"Thank goodness."

But I couldn't help but think of the real damage my magic had caused. I tried to keep my worries inside, plying myself by unwinding and winding my braid, but by his second sip of tea, I could feel magic crawling under my skin.

"I know we've just finished work," I said, "but can you teach me how to cast a blessing now?"

Any alertness in his eyes faded away. "It—it isn't something you can learn to do so fast."

"Then *when* shall I learn?" I pressed. Papa's heart would only grow weaker.

Xavier's gaze arced across the ceiling as if it could bring him an answer. "Well, if you like, I can show you what a blessing would look like." He held out a finger in warning. "But remember what I said. This kind of magic takes great control and great intention. With yours as . . . spirited as it is, it could take weeks of practice—"

"You saw my father; I can't sit here and make play-magic potions for *weeks* while he's so ill!"

Xavier rubbed a hand against his arm. "Those potions will teach you how to tame your power," he said. "If you can learn to direct your magic with little enchantments, a great spell like a blessing will be feasible one day."

I scoffed. "I did horribly with the potion, though."

His lips twisted in a thoughtful frown. "I don't know if I'd say *horribly*. Your power was just excessive. Your potion was effective, I suppose. With no sense of taste, it's hard to become nauseous. It just became . . . too much. I intend to read more about this as soon as I can—"

"But the blessing?"

"Right," he said, "your magic wished him ill, so you must wish good things upon him. Think of a strong, affirmative statement. Something, like, 'May you . . .'" He waved his hand at me. "It's better if you're the one to come up with the spell. The syntax should be unique to you. That's why it needs to be spoken in your voice, after all. It wouldn't work if *my* words were coming out of your mouth."

I wished Papa all the best in the world. I wished for him the peace he provided to me with encouraging words and consoling hugs. The confidence to know that he would live a long, happy life at my side. The freedom of a life unhindered by this curse. My mother had left him with loneliness and fear and doubt. Now that I was grown, I wanted to give him everything she had taken from him.

"May every beat of your heart be filled with peace, confidence, and freedom," I murmured.

Xavier's eyes twinkled. He nodded. "Beautiful. A blessing

is so difficult to cast because one must deeply love, or convince themselves that they love, the person they bless. Concentrate on your love for him, and you'll feel, with unshakable certainty, that the thing you wish will come true. Hold on to all of that peace, confidence, and freedom within *you* as you prepare to give it to him."

I placed myself in the chair across from him and shut my eyes. In my mind, Papa sat before me. I let my shoulders go slack and took slow, deep breaths. For once, my magic felt like a part of me—not some foreign body, not a creature warring against me. "May every beat of your heart be filled with peace, confidence, and freedom."

I opened one eye, as I used to do when I played hide-and-seek with Xavier. "Is—is that enough?" I asked. "Could I have lifted his curse just now, without knowing it?"

"No. You must lay your hands on him. And as I've said, you must train your magic to be able to carry out your will."

"How will I know when I'm capable of that?"

"When you say the blessing, if your magic does as you say, you'll feel it in your hands." He flexed his gloved fingers. "It feels like your hands are made of stardust. They'll sort of fizzle and burn. It's very strange."

I cocked my head, my eyes narrowing. "You've cast a blessing before?"

"Yes. Once." His voice was soft.

"What sort of blessing was it?"

He huffed through his nostrils. "You're very inquisitive, Miss Lucas."

"Impertinent, you mean?"

He shook his head. "You're like me. You're curious." Xavier rose to his full, excessive height, stretching his arms and rubbing his eyes like a child waking from a nap. "Come, I'll show you some books on blessings. I've used them before."

I trailed behind him up the winding stairwell, which was punctuated every now and again by sunlight filtering through its tiny windows. "Shall I guess who you blessed, then, or shall you tell me?" I asked.

He sighed, stepping onto the second-floor landing and then turning to face me. "I propose a game."

My brow furrowed. "A game?"

"Yes. If you wish so dearly to know all my secrets, you must first share something about yourself."

I scoffed. "I must? And I'm to go *first*?"

Xavier rolled his eyes. "All right, then. I blessed Inés before she left for Álbila."

He made for the library, and I trailed behind him as fast as I could.

"And why did she—?"

Inside the library, he stopped me with a raised hand. "We had a bargain."

"You already know everything about me. Red hair. Wild magic. Nosy. Can still beat you in a footrace."

As I ticked things off on my fingers, he fished around in his jacket pocket, removing a gold band.

"Whose was this?" he asked.

My heart sank. A book flung itself off one of the shelves.

Xavier raised an eyebrow. "Now I'm even *more* curious."

"It was my mother's," I murmured as the book swiftly replaced itself. A pit formed in my stomach at the thought of her—and of him, accepting payment from me yesterday as if we were complete strangers.

He set the ring flat on the oak table. "Thank you," he said, his voice gentler—no longer teasing. "Your turn."

He left it there and approached the bookshelf nearest the fireplace, running his finger along the spines. I ambled towards the emptier desk, where a sketched family portrait sat in a silver frame. Three smiling girls, hugging their embarrassed, blushing brother.

"What sort of blessing did you give Inés?" I asked.

A stack of books thudded on the desk at my side, causing me to clutch my chest.

"Sorry," he murmured. He held out the chair for me, and I sat.

I fanned the books out on the table. Each was jewel-toned, worn at the edges, and bore a title in silver print: *A Complete Guide to Blessings and Curses. A Critical Study of the Power of Voice and Intention. Speak No Evil.*

Xavier leaned over my shoulder, laying his long fingers

against the cover of the latter. His sleeve brushed mine, and his hair hung down as he bent his head. My face prickled with warmth as he leaned by me. He smelled of oranges and cloves, like a nice, wintry tea.

"I blessed Inés with courage," he said, drawing back the cover and flipping through pages.

She'd always been quiet, even around her own family. Xavier was the one who could always make her smile. Now that they were apart . . . it made sense that he would want to give her the gift of bravery in his absence.

He pointed to a chapter heading: *Visualization.* "I pictured her talking to strangers. Walking fearlessly through the marketplace. Standing up to bullies. In my mind, I could see the scenes vividly. I could smell the night air, hear the crowds, feel her heartbeat. It was easy to imagine it being the truth. I held her hands in mine and felt that intention flowing from me to her."

Even now, he spoke so tenderly of her. He glanced at the sketch on the desk and sighed.

I hated seeing Xavier so sad, especially in this room. Although he'd changed a great deal, it just felt . . . wrong.

We had laughed in this room. We'd read here for hours and hours. I remembered my stomach aching from lying on the rug for so long. The smell of the pages, the sound of them whipping back and forth as he and I read as fast as we could. The crackle of the hearth and the heat of the fireplace against our cheeks.

"Do you remember the contests we used to have?" I piped up. "To see who could read the fastest?"

As I'd hoped, he looked back to me, raising a brow. "I remember you cheating."

A laugh burst from me, far too loud in the big room. Little sparks fizzled in the air, so small and quick I wondered if I'd imagined them. "*I* cheated? There's no possible way you finished a five-hundred-page novel in thirty minutes."

"Nor was it possible for *you* to have read an entire textbook about using root vegetables in potions. Including the footnotes and appendices."

I bit my lip and primly turned my attention back to the textbooks before me now. "Perhaps I skimmed a little bit. But I couldn't let you win."

"Oh, I know." He lifted the ring from the table opposite from mine and examined it in the lamplight. "Did your father ever tell you anything about your mother? You . . . didn't like to talk about her, growing up."

Magic twisted my stomach like a wet rag. My smile faded. I *still* didn't like talking about her. But I'd made a bargain. "Papa said that she used to pray that I would grow up to be a witch like her." I swallowed to hold my nausea at bay.

Xavier nodded slowly, glancing towards the door. He absently reached into his pocket and procured two small pearl earrings and then my tiny bag of coins. He laid them all beside the ring.

"I shouldn't have taken these," he murmured. "You're

already giving me enough."

A shiver rolled down my back. I was paying him with my magic, after all. And that was a good thing, I promised myself. I wouldn't miss my magic. I *wouldn't*.

Delicately, I cradled the earrings in my hands. Papa had given them to me for my birthday, along with the sweetest, softest lemon cake.

When I looked up again, Xavier was nearly out the door.

"Thank you, Xavier!" I called.

He didn't look back. "Best of luck with your studies, Miss Lucas." And he shut the door behind him.

Leaning in my chair, I scowled down at the earrings. "What an odd man," I muttered. He was kind to give me back my possessions. But he hadn't offered to let me keep my power after the blessing was complete. A gift more precious than gold or jewelry, most said. I'd offered it up so easily.

And he'd accepted it just as easily.

Watch him, Madam Ben Ammar had said.

That night, magic sizzled in my belly, like a coal in a fireplace too stubborn to go out. Below me, the old house creaked and rattled like it was breathing, but that sound was more calming than unsettling. My magic had no reason to be so restless—or to leave *me* so restless. Bathed in the smell of the flowers I'd gathered from the floor, I lay in bed and stared at the domed ceiling of the tower room, pressing my hand to my stomach. White stars sparkled overhead in the black of the enchanted ceiling.

It was far too late to ask Xavier how to reckon with my magic.

Instead, I lit my lamp and slid onto the floorboards, now covered with books I'd borrowed from Xavier's library, all of them new to me, and some of them translations of Albilan books. Opening a translated theory book titled *Speak No Evil*, I turned to the page I'd marked with a lavender sprig.

Blessings: this type of spell is the most difficult of all. Practicing the incantation alone will not suffice. The caster must have complete control over their powers.

At this, I sighed and exchanged this tome for another, simpler one: *On the Instruction of Young Magicians*.

I tried all of the author's methods for soothing uneasy magic. Short inhalations and long exhalations. Picturing a walk through a forest. Imagining magic seeping through my head, down my spine, and into my toes, and then creeping back up.

A faint clanging sound from downstairs shocked me out of my meditations. I jerked to my feet and swept my lamp off the table, scurrying out the door. I paused in the stairwell, silent but for the thrumming of my own heart. Perhaps I'd imagined the sound—but no, there was more: clinking glass, a knife chopping against a wooden block. Xavier humming.

Descending the tight coil of stairs, I stopped on the ground floor, treading across to the kitchen. Xavier stood in the lamplight, hunched over a cauldron on the stove. A sickly-sweet smell like burnt sugar wafted through the air.

"Xavier?"

He flinched and turned, eyes wide and bloodshot, his damp hair drooping over his brow. His white shirt was neatly tucked into his trousers but stained with sweat and purple drops from the potion. He had a black leather notebook pressed tight against his heart.

"What are you doing?" I asked.

"Nothing." He shoved the book in a drawer and then leaned against it, frowning at me. "And—and you, Miss Lucas? What are you doing up at this hour?"

I took a cautious step into the circle of lamplight surrounding his workstation in the kitchen. "I was reading, and I heard noises."

He moved in front of the stove, blocking it from my view. "I'm just working on a potion," he said.

My eyes narrowed. "In the middle of the night?"

"I work during the day, I teach you in the evening, and I make more potions at night," he rattled off, his voice hard. "If you'd allow me to continue?"

He'd been so kind this afternoon. I had seen a glimmer of his old self—now I was more confused than ever.

Without waiting for my response, he turned back to his potion. He poured the contents of a small ceramic bowl into the cauldron.

I marched over to his side and inspected the ingredients on

the countertops. Leaves of peppermint, a jar of brown sugar, finely chopped sunflower petals. "I could help—"

"No!" He stuck out his arm as a barrier and I stepped away, shielding myself with my little lamp. He must have seen the shock in my eyes, for he sighed and said, "I—I'm sorry. I mean to say that no, I don't want your help."

I flinched, first at his rudeness and then at the memory of my "help" this morning. "I know I'm a menace, but you've seen me chop herbs perfectly well."

"I'm fine." He kept his back turned, swirling the long stirring stick through the thick violet liquid in the cauldron.

Be cautious around him, my magic warned, using Madam Ben Ammar's voice.

"What kind of potion is it?" I murmured.

"It's the cure I'm due to give the Council by Midsummer." Out of the corner of his eyes, for the briefest moment, he threw me an irritable glare. "Please go back to bed, Miss Lucas." Before I could reply, he pointed to the shelves with his left hand. "Fetch yourself some sleeping draught if you need it. Take a small dose."

My hands and my stomach curled tight. "Arse," I said under my breath.

Safe in my little halo of lamplight, I swept into the corridor and up the stairs, stopping a few steps up to listen. His chanting and humming resumed. A spoon clanked against the metal of the cauldron.

The sounds from below echoed in my head as I returned

to my bedroom. I took one step closer to my bed, but gasped when I caught sight of myself in my mirror. Large, peach-colored begonias bloomed in the tangled curls of my hair. One by one, I tore them out and tossed them to the floor.

Begonias, I thought. *A warning of evil to come.*

7

The next morning, I found Xavier in the kitchen, drap-ing a cloth over a wicker basket.

I stopped in the doorway, unsure if interrupting him in this task would also upset him. If his odd behavior from the night before was an aberration or the norm. Lifting his head, he caught sight of me and promptly turned pink as a rose petal. He lowered his gaze again, like I'd caught him in the middle of something unseemly.

"Good morning," he said, more to the basket than to me.

I dared to take a few steps closer. "Good morning."

He took one deep breath, and then his words came out in a flood. "Miss Lucas, I'm dreadfully sorry for my behavior last night. You didn't deserve to be shouted at like that, and I'm ashamed of myself."

I folded my arms and stood at the other end of the kitchen counter, watching his face carefully. He looked exhausted.

Hopeless. He seemed more and more to be a different Xavier altogether from the one I saw last night.

"Do you spend all your nights making potions?" I asked.

His eyes met mine once more. They were still red and surrounded by dark rings. "Yes, I work all night."

He didn't look away. So this was the truth. *And* it wasn't punctuated by another question or a biting remark or an accusation. Perhaps my luck would continue.

"Why were you hiding your work from me?"

When he glanced down, I bristled, waiting for a lie.

"This project for the Council, it's . . . delicate. They wish to keep it a secret."

Xavier glared at the wooden floor as if it had offended him. He certainly had difficulty lying. The trouble was that I couldn't tell which part of what he'd said was the lie.

"Midsummer's in nine days," I said. "It must make you anxious, having your deadline so soon."

"Yes, well." He clapped his hands and straightened his back, like a mechanical toy that had just been reset. He laid his fingertips against the wicker basket. "No time to waste, then. I have a lesson planned for you outside."

I raised my brows. "Are we having a picnic?"

"Not exactly." He lifted the basket and made for the front door, beckoning me with a jerk of his head.

I followed at his heels. He set the basket on the floor beside him and then touched one hand to the door, as he had done when he made the portal to my home.

"Wait a moment," I said. "If we're leaving, what's to be done about the shop? What about the customers?"

"I—I figured we could give our schedule a slight change. Besides, we won't be gone for more than half an hour, I promise."

A schedule change? Perhaps this *was* a new Xavier.

He bowed his head to the door as if in prayer. As before, he breathed slowly, deeply. His eyes drooped shut. Xavier sang to the door, each syllable whispered and soft and hypnotic. Then, with his chest heaving, he pulled the door open with a *click*.

Instead of the grassy hill and the muddy path leading to Williamston, the doorway led to a plain, with beautiful, leafy trees on the horizon, whispering to one another in the breeze. Stepping through onto the soft earth, I breathed in the scent of the grass, damp with dew, and felt the wind nip at my cheeks.

Fat clouds nearly kissed the smooth, green horizon. Every now and again the skyline was interrupted by jagged, brown peaks. In fact, we were standing on such a peak—after walking a good distance, I found a beautiful, glimmering lake lying at the bottom of a steep cliff.

Stray curls broke from my braid, and my skirts fluttered in the wind, but I didn't mind. I watched the sunshine twinkling on the perfect, glassy surface of the lake, more like a puddle from so high up.

"This is marvelous!" I cried, letting my voice bounce down the stone walls below.

The grass rustled as Xavier strode to my side, basket in hand. He was distractingly handsome with his long, black hair tickling his face. Was that sun or a blush burning my cheeks?

"You like it?" he asked.

"Oh, yes!"

I bent down, slipping off my glove so that the blades of emerald-green grass could caress my fingertips. I breathed in the dew and tipped my head towards the glorious, warm sunlight. The greater part of my apprenticeships had been spent indoors, which had always seemed so strange to me. We magicians were made of the earth, of sunlight and of nature itself. When I could smell the grass, feel the wind on my cheeks, the sun on my skin, hear the birds singing to each other—I felt *whole*.

"We used to take family picnics here," he said, drawing me out of my reverie. I stood up and watched him as I slid my glove back on. His skin was pale gold in the sunshine, but the shadows underneath his eyes had gotten darker. "I remembered how empty it was. No people, not many obstacles. It's the perfect place to release your emotions."

He bent down to the basket he'd placed in the grass, pulling back the fabric cover and removing a pink porcelain rabbit. He set the heavy, gaudy decoration in my hands.

"Is . . . is this a magic rabbit?" I asked, not certain if he was joking.

"There's nothing special about it at all. I find it horribly ugly, and I'd like for you to break it."

My forehead pinched. "And this is training?"

"Magic becomes restless when feelings are stifled. So you'll release those emotions in an uncontrolled way at first, letting your magic run free out here where you can't harm anyone. Then, we'll try to make your magic manifest another way—a way you choose. Over time, it'll obey you faster and faster."

I pivoted towards the lip of the cliff, many paces away, glaring at the garish, porcelain rabbit in my gloved hands. "So I'm to be . . . angry?"

"That's all."

He stood a few feet from me, his hands behind his back. His hair danced in the wind, but his pale face remained passive, emotionless. Like he had no heart at all.

The slithering fire inside my chest rumbled like thunder. He didn't understand how *evil* my magic was. It wasn't some petulant child that needed some exercise. It had nearly killed my father with a touch, and here Xavier stood, looking on serenely, watching his little experiment unfold.

"Will you express your magic, too?" I asked.

His gaze flitted to mine. "I don't believe that will be necessary."

"Why not?" I pressed. "You said not to suppress your feel-ings. That it harms your magic."

He paled and didn't say anything.

I took a tentative step closer to him. "Last night, I saw panic in your eyes. Fear. Rage. It was that potion, and me—me being so close to it. It angered you."

Xavier stared at the grass. "It wasn't your fault."

"But you *were* upset."

He pressed his lips. "Would it help your training if I were to be angry as well?"

Really, I wanted to see what hid beneath this strange, unfeeling mask of his.

"It would help me," I said.

He removed a yellow-brown teacup from the basket and walked in time with me to the edge of the cliff.

"We could count to three," I suggested.

He looked like he'd blow away if I bumped into him. His hands shook as he held the cup.

"Yes," he said, "I'll count. Focus on what angers you. Let it grow, and then, on three, let it out."

I shut my eyes.

The way the people in town used to back away from me, like I was a rabid animal. Papa spitting up those flowers—all my fault. The poison of my magic coursing through his body.

"One."

Xavier's harsh tone last night. His glare; his hand pushing

me from the cauldron. His back, turned to me. His refusal to let me help. His impossible, stubborn secrecy. How he hadn't spoken to me in five years.

"Two."

My mother, vanishing from our lives, abandoning Papa and me, leaving him working himself to the bone to support me. The harm she'd done to the community. The Councilmembers watching me, punishing me. My teachers, noting that *She may be hard to teach, like her mother.* The nights I'd heard Papa crying. The gaping hole Mother had left in our household. She'd broken my father's heart, and now I'd destroyed it with my magic.

"Three."

I hurled the porcelain rabbit off the lip of the cliff, watching it bounce and then fall apart magnificently against the rocks. Xavier's teacup joined the mess of pink shards below.

The two of us reached into the basket again—I took a pot meant for serving sugar, and he removed the teacup's matching plate.

"Shout this time," he said, his chest heaving. "I'll do the same."

I didn't wait for him to count; I hurled the sugar bowl over the edge with a grunt.

"No, shout," he pushed. "You can't hold in your anger, it'll only hurt—"

"I'm trying!" I snapped, and tossed a glass paperweight

as hard as I could. It cracked as it landed, and I took a deep breath and screamed into the abyss. The shrill sound echoed and returned to me and was then matched by another cry of pure rage. I hardly recognized the boy at my side. Red-faced, hands clenched, eyes squeezed shut. This was truly him. His fear, his forced smiles, his weariness—they were all hiding *this*.

"Why are you lying to me?" I asked.

His eyes flew open. "I'm not—"

"You are! About that potion. And you've been so guarded. Madam Ben Ammar warned me to be careful around you. Why can't you just tell me what's wrong?"

He grimaced. "It's complicated."

"It's not right of you"—I threw an old clock down the cliffside—"to keep me in the dark! Not when we've made a vow. We aren't children anymore."

He snatched a flowerpot from the pile and flicked it with his wrist like a discus. It clattered against the cliffside. "You have nothing to do with this. Not with my anger, not with my past—none of it."

I heaved a pea-green teapot over the edge with a huff. "But I did, once! I *was* a part of your past—"

"Am I obliged to bare every part of my soul to you?"

"Yes!" I held my hand against my forehead, white, angry heat pulsing behind my eyes. "We were best friends, once! We told each other everything."

He bowed his head, his eyes closed tight again, like he

was trying to remember something—or forget something. "You're right. We *aren't* children anymore. We're very different people." He set his jaw and looked at the brilliant horizon. "Why didn't you visit me?"

The words were disjointed and ill-fitting, a flower growing in a field full of weeds.

"I—what?"

Xavier turned his head towards me but kept his gaze lowered—half of the gesture of looking at me. "You must have come home to see your father, even during your apprenticeships. For holidays and such. You . . . you never stopped by."

His voice was so small. It had deepened since we last visited years ago, but there was a trace of the old cadence of his speech in there. He had always been soft-spoken.

"*You* stopped writing to me," I murmured. "I wrote to you and you never replied. I thought you hated me."

He flinched like I'd struck him.

There was more he wasn't saying. I took a step closer. "Why didn't you write?"

Xavier curled his fingers into tight, black-gloved fists. "Father was worried that you'd be a bad influence on me."

My brow furrowed. "But my magic wasn't so wild then—"

"It was your mother," he said, and this time, he dared to meet my eyes. His mouth was pressed tight.

Part of me had always wondered and feared that this was the case.

He went on, twisting the knife. "She'd . . . she'd poisoned a hundred people in the district."

I knew the case well; Madam Albright had shared the reports with me, especially when it seemed clear that they were connected to my mother.

"I've never even spoken to her," I said. I balled up my hands to stop them from trembling. "Why would that keep you from answering my letters?"

"Because I'm a Morwyn!" His voice echoed across the valley. He winced, as if startled by his own voice. "Father . . . Father forbade me from writing. He said friendship with you would reflect poorly on the family name."

Rage dripped down my back like hot wax. His father, who'd welcomed Papa and me as guests and let me borrow his books. He was just another person who saw me as no better than my mother. Even when I was a child. Even when he *knew* me. And he'd tainted Xavier's view of me, too. He'd fractured the relationship we'd once had.

My magic groaned in my ribs like an old, rusty door hinge. My mother hadn't only ruined my family. She'd poisoned the longest, truest friendship I'd known my whole life. And she hadn't even *been* here to do it. I pressed my hand against my pounding heart.

"I'm sorry, Miss Lucas, I—are you all right?"

Even in his soft tones, the title cut me, emphasizing the distance between us. I grimaced.

Wind roared through the trees on the horizon, bending their branches. I could feel my control slipping. Heat blossoming in my chest. A voice hissing in my ear. Here it was again, the proof that my magic and my emotions would always be stronger than my will; that I was meant only to cause destruction.

"Please take me home," I said, my voice quivering.

Xavier shook his head. His eyes were filled with something altogether worse than anger: pity. "We need to continue the lesson." He gestured at the swaying trees around him. "Is it your mother that upsets you so?"

He was such a fool. To try to pin all my grief, all my rage, onto *her*, when I bore so much more hurt than that. It was him; it was *everything*. My failures, my father, the years I'd lost with Xavier, and for these wounds to be opened for my own *education*?

My magic reached a boiling point, spouting from me in a scratchy, desperate scream: "Leave me alone!"

Lightning flashed white on the horizon. Thunder rumbled like rapid drumbeats, and rain fell in buckets. I gasped at the sudden shock of the cold water. Xavier stooped to riffle though the picnic basket; meanwhile, I pressed my already-damp sleeve to my eyes as I began to tremble with tears. Even the warm sunshine—the comforting source of all magic— was now hidden away by dark clouds.

I was hopeless. A simple nausea potion was too much for my magic, and now an exercise that involved nothing more than shouting and breaking things had ended in disaster, too.

"I can't do this," I whimpered, my voice drowned in the roar of the rain.

Xavier returned with an umbrella, opening it with a *pop* and holding it over my head. I instinctively drew closer to avoid the rain, but as I looked up at him, I realized there was only an inch between us. My breath made the hair resting on his collar flutter.

"You've done wonderfully, Miss Lucas," he said. He held a hand out into the rain, letting the drops sparkle against his glove. "Look at this! Your raw magic."

Resentment boiled in me. We were so close, and my heart was racing so fast, I was certain he could hear my pulse over the drumming rain. "*Your* magic, you mean. Is that what this was? A chance for you to see what sort of tricks you'll be able to perform one day?"

His proud smile smoothed into a frown. "No, of course not. And you'll recall that you offered your magic to me—"

"My circumstances were dire!" I cried. Something snapped inside of me, making more tears fall. Thunder shook the ground. My circumstances were *still* dire.

I did not regret the trade I'd made with him. But more and more, I wondered what sort of man Xavier was.

As I stood there in the storm I'd caused, I felt more certain than ever that casting a blessing on my father would prove impossible.

"I'm sorry."

I deigned to look at him. I hoped he could feel the fire in my stare.

But Xavier's eyes were soft and sad. "I wanted so dearly to write—"

"If you cared so much about your family's reputation," I said, "why have you taken me on now? Is it only for my magic?"

He shook his head, his wet hair flicking back and forth. "No, no, I—I missed you. I truly did. The past few years, they've been so quiet." Xavier trailed off, digging in his pocket. A blush bloomed in his cheeks. "I'm afraid I've already given you my handkerchief."

I laughed. I could scarcely believe myself, that I still had some kernel of levity left in me. I covered my mouth with the cracked leather of my gardening gloves and watched the rain stick to the blades of grass.

"I wish I'd been braver," he said. "I wish I'd replied to your letters, no matter what Father had said."

With all the emotion and magic that had left me, I felt hollowed out. "You were just a child. It's all right."

"No. It's ridiculous that he'd think that of you."

I wasn't certain. Perhaps that's why my magic was so uneasy, so volatile.

He touched my arm. A chill swept through me, making my heart quicken and my head lift to meet his gaze. I'd forgotten how near we were. If I stood on my toes, my cheek would have brushed against his.

"It's not *her* magic that's in you. It's your own. And you'll heal your father soon, I know it."

It's not her *magic.* I pressed my palm to my chest. My magic might not listen to me often, but it was mine. Mine to fear, but also mine to control. "Could making a rainstorm heal him?" I grumbled. My voice was small and confined as I tried to fit beneath the umbrella and not press up against his chest all at once.

"It's a start," Xavier said. He was no longer blushing—perhaps this closeness didn't trouble him as much as it did me. Yet he couldn't meet my gaze. "Tell your magic to do something else—whatever you want of it."

"It won't listen to me."

"It's worth a try."

Perhaps he was right. And if I were to put my magic to the test, this was the best place to do it.

I shut my eyes and tightened my fists. I pictured the rolling hills, the blue skies. Something tugged in my ribs, like a horse resisting its reins. I held out a hand, trying to wipe away the storm clouds—but it was as if I were trying to pass my hand through stone. The effort made my muscles quake.

"It's all right if it's something simple," Xavier said. "The hope is just for your magic to bend to you."

"What if it won't?" I whispered.

"Then we'll try again some other day." His voice was sure, comforting.

I breathed out in a steady stream. I thought of this new way of managing my magic—that I could cry without fear or shame. That my emotions were nothing to fear. *Very well, magic,* I thought. *You're with me. You're around me. That's all right. But you'll do what I tell you to.*

Under the shelter of the umbrella, I bent low to the ground, brushing the blades of grass with my gloved fingertips. As before, I dug my hands into the earth and breathed in the familiar scent, dark and dusty and warm, the smell of spring mornings and summer evenings. Papa's dirt-speckled hands. The gardens he had crafted for people in Williamston. Our own garden: a rainbow of flowers. The blossoms my magic had grown in Xavier's house. An illustration in *Waverly's*, torn at the corner from too much reading.

My anger and my magic crackled in the air around me and lifted the hairs on the back of my neck, but I let the energy flow, sending it into the ground instead.

I pictured a flower: one small white bloom. *Carpet of Snow to alleviate anger,* said *Waverly's*. I'd never seen it in person; it grew mostly on the coast of a faraway ocean. All I wanted was one little piece of proof that my magic would obey me long enough to heal my father.

My lungs filled with cool air, and goosebumps tickled my arms in cold waves. I pried open my eyes. Dotting the grass all the way to the far-off trees were little white flowers, in the shape of round, messy X's, with a little dot of green in the middle. I caressed the soft petals and removed a bloom from the grass, twirling its stem between my fingertips.

Xavier was grinning as brightly as I'd seen him do since we'd reunited. "Well done, Miss Lucas," he exclaimed. "I'd bet this was the precise flower you wanted to conjure! And it isn't even local flora!"

I wiped the sweat from my forehead with the back of my work glove, my chest heaving. "Yes, well. I only wanted one."

I wasn't certain that all the ranting and raving and theatrics was worth the beauty at our feet, but there was a new swell of pride making a home in my heart. I let it live there for a while. My magic had listened to me. For a moment, I'd been its mistress. For a moment, the worst it could do was grow too many flowers.

"I'm sorry I pushed you like that, when you said you wished to go home," he said. He rubbed the back of his neck and gazed out over the cliff at the lake below. The rain had made mist rise above the water's surface. "And you were right. I ought not to be so secretive. There are things I dearly wish that I could tell you."

I watched his profile, all sharp angles and severity, like a marble bust. "Why won't you?"

The statue's marble skin flushed pink. He rolled his bottom lip under his teeth. "I'm afraid you won't see me the same way after."

My stomach sank.

"You needn't bare your whole soul to me," I said. "I shouldn't pry like I do. Papa said they made up that saying about curiosity killing the cat in my honor."

Xavier smiled. "Mother said something similar about me. I liked to spy on her meetings with other magicians, even when I didn't understand what was happening. I just liked the thrill of it." His eyes searched the horizon, and his fond look faded away. "I love my family more than anything in the world. But I don't think I've earned the privilege of their company these days."

"Earned it? They're your family."

"Yes. And it's better that people don't associate them with me right now."

I said nothing. I yearned to hound him with more questions, but I knew that what little he did divulge was precious and would not come again for a long while.

My patience was rewarded as he said, "One day I'll tell you the story in its entirety. Not because you've earned it, but because I'll finally have mustered up the courage to discuss it."

The rain continued to patter against the earth, sticking to the flower petals like little crystal beads. A flock of geese landed on the glassy lake below.

"It's beautiful here," I mentioned.

"It is."

We stood in silence, huddled safe beneath the umbrella.

Amid the drumming of raindrops, birds sang to one another.

After a moment, Xavier said, "I'm happy to open a portal here for you another time. You could express your magic whenever you like."

I smiled, and wanted to quip, *Perhaps I'll come here when I'm cross at you again,* but looking at him, I suddenly lost my train of thought.

His eyes were so lovely. Attentive. Gentle. They were the deep brown of wood soaked by rain.

A bit dazed, I just said, "Thank you."

Side by side, watching the beauty before us, I was content to stay there a little longer, even if our lesson was over. The two of us, and the quiet—for once it felt like I didn't have anything to fear.

8

Friday came; the day when Xavier and I would sell his potions and tonics at the nearest market. While I was eager to see my father on the weekend, I felt a pang of sadness that I'd have to leave Xavier. I'd already become so used to his presence. We had grown out of the relationship we'd once had, but with every dinner spent together, with every lesson and every laugh, something new was starting to bloom in its place.

I sat on the floor of my tower room, surrounded by books and flowers. Tomorrow, I'd see my father again. Madam Ben Ammar had written to us, saying she would be there to oversee my first attempt at a blessing—and to gauge Xavier's skills as my teacher. I had much to prove to them both.

I'd flipped open three different books to their diagrams on casting blessings. One showed a man holding his hands against another man's back. One showed a witch touching both hands to a child's head. In every illustration, I noticed, the caster pressed their bare hands to the patient's skin.

I glanced down at my own uncovered hands. Would I do more harm than good if I touched him, even if I was casting a blessing?

There was a knock on the door. "Miss Lucas?" asked Xavier. "We'll be leaving for the market shortly."

I hopped to my feet, slipped on my gloves, and then threw open the bedroom door. Out on the landing, Xavier started.

"I was doing some research," I said. "Must I use my bare hands when I bless Papa? All the books say it's important. But I fear I'd hurt him again."

He hummed in thought. "I think you must—but I believe that once your magic is under control, it won't be able to harm him."

I didn't have that kind of faith in my magic. In myself. But *he* did. Maybe that was enough.

Something caught my eye—a cream-colored envelope pinched between his fingers.

"What's that?" I asked.

"I found it in a drawer. It looks like I was all ready to send it, when . . ." Xavier trailed off, pressing the envelope into my gloved hand. "I hope there's nothing too embarrassing in there."

The letter was for me, according to the messy scrawl on the front. But it was to an address in Oakridge—Madam

Albright's address, from years ago. I tore open the envelope, and as I unfurled the letter, something dropped onto my boot. I bent down and scooped up a small dried forget-me-not shaped like a bright blue star.

Nostalgia filled me to bursting as I looked at his looping handwriting. He tried to write like his father, he'd once said. *Illegibly?* I'd replied.

To My Clara, it read,

> *I miss you terribly. Father shouted at me again. I wish you were here. You would know what to say to make me feel better.*
>
> *I make so many mistakes when I do magic. Father says I'm lazy and that I spend too much time playing instead of studying. And last night, we had a party for magicians, and there were so many people, and I hated it. I wanted to hide. I asked Father if I could go to my room and he shouted at me then, too. He said I embarrass him. That I need to grow up and be brave around strangers.*
>
> *When I'm older, I don't want to be like him. But I do want to be a wizard. You could be my partner after we finish our studies. You can diagnose our patients and I'll make the potions. Father makes me greet customers now, and I know a lot of them, but I hate having to say hello to so many people over and over. They ask the same questions about how old I am or how tall I've gotten or if I've made my first potion yet.*
>
> *How is Oakridge? I'm glad it isn't too far from us. Perhaps you can come to visit for Midsummer or the first day of spring. Or*

*maybe Father will let me visit, if I do well in my studies. Do they
have a library there? Do you have time to read anything for fun?*

*I hope you haven't forgotten me. Today in the garden I found
this forget-me-not, and I thought of you, since it's your favorite.*

*Please reply with my favorite flower so I know it's really you
who's gotten this letter!*

Your friend,

Xavier

He *had* written to me. He'd wanted to. He'd missed me.
He'd *needed* me.

I remembered how he trembled when he stood before his
father. How fiercely he held my hand. We would hide together
in the garden, where it was quiet. Happy among the bluebells.

Back in the present, back on the landing, the strange, soft
perfume of flowers wrapped around me. I frowned. My braid
was loose and scratchy, and when I touched it, I found it filled
with bluebells, unwinding my tightly tamed curls.

Waverly's said that they were useful in triggering memory.
That they were markers of eternal faithfulness.

Xavier's eyes grew wide. "Did—did you ask those to
grow?"

I shook my head adamantly. "The letter asked me to send
you your favorite flowers, and—"

"And you remembered bluebells! It's no coincidence.
Your magic *is* listening to you, at least subconsciously!"

Hope rose in me like a hot-air balloon. I held the envelope tight in my hands. "Teach me something else, then! Let me try to create the portal to the market!"

He bit his lip in thought, but slowly gave in to a smile. "All right," he said. "We may as well try."

Xavier rested his hand upon the twisting iron vines fixed to a nearby sconce. His eyes glimmered, brown and gold. His small, timid smile pressed a dimple into his cheek.

"Would you like to . . . ?" He tipped his head towards the sconce.

I grinned. A nagging voice that sounded like Madam Albright told me that sliding down the stairs was not very delicate of me, but if I didn't do this now, Xavier might not do anything so silly ever again.

"You first," I said.

He chuckled and tugged on the iron fixture of the sconce. There was a loud *thump*, and the stones of the staircase melted together into one long, winding slope. He slipped off his shoes, and I gave him space, my back pressed to the door. Happiness filled me up, like the sunshine through the window had become a part of me, down to my marrow. The mischief in his eyes, the grin on his face—it was like before. When things were simpler.

With his shoes in hand, he took a few steps back and then charged forwards, sliding down the slope in a standing position.

"You didn't go headfirst!" I called down after him.

"I lost a tooth last time!" he hollered back.

I threw my head back, laughing. I remembered that day. Blood and screaming and his parents rolling their eyes and tending to their boy with a simple spell. They'd made it seem like, with magic, anything was possible.

After tucking the letter in my pocket, I plopped down at the top of the stairs, my pale green skirts puffing around me like a pastry. With one great push, I zipped down the spiral slide, letting out a peal of laughter. Wind whipped against my cheeks and tugged hair from my braid, and then suddenly, in one heart-thrilling moment, I was tumbling across the stone floor.

Somewhere over me, Xavier asked, "Are you all right?"

I lay on my back, watching his tall, far-too-pale figure spinning above me. The world shifted back into focus as my heart skipped delightedly against my ribs. "I'm fine!"

His hands met mine, and he pulled me to my feet, both of us trying and failing to smother laughter. I smoothed my hair down and dusted off the wrinkled bustle of my skirt, discovering that I was covered in yellow rose petals. Which had come from nowhere.

Yellow roses—for friendship and happiness.

"Well," said Xavier, "I suppose I didn't need to help you up. You *rose* all by yourself."

I looked to the petals. And back to him. He had the proudest grin on his face.

He'd made a pun. The boy who insisted on calling me *Miss Lucas* and bowing when he greeted me in the morning had made a *pun*.

I rolled my eyes. "You aren't funny."

His smile didn't fade. "But you're laughing."

"It's a pity laugh."

Xavier touched a hand to his chest. "Thank you, Miss Lucas, for being so charitable towards my poor sense of humor."

I tried and failed to tamp down laughter. "More of that and I'm going to step on your foot."

With a laugh, he strode around me, far away from my muddy boots.

I followed him into the shop. Beside the front door were several crates filled with potions, powders, perfumes, and teas. I'd always liked market days with my teachers—meeting new people, getting to see the other vendors and their wares, tasting different foods. But it appeared Xavier expected we'd have many customers to serve. I doubted he would want me wandering about in search of sweets.

"Have you been to the market at Plumford before?" he asked.

"With Papa, a few times."

"Good. Now let's see if you can create a portal there."

I took a calming breath, squeezing my apron in my hands. "How do I start?"

"Can you remember how Plumford looks?"

I nodded.

"Place one hand on the door and the other on the handle," he instructed. As I did so, he added, "It helps to center you. You need to feel certain. Confident. Feel the metal in your hand. Your palm against the wood."

With my magic, I was rarely confident. I closed my eyes and focused on my breath, like Madam Ben Ammar had taught me. Breathing in steady as a flowing stream, breathing out like extinguishing a candle.

"Imagine the marketplace," said Xavier. "The smells, the sounds, the sights. Make it real in your mind."

Papa had taken me there for my birthday when I was small. It had been bitterly cold that day, but I hadn't minded. Now, standing before Xavier's door, I could smell the spiced wine, the sugared plums, the ginger, the caramels. I could hear vendors shouting to one another. Children squealing as they chased each other across open, grassy spaces. The canary-yellow tents and the bright red peppers imported from far away.

"Hold on to that image," he said, "and now imagine the idea of journey, arrival, completion, and success. Speak those ideas aloud."

I glanced back at him, unsure. "You sing when you make your portal spells. In Albilan."

His eyes twinkled. "Ah, yes. It's a trick my mother taught

me. I think of her songs. Of our trips to visit my grandparents abroad. You, erm, don't have to sing, of course. You just have to think about traveling."

"Right," I murmured. Staring back at the deep green of the door, I thought of my own travels. Papa and I couldn't afford to leave the country; we hadn't even been to the capital city. But we'd had other adventures. Memories I held just as close.

"Journey." The off-key songs I'd sung with Papa as we rode a wagon down to my very first apprenticeship in Oakridge.

"Arrival."

The long, tight embrace I'd given him just before I stepped into Madam Ben Ammar's house. My heart squeezed. What I would give to embrace him like that now!

"Completion."

This time, I pictured something that hadn't come true—not yet. I would speak the blessing, and Papa's heart would be healed. He would wrap his arms around me without fear of being harmed.

"Success."

The thrill of three days before—opening my eyes and seeing a field of beautiful, foreign flowers. Flowers I'd *wanted* to be there. The warmth of pride in my chest. For a few minutes, I'd successfully controlled my magic.

I knew I'd be able to do it again.

"Now, specify—imagine that you're there. And when you're ready, open the door," said Xavier.

I could picture it so clearly. I knew full well that when I drew back that door, we would be square in the middle of a bustling, fragrant market, and Xavier would beam with pride.

Eagerly, I tugged it open.

Outside was an empty field.

"I—I don't know what I did wrong," I said.

He peeked over my shoulder. "It was your first portal," he said. "You should be proud of yourself. On my first try, the door opened onto a great black abyss."

"It may as well be an abyss."

He squinted at the horizon and covered his eyes as sunlight streamed into the shop. "Wait a moment. Do you see that tree over there?"

I peered at what seemed to be a scraggly bush in the distance.

"That's the old oak tree outside of the market!" He laughed and touched my arm.

Before I could register this, he drew back and glanced hastily at the doorway. "You took us too far! The market is over there!"

Looking closer, I could see the shop tents, like little blots of paint. Even from here, I could hear merchants shouting and see shoppers bustling around. I gasped. "I did it?"

"You did it," he said, nodding.

I whooped with delight and hopped in place in front of the open door. "Bravo, magic!" I declared. It fizzled through me, making tiny sparks flit in the air around me like fireflies.

"I would never diminish your accomplishment, Miss Lucas," said Xavier, "but it would be better if we were a bit closer to the market itself. Do you mind if I make a new portal?"

The embers vanished at once. "Well . . . no, I don't mind, but I don't want you to exhaust yourself." Thanks to his sleepless nights, the smallest spells were leaving him breathless and weary. When he made portals before, he'd nearly swooned from the effort.

He frowned. "I can handle a simple portal spell. It'd be better than carrying our wares all that way, anyhow."

Before I could open my mouth to argue, he drew the door shut, pressed his forehead against it, and softly hummed. When he opened the door again, we were flooded by sounds and smells. Noisy vendors, parents shouting at their children to behave, and horses whinnying. Fresh pastries, smoke, and wet grass.

But I was distracted from all of them as Xavier fell into a nearby chair, holding a trembling hand to his temple. Blood dripped from his nose.

"Xavier!" I exclaimed, fishing his handkerchief from my pocket and pressing it beneath his nose. He blushed from his widow's peak to the sliver of skin between his chin and his collar and then nudged my hand aside, holding the piece of cloth on his own.

"I'm fine," he grumbled. With his eyes still shut tight, he waved an arm towards the stack of boxes. "Take that roll of canvas outside. There'll be an empty space in the grass."

I tore my eyes from him and reluctantly picked up the long, tightly rolled canvas.

"It's already enchanted," he explained, voice muffled beneath the handkerchief. "Unroll it like a picnic blanket and it will form a tent on its own. Go on—don't worry about me."

I did as he said and carried the fabric out the door, stepping onto the damp grass. The longer I stayed behind, the more embarrassed he was bound to be.

Alone for a moment, I basked in the sunshine, imagining that I was simply part of the crowd of people milling around me. Folks tended to their stalls, wrapping glassware or boxing up beautiful pastries, while others peeked into tents or left with gifts or the week's shopping. The sound of people chattering was as lovely and familiar to me as birdsong. Shoppers nodded courteously as they passed, and a child waved as she rushed after her mother.

They couldn't see the magic burning inside of me. They couldn't see the mistakes I'd made, or where I'd come from, or that I had a witch for a mother and a father I'd cursed. I was ordinary.

Well, except for the enchanted tent I carried in my arms. I glanced back behind me, where Xavier remained in a chair, his handkerchief still pressed to his bloody nose.

Stepping away from the door, I whipped the canvas like a bedsheet. It fluttered back to the ground, and with a stiff *pop!* it became a tent with three walls and a pointed roof. Peering within, I found a counter, three shelves for merchandise, a coatrack, and even a clock hanging from the tight, ivory-colored fabric. On the outside, a wooden sign hung over the mouth of the tent: *Master Morwyn's Magical Goods and Services.*

"Quite an enchantment for someone who gets a nosebleed from a portal spell," I muttered.

I wondered if something had happened to him to leave him in such a state. If his emotions had become so stifled that his magic was starting to retaliate against him. Otherwise, it didn't make sense. The Morwyns were known for their power. *Xavier* was known for his power. That he'd become an official wizard *and* a Councilmember all at the age of fifteen was unprecedented. Why, then, was his magic ailing him this way?

My stomach dipped.

The day the Council had first visited me, they had proposed a spell that would bind my magic, weaken it—and make it painful to use.

Xavier had protested.

Perhaps his magic had been bound, too. Perhaps *that* was why he had been so ready to make the vow, to take my magic as payment for his help. After being burdened with stifled, agonizing magic, he would finally have the opposite problem. Unbridled power.

But why would the Council bind his magic at all?

I walked back to the emerald-colored doorway standing isolated in the grass. Xavier was still in his chair, one hand against his nose, the other on his forehead. The worrying half of me urged me to make certain that he'd be all right. My much-quieter common sense told me to leave the poor man alone. I listened to the latter and wordlessly carried the crates of potions out into the tent.

As I placed the bottles and boxes along the shelves inside the stand, Xavier appeared, slouching, in the entryway.

"I'm sorry about that," he said.

I lowered my gaze to the grass. "I confess I'm worried for you." When he opened his mouth, I held up a hand. "You have to admit it's cause for concern, seeing you tire so easily." My own magic tightened its grip on my stomach. "The Council bound your magic, didn't they?"

He stared unblinking at me and worked his lip beneath his teeth. Then he said, "I—they . . . yes."

Despite the summer heat, ice seemed to fill my veins. Along with pity, I felt the smallest light of hope. If they had done this to Xavier, perhaps his magic used to be like mine. Perhaps I wasn't the only one like this.

"Was it as wild as mine is?" I asked. "Did they bind it as a means of controlling it?"

He gave a stiff nod, locks of dark hair drooping over his eyes. "Yes. My magic . . . gave me a great deal of trouble."

So he *was* like me. Xavier the powerful, the prodigy, the certified wizard—his magic had been wild, too.

If he had only told me sooner, we could have found comfort in this shared misery. Maybe he was too ashamed to speak of it. *What kind of Morwyn am I?* he'd say. *To have uncontrollable magic?*

"Well," I said softly, "I'm sorry the Council put you through that."

Xavier waved a hand. "It's nothing."

"It's not nothing," I said. "I know what it's like to have disobedient magic, and it's awful. Humiliating. Frightening."

I curled my hands against the countertop. I feared my magic enough as it was. If every attempted spell made me feel as weary as Xavier looked, I was certain I would dread using my magic. Even if every enchantment was for a good cause. "I think you have every right to be frustrated."

A half-smile began to dawn on his face. "Thank you, Miss Lucas. You're very kind."

Then he gasped and turned on his heel. An old lady in a worn orange shawl smiled meekly up at him as she tugged on his sleeve.

"Oh, excuse me, young man," she said. "I was just looking for the wizard."

He laughed, holding a hand to his heart. "That would be me. Come in—my apprentice and I will help you."

9

Customers were even more eager to visit our little tent than they had been at the storefront.

An old man thanked me profusely for the potion I gave him to ease his back pain. A woman bought an anti-inflammatory tonic and fondly mentioned that Xavier's mother had helped her prepare for the birth of her daughter.

It seemed that everyone who came had a story about the wonders the Morwyns had done. Standing there with Xavier, I allowed myself to imagine a world where *I* was responsible for helping so many people. Where I could see the faces of the people I'd healed, and shake hands with them.

After packing up a box of salves for a harried family of five, I stood in the entryway, watching the father pull their wooden cart full of groceries. The three daughters skipped along, laughing and singing at the top of their lungs. They reminded me of Xavier's sisters. When I looked back at him, at the pain in his eyes, I could tell he thought the same. "All this talk of the great Morwyn family," I said, entering our tent once more. "Does it feel like you're living in their shadow?"

Xavier's shoulders slouched as he leaned forwards on the countertop. "I—I'm proud to be one of them. I love hearing how they've helped people, but I just don't think I'll ever . . ." He trailed off, shaking his head. "Never mind."

"You can tell me," I said. I walked across the grassy floor to face him at the counter. I reached over, giving his arm a light nudge. "You have seen a great deal of *my* emotional turmoil. I won't tease you, I promise."

He ran his pale fingers through his hair and kept his gaze averted. "I miss them very much. I really do. But . . . it's good, too. Being away from him."

My heart fell. "You mentioned your father in that old letter. I take it your relationship with him is much the same?"

The shadows under his eyes seemed to darken as he looked at me. "This isolation was his idea, you know. He said I needed to be free from distraction while I worked on my assignment for the Council." Xavier laughed humorlessly. "I wonder what he'd think if he knew that I've taken on an apprentice."

I bristled. "We already know what he'd think."

Xavier's pupils shrank. "Curse me, I'm sorry, I didn't mean—it's not you, Clara. He doesn't like anybody. He doesn't like *me*."

If he were someone else, I might have pushed against this. But I knew his father's temperament. And I knew what it was like to have a parent who did not want you.

"I'm sorry," I said. "I wish I could have been there for you. For all those years."

"So do I."

Silence stretched between us, heavy and sad. Thinking of the time we could have spent together ached, almost as if something had died between us. Like we were mourning some life we never got to live together.

But we were together now.

I smiled at him. "You called me Clara," I murmured.

Our eyes met. Despite the secrets, the shyness, the outbursts—there was such tenderness in his eyes. They'd always been so kind.

"Is that all right?" he asked.

"Yes."

He nodded. "I suppose that makes us friends."

I laughed so loudly that he jumped. "We've only *now* become friends?"

"I just meant that we're more than just apprentice and teacher. I—I don't mean *more* than. That is to say, I—" He stopped himself mid-ramble. His cheeks were growing pinker and pinker, and my heart fluttered. "I should get us something to eat. Together. If you want."

"That sounds nice." I patted the countertop. "I'll keep an eye on things while you're gone."

"All right."

"All right."

Still blushing, Xavier lifted his jacket off the coatrack. He lingered in the entryway of the tent for just a moment. "I don't regret it, by the way. Being your teacher." He smiled at me. "Father's wrong about you. You're an excellent witch."

Before I could reply, he darted out of the tent.

Standing behind the shop counter, happiness glowed within me like a warm ember. More and more, the boy I remembered was reappearing. And my magic was listening to me. There was hope for the both of us.

I'd helped multiple customers today, all without incident. The tent was standing tall—nothing broken, nothing burnt down. And tomorrow, I would go home and heal my father. My magic was strong, and I was even stronger.

I looked up to see a man enter the tent.

He quietly perused a shelf of potions, inspecting the label of one and then another.

"Can I help you, sir?" I asked.

The man's movements were slow as he set aside the phial and approached the counter. His shoulders sagged, and his eyes—they were ringed with shadows, just like Xavier's. The comparison made my heart twinge.

"I—I've heard that there are potions to help with . . ." He lowered his gaze, his soft, scratchy voice even gentler as he finished. "Melancholy."

At once I thought of a textbook from one of my

apprenticeships, *The Art of Modern Healing*. In the very back was a small addendum with just a couple of paragraphs, titled *Issues of the Heart*. There were a few terms I'd memorized in case I was to be tested on such things.

Melancholy, the book had said, *marked by fatigue, an uncharacteristic lack of interest in activities, a fogginess of the head, numbness of the spirit, and extended periods of sorrow.*

But my teachers never spoke of such matters. Problems of one's heart were outside our domain, the Council said.

It was why potions like Euphoria were illegal.

It was why potions like Euphoria were sought out.

I swallowed. "There . . . there is no treatment for that, sir. I'm sorry—"

He carefully removed a few golden coins from his wallet and placed them on the counter. "Please, ma'am. I've heard others say that such a potion exists. Is . . . is this enough? I could pay you more later."

Madam Ben Ammar had asked me to be on the lookout. To report to her about this potion. Could it be spreading *here*? Could someone be selling it close by?

"Is it Euphoria you're looking for?" I asked him.

His eyes widened. "Yes. Do you have some?"

I hid my hands under the counter as they began to shake. "That potion is contraband." My magic chanted *her* name in my ear, and the hair on my neck stood on end, like someone had crept up behind me. "Who told you about it?"

He swept his money back into his wallet. His eyes had grown dark and somber. "Never mind."

Xavier stepped into the tent, carrying two small paper bags in one hand. He must have seen the worry on my face, for he frowned at the man between us almost immediately.

"I'm the owner of this shop, sir," said Xavier. "I apologize for my absence—is there something I can help you with?"

He shook his head. "I don't think you have what I'm looking for."

The hopelessness in his voice chilled me.

"Do we have anything at all to help with melancholy?" I asked.

Xavier blanched. "I—I'm sorry, sir. Such a potion doesn't exist. Not yet, anyhow—"

"It exists," the man said coldly. "I *know* it does."

He stormed past, making his way towards the entrance of the tent. But Xavier stopped him with a hand on his shoulder.

"Are you referring to Euphoria?"

My heart leapt into my throat. I supposed it made sense that he knew about this potion, as a Councilmember. But I thought of Madam Ben Ammar's distrust of him, and of the night he'd spent shielding the bubbling cauldron from my view. Surely he'd not sell something illegal. Let alone in the middle of the marketplace . . .

"Yes." The customer's shoulders trembled. His eyes glimmered with tears. "Please, I . . . I need help."

"It's not safe to take it. After a few days—"

"I know," he murmured. His eyes seemed so distant, so empty, like he was barely there at all. "Please, sir."

"I'm sorry," Xavier told the man again. "There's nothing I can do. And I beg you—do not go looking for this potion. The happiness it gives is not worth the consequences."

The man stared wordlessly at the two of us and then, as silently as a ghost, he slipped out of the tent.

After a moment, Xavier draped the flaps of the tent shut. He slumped onto an old crate in place of a chair. "Curse me, what a mess."

"Should we tell the Council?"

"I'll send them a note," he mumbled.

The silence was thick and heavy around us. Xavier stared blankly ahead of him, his posture sagging with fatigue—and sadness.

"You know quite a lot about Euphoria," I said.

He nodded slowly. "My project for the Council—I'm trying to make the cure for its effects."

My brow furrowed. "Madam Ben Ammar said it was a joy potion—and something about dandelions?"

"Well, it . . . it's not really *joy* they're feeling. If it was meant to treat melancholy, it doesn't succeed. It just gives the patient a false sensation of happiness for a day. On the second day, it escalates to delirium, and dandelion buds grow on the skin. By the third day, the final stage, the dandelions start to blossom, and patients enter a dreamlike, sleepwalking state. We've been unable to wake them."

"What—what is done for them then?"

His voice grew softer and softer. "They can eat and drink, thankfully, but they've lost themselves. They cannot hear or see anything but the dream playing itself in their heads. Their bodies are there, but their spirits, their very selves, it's . . . it's like they're gone."

No wonder he was so adamant against its usage. And no wonder Madam Ben Ammar was hunting it down with such fervor. It was dangerous indeed, and more so because it was so desirable. A potion that provided instant escape.

"What is the Council doing about this?" I asked.

"We're working on creating the cure."

I frowned. "We?"

"Other Councilmembers are experimenting with possible cures, too. But I differ because I have a deadline. I'm to create the potion by Midsummer."

This was absurd. "You—you're *sixteen*. Why are you expected to—"

"Because I'm a Morwyn," he said.

"Was this your father's idea?"

"He's the one who proposed I be given the deadline. He wants me to make it before anyone else does."

I hated it. I hated him having to carry such a burden. It was cruel, placing the fate of others' lives and happiness in the hands of one boy. All for the sake of family honor.

"And what if you fail?" I asked. "What would happen then?"

He lifted his head, his gaze meeting mine. "If I fail, the Council will take my powers from me."

My eyes widened. "What? But—why would they do such a thing? And with your powers already bound—how are you supposed to make such an important potion under those conditions?"

"It's all very complicated," he muttered.

I understood his anxiety. His sleeplessness. His doubt. A future without magic loomed before him. That is, until I came along.

No, I thought, *he is not exactly the same Xavier as before.*

"Is that why you wanted my power?" I asked, my voice growing fainter. "Because you fear you'll lose your own?"

He exhaled, not out of frustration, but softly, like he could finally breathe easily again. "Yes," he said.

So this was the truth. He was so confident that he'd fail, he had already begun to plan what he'd do if he lost his magic. "Do you have so little faith in yourself, then?"

"It's hopeless." He shook his head, not daring to face me. "I've spent every night for three months on this project. I give one draught to a patient; it doesn't work; I try another—it's useless. I make the perfect potion; I can *feel* my magic buzzing inside of the bottle . . . but it does nothing. It's a fool's errand."

I couldn't bear to see him so hopeless. I approached him, my fingertips grazing his arm. "Unless . . ."

He frowned at me. "Unless?"

"I could help you with the potion," I said.

His furrowed brow smoothed. "It's very kind of you to offer," he said softly. "But you have important matters of your own. You need to bless your father."

"I could learn to train my magic by helping you," I said. "I know I'm a bit of a mess myself, but my magic is starting to listen to me. And besides, you could use some help, even if I'm just chopping ingredients."

He bit his lip until it turned white. "What do you want in return?"

I frowned. "Nothing. If we really are friends, like you said, then this is precisely the sort of thing a friend should help with."

He slowly, cautiously smiled. "Thank you. On Monday, I'll show you the work I've been doing."

"Not tonight?"

Xavier shook his head. "You've had a long week, and you've worked very hard. Spend the night at home. I'll be by in the morning to oversee the blessing."

He turned to the paper bags beside him, lifting the smaller one and holding it out to me. "Here, I, erm. I got you a present. To wish you luck. Not that you'll need luck, but . . ."

Inside the bag was a pair of black cotton gloves,

embroidered with intricate vines and flowers. I gasped delightedly and immediately tore off my gardening gloves to try on these new ones.

"They're absolutely lovely," I cooed, admiring them by the light of the lamps hanging in the enchanted tent.

"I thought you deserved something better than the gardening gloves," he said.

He had confidence in what I'd learned; in what I would do. Perhaps he truly believed that I could succeed in blessing Papa.

Of course he's happy, said my magic. *If you succeed, he'll have strong magic again.*

My throat pinched tight, and my hands fell to my side. "What will happen, then, if I succeed in blessing him? With the vow, I mean. Will my power just zip right into your chest?"

He averted his gaze. "I'm not certain about the zipping bit, but . . . yes, essentially."

For a few, bright hours, we had felt like partners. We had worked side by side, been equals. When we were children and played at being magicians, we'd pictured having our own shop together: *Morwyn and Lucas.*

I never could have imagined then how such a simple wish could become so complicated and impossible.

10

That evening, when Xavier opened the portal into my house, I was too excited to even say goodbye.

I leapt across the stoop and into the sitting room, my heart incandescent. The second I saw Papa in his chair, hunched over a book, I barreled towards him, tossing aside my carpet bag. Upon catching sight of the finger-length scars along his cheek, though, I paused a few inches away from his chair.

He popped up his head, his eyes owl-like behind his reading glasses. "Bless me seven times, look who it is!" Wedging the book between the cushion and the arm of the chair, he uncurled himself and stepped towards me, his arms open wide.

I stepped back, my pulse racing. Papa's face fell. "I'm sorry," I said. "It's just . . . it's my magic. I don't want it to hurt you."

Cries of pain and images of azaleas filled my mind.

But Papa swept up my hand, kissing the back of my glove.

"Your Greatness," he said, bending in a stiff bow.

I reveled in the title, even if it wasn't accurate just yet. When I laughed, evening light streamed even brighter through the windows, the color of tiger lilies.

You're giving away that title, my magic whispered.

"You—you look better," I said, trying desperately to drown out that awful voice.

"I feel much better. Robin has done wonders for me. They—Robin!" called Papa over his shoulder. "Come see; a witch has come to call!" He turned back to me, his button nose wrinkled mischievously as he examined my gloves. "Oh! These are new. And sophisticated."

I squeezed his hand tight, feeling every callus through the fabric. "Xavier bought them for me."

He raised his eyebrows. "Have you been a model student, then, to be getting gifts from your teacher on your first week?"

Something about the playful look in his eyes made my cheeks grow warm. "I've been working hard."

Robin slid into view, their hands pinned on either side of the kitchen doorframe. Clearly, they had been practicing transformation spells. Their face was more angular, their hair was now midnight blue, and they were much taller than before, having to stoop to get through the doorway.

"Oh! Hello, Miss Lucas," they said breathlessly. They pivoted towards Papa. "Did you say Madam Ben Ammar was here?"

"I meant Clara, actually," Papa said, beaming at me. "What sorts of things have you learned, my dear?"

I shook my head and held his hand as tightly as I could—the safest bit of affection I could give him. "That doesn't matter," I said. "*You're* the one I've been fretting over!"

Papa scoffed. "You needn't have. Robin takes great care of me."

I bowed my head to the apprentice magician and then helped Papa back into his chair. "How has he been, Robin?"

"You're talking like I'm not here," Papa mumbled.

Robin joined us in the living room with a potion case. As they unlatched it, they smiled at me. "Truthfully, he seems better and better as each day goes by."

"And still you won't let me leave the house!" Papa rolled his eyes.

Robin blew out through their nose in a sort-of laugh. "Madam Ben Ammar demanded bed rest, and if I can't keep you to your bed, I'll at least keep you to your house, Albert."

They removed two bottles from the potion case and showed them to me. "He stopped coughing up the flowers by the end of Monday. But he has stomach pains," they explained, "so I give him this every six hours, and he's been eating very carefully—"

"Soup, Clara," said Papa. "*So* much soup."

Robin grimaced. "I thought it best."

"Don't listen to my father. I'm certain you're an excellent caretaker."

"I can't remember the last time I had a cherry tart," Papa said wistfully.

I felt like two people at once, loving and hating his lack of sincerity all at the same time. I sighed heavily. "Perhaps your warden will allow you to do some baking," I said, raising a brow at Robin.

They nodded. "That should be all right." They riffled through their box of potions, procuring a little pad of paper. I smiled, remembering something.

"Madam Ben Ammar makes you take a lot of notes, doesn't she?"

Robin looked at me over their shoulder, their dark brown eyes crinkling. "She's very thorough. But it's a good habit for me to get into."

"Do you like working with her?" I asked. My time with her had been lovely—I deeply regretted how I had failed her.

Robin beamed. "Oh, yes, I love it. She's patient and smart, and she's transgender like me. It's nice to have a mentor who understands me so well."

My heart lifted. Robin needed Madam Ben Ammar, and the two of them were a good fit, teacher and student. "That's wonderful," I said. "She's probably the smartest person I know."

"Absolutely." Their eyes twinkled in a fond smile, and they turned back to their potion case. They hurriedly marked something down in their notebook, and then muttered,

"Oh!" before handing me another bottle, filled with bright orange liquid. "Your father's been taking this, too. For his heart."

There: the sting of reality that dampened all of the niceties and undercut Papa's quips and jokes. He lowered his gaze to the floor.

"How is it?" I whispered.

"It's doing better," Robin began, but this was not nearly enough to soothe me. Magic grasped my stomach in its fists.

You're killing him, it said.

"It's the poison from the flowers. His pulse is still weak," said Robin, like that was their fault, not mine. "He can get lightheaded, and he's too pale for my liking. But that's why I've tried to keep him sitting down as much as possible. I check his heart rate every hour, at least."

I sank onto the sofa, watching my father's face and the dark shadows around his eyes. I bunched my skirts in my hands and found breathing to be far more difficult than usual.

Robin knelt down at Papa's side, checking their pocket watch as they took his pulse. "With the flowers gone, it's only their poison that's concerning us now. But even that seems to be getting better and better." Their cheek dimpled with a hopeful smile. "Time and magic can do wonders." Robin gave Papa's hand a little pat. "Excellent heartbeat."

Papa grinned. "I try." He turned towards Robin, playfulness making his eyes wrinkle at the corners. "Now then, my one and only daughter has finally returned home from her long apprenticeship with a faraway wizard. You don't suppose she could handle me on her own, do you?"

I rolled my eyes. "Don't try to get rid of your healer so soon. You're welcome to stay the weekend if you'd like, Robin. We'd love to have you."

They chewed on their lip. "I *ought* to stay," they said. "I usually visit my mothers on the weekends. It's been a while. But I don't want to leave you here—"

Papa waved his hand in a shooing motion. "Go back to Queensborough! Clara will be able to tend to me."

I failed to have as much confidence as he did. "What does Madam Ben Ammar say about his progress?" I asked.

"She stopped by two days ago and thinks he's doing better. Since it was your touch that afflicted him, I assume that as long as you keep your hands covered, everything should be all right."

I looked down at my gloved palms, thinking of the blessing, of the illustrations. Of a future where my magic wouldn't hurt anyone. But that future didn't exist, really. There was only the possibility of losing my magic forever. At least then, it would no longer be able to hurt anyone.

"Master Morwyn has been teaching me to cast a blessing," I told Robin.

They nodded. "Madam Ben Ammar told me so. I'll admit I was surprised . . . blessings are extremely advanced. I've only seen Madam Ben Ammar perform one once. She was exhausted afterward."

I grimaced. "I know it's a complicated spell. But it seems to be Papa's only hope of recovering fully."

One more day. Papa nestled against the back of the worn chair, his eyelids drooping.

"Are you all right?" I asked him.

He moved his head in a slow nod, smiling. "Just a little tired, that's all."

Robin set the two potions on the table, the green for his stomach and the orange for his heart. They touched the bottle with the orange potion. "A spoonful in the morning and before bed," they instructed. They dug through their jumbled-up potion case and procured Madam Ben Ammar's sky-blue card. "I know you'll see her tomorrow, but . . . just in case."

I nodded. Papa's eyes were closed now, and he was breathing heavily—but not labored breaths, just sleepy ones. "Do you think we'll be all right on our own for the night?" I whispered to Robin.

"I *can* stay."

Seeing Papa asleep in his chair like this reminded me of lazy Sunday afternoons. I'd read to him from a novel, he'd fall asleep, and I would scold him for not paying attention.

Robin deserved a moment of peace like that. A moment of quiet with their family.

"You should go see your mothers. You've done so much for Papa and me." My eyes prickled with tears. I took a deep, steadying breath. "Thank you."

Robin wished me farewell with their robust handshake. They took their potions and their bag over the stoop and through the door, now attached to a living room in Queensborough. As soon as it closed behind them with a *click*, Papa's eyes flew open. He giggled.

"You're a child," I said, squeezing his hand.

He leaned closer to me with a conspiratorial grin. He may have been feigning sleep, but his eyes were truly tired, darkened with shadows beneath. "So, what do you think of young Master Morwyn? Has he changed greatly?"

I curled into a ball on the sofa, my knees against my chest. Thinking of Xavier—it made cold seep into my bones. His secrets. Our bargain. The fact that if I were to succeed in blessing Papa, Xavier would get all my magic. What then?

"Clara?"

I blinked. "What were we talking about?"

"Xavier. Do you like him as your teacher?"

My finger lazily traced figure eights against the worn, wine-colored fabric of the sofa. "He's a good teacher. Very knowledgeable. He helped me research blessings. And he's kind, too. He doesn't get cross with me when I do something silly. I don't think he *can* get cross."

No, that wasn't right. Brewing up that potion in the

night, his eyes blazing as he threw out an arm to keep me from touching the brew. His skin, flushed as he bellowed and hurled porcelain off a cliffside. He did have anger inside him—like a seed that was only just starting to grow. What had caused it? What had planted it there? And would he ever tell me about it?

"You're awfully pensive," Papa noted. He reached to touch my hand, but I pulled away. He sighed. "You used to shy away from me like that when you were younger. You didn't care much for me for a good two years."

I winced. "I was ten. I was foolish."

"No. You were just trying to impress your friends. And I was a little . . . overbearing." He rolled his eyes at himself. "And now I've been cursed with an overbearing daughter!"

"Don't say 'cursed,'" I snapped.

His blue eyes widened. "I didn't mean that, blossom—I'm sorry."

I wondered if he *did* mean it, just a little bit. If he hated how much I worried. If he thought I still hated him like I had when I was younger. If he thought I was wicked like my mother.

"Clara Lucas," he chimed, singsong, to get my attention. I lifted my head again. "Just tell me this. Are you happy with Xavier?"

I laughed—sort of like how Xavier did: soft and one-note.

"Oh, yes," I said, the answer spilling out of me before I

could even think about it. I'd laughed and smiled with him more than I had in any other apprenticeship. "He's horribly shy and afraid of everything. Afraid of himself, like he's worried he'll say something foolish at any moment. He blushes more than I do." I snickered and smoothed the stray hairs of my braid. "He likes to hear about me, about you. And he'll tell the most ridiculous jokes—we spent ten minutes making puns about potion ingredients one day, and he had the silliest grin on his face. . . ."

Like the one Papa was wearing now. His eyes were like the sky, bright and clear. "You're fond of him!"

It was as if he'd doused me in cold water. I sputtered. "He's *my teacher*, Papa!"

"He was your friend first."

I sat further back into the sofa. "Things are different now."

"But you like him?"

"Yes, he's a kind man. A good friend. A partner." The word made me think of the dreams we'd had as children, and of our secret, dark promise, marked by the ring on my hand.

Papa counted on his fingers. "Kind. Friend. Partner. All good traits in a husband."

"Papa, *please!*"

"If you're worrying about rushing things, don't—I married your mother after only a few months."

Magic fizzled from my stomach straight up my spine. There she was again, in his words, in his memories, in my magic, in my blood. She was an invasive plant, her roots

150

spreading all throughout my life. Thunder shook the house.

Papa yelped in surprise and clutched at his chest. I leapt up from the sofa at once, carefully draping a blanket over him and feeling his pulse.

"Is it your heart, Papa?"

He shook his head and took a long, calming breath. "Just the thunder. I'm only startled."

His hand reached for me, and when I took a step away from him, his forehead furrowed.

"Rest for a bit," I murmured, striding towards the kitchen. "I'll make you some scones and tea for when you wake."

From behind me, he called out, "Have I upset you, dear?"

"No, no," I said, striving to keep my voice light.

Alone in the kitchen, the voice of my magic slithered about in a tight spiral in my head.

You have her power in your veins. You're too weak to control it. You'll never save him. You'll have no mother and no father.

I gripped the side of the table in the kitchen, my arms quaking and tears beading in my eyes. The voice was loud, so insistent and so *true*. But I'd worked hard to tell my magic to be quiet, to use the lessons I'd learned with Xavier and all the others.

You are going to heal your father, he'd said. There'd been such conviction in his voice. His eyes, certain and warm.

He hadn't been lying. He believed in me.

In the maelstrom of my magic, I clung to this fact as tight as I could.

11

Confidence is important, Xavier had said.

I had to believe that my blessing would work.

The next morning, I waited in the living room shortly after the sun had risen. With trembling fingers, I flipped through the pages of another book about blessings. I pressed my palm against the words as if the paper was Papa's heart.

I shut my eyes and imagined him healthy, exuberant, playful. I'd lift my hands off his chest, and he'd spring to his feet, grinning and declaring he could run for miles.

The knock on the front door startled me back into reality.

I leapt up and pulled back my hair and smoothed my skirts before flinging open the door.

Madam Ben Ammar was there, smiling. "Hello, dear."

I curtsied to her and then let her in. The disappointment sitting in my chest was so odd. I was delighted to see her, of course. And I shouldn't have been *missing* Xavier; I'd spent all week with him, for goodness' sake.

Madam Ben Ammar set aside her potion case and then unfastened her long, gossamer cloak, the color of the night sky. As she slung it over our coatrack, she said, "Robin told me you sent them back to Queensborough."

"We both thought they could use the day off," I said.

"Without a doubt. The poor dear works so very hard." She winked at me. "I'm sure you've taken excellent care of your father in Robin's stead."

Doubt and magic whispered horrible things to me as I led her to a chair. *You're nothing,* it said. *Your father will die because of you.*

"Papa's in his room, sleeping," I said, loud enough to smother the whispers of my magic. "He had a stomachache last night. I suspect I spoiled him by making scones. And his heart . . . he looks so pale, and sometimes I can tell he has a hard time staying awake." I wound and unwound the end of my braid.

Madam Ben Ammar's gloved hand reached out and stilled me. "You're a smart student and a caring healer, as you have been ever since I first met you. I *know* you're taking good care of him." She retracted her hand into her lap, quirking a dark eyebrow. "And where is Master Morwyn? Does he intend for his student to perform a blessing on her own?"

Her tone was cold—as it always was when she spoke of him.

"I'm certain he's on his way. Why . . . why don't you trust him?" I asked her softly.

She stared at the ceiling the way some people did when they prayed. "Let's just say I find it very strange that, while I had to practice as a witch for five years before joining the Council, he only had to practice a month. I respect the decision of my Council, but—"

"The Morwyn name," I murmured. For a moment, I felt a twinge of jealousy. If I had been born into the Council's favorite family, would I have been a witch by now?

Madam Ben Ammar curled and uncurled her hands into fists. "He is entitled, immature, completely full of himself, and absolutely reckless."

"He has not behaved that way towards me," I said.

She snapped her head back down, leveling her gaze. "He has demonstrated such behavior to the Council, Miss Lucas."

"How?" I pressed. "The whole Council seems to hate him, and you told me to watch him closely! But what am I supposed to look for? The man is as ruthless as a rose petal. Well, he did shout at me once, but it was only because I interrupted him working on the Euphoria cure."

Her eyes searched mine. Her jaw tightened. "That's what he said he was making?" she asked.

I nodded. "A man came to him asking for Euphoria at the market, and Master Morwyn was adamant that he did not carry it. He told me he was working on a cure, and that it was due on Midsummer, or he'd lose his powers."

"That's all he said?"

"Yes." My brow furrowed. "Is . . . is there something you're not telling me? Is there something *he's* not telling me?"

"I'm a Councilmember, Clara. I'm bound to secrecy." She gave my hand a gentle squeeze. "I find it odd, that's all. That he would take on a student, even in the middle of his assignment. And that he chose a pupil with such strong magic."

She thought he was using me.

And she was right.

"I asked for his help in the first place," I said softly. "We grew up together. I knew him—I know him."

"I know that. But everyone changes with time." She sighed. "I understand that you want to defend him. I don't know what your feelings are for him—"

"He *is* a good teacher," I said, my face aflame. "He's helped me with my anger. My magic, it—it hasn't hurt anyone all week." I smiled sadly. "I know it's still wild. But he gives me hope. That perhaps I *am* strong enough, good enough to heal Papa. For the first time, I feel like I could use my magic well."

For the first time, too, I knew that my magic would not last. This boy who had helped me had also accepted my power as payment. Once he had my magic . . . what would he use it for?

There was another knock on the door.

"Excuse me," I said to the witch.

155

When I pulled open the door, Xavier was there, the entry-way to his shop behind him. He had his potion case in one hand and a bouquet of red peonies in the other.

This was the boy the Council could not trust?

"Good morning, Clar—Miss Lucas," he said. He stiffly held out the bouquet. "This is for you."

"Oh!" I accepted the wilting flowers and stepped back, allowing him in. A blush brightened his cheeks, and he worked his lip under his teeth.

He gestured to the flowers. "Red peonies—"

"—for good luck," we finished in one voice.

"Master Morwyn," said Madam Ben Ammar, making the two of us jolt. "Is this a social visit, or have you come to oversee Miss Lucas perform the blessing?"

"I—I'm here for the blessing." He bowed to Madam Ben Ammar. "Good morning, Your Greatness."

She gave him a curt nod. "I trust you've been treating Miss Lucas with the utmost respect and care."

Xavier glanced back to me for just a moment, the blush fading fast from his face. "I endeavor to that end, madam."

The door to Papa's room creaked open. He shuffled into the hallway, wearing his nicest, buttercup-yellow shirt. He smiled at Madam Ben Ammar and Xavier.

"So many guests! I hope Clara's gotten you tea," he said.

I hastily tucked the flowers into a vase already occupied by hydrangeas from our garden. "I will in a moment, Papa." I spun back to Xavier. "Do you think I could attempt to perform the blessing now? With you here beside me?"

He nodded. "As soon as you're ready."

I'd *never* feel brave enough. My magic was armed with frightening images of all the ways the spell could go horribly wrong. And if it worked, my power would now belong to Xavier. Someone I wanted so dearly to trust—perhaps against all evidence to the contrary. But I said, "Let's begin."

Papa sat on the sofa, looking up at the three of us. His eyes were wide and hopeful. He was like so many people I knew who thought of magic as a marvel, as a miracle—not a monstrosity, like it was for me.

I placed myself beside him, my fingers shaking as I plucked off my gloves. Out of the corner of my eye, I saw Madam Ben Ammar's hands clench tight against the fabric of her gown.

"Clara?" asked Papa. "Have you got a vow on your finger?"

My heart somersaulted. I pulled my hand back into my lap, as if doing so could somehow make Papa forget he'd seen it. "I—it's nothing, Papa. I made a promise. . . . I made a promise that . . ." I fumbled for words and glanced back to Xavier for rescue. His skin had gone ashen.

"We—we gave each other a pledge to stay friends, no matter what," he said. "To commemorate our friendship. That's all."

Well. It was much better than what *I* could have come up with.

Papa grinned. "How charming!"

Madam Ben Ammar cleared her throat. When I turned

back to her, her eyes were still narrowed at my hand. "Shall we proceed, then?"

As best as I could, I concentrated on the blessing, letting the words run through my head over and over.

"First, harness an emotion," Xavier instructed from behind me. "Combine it with your confidence and with your magic."

Harness an emotion. Looking into Papa's eyes did the trick.

They were bloodshot; watery; tired. My magic had kept him from sleeping well. It likely was plaguing his thoughts as much as his body. Sorrow and pain and hate sent magic coursing white-hot through me like water from a burst dam. We needed all of my magic, now; all of its strength.

"I need to touch your heart, Papa," I told him. Magic rose in me, filling my head like steam. I clung to it. I encouraged it with images of Papa breathing well, of any poison left in him leaving his body.

He unbuttoned the first two buttons of his collar, leaving a little exposed skin just over his heart. He was freckled, like me.

I swallowed a lump in my throat and felt my nose prickle. "I'm scared," I whispered to him. "What if my touch hurts you?"

"It could also heal me," he said softly. He smiled. "Your magic is *yours*. *You* tell it what to do."

He was right. I was its mistress.

"Focus on your breath, Miss Lucas," Xavier meekly piped up.

I breathed deeply, catching my father's familiar old-leather-and-cinnamon smell.

"Papa," I said, willing every syllable to be full of my power and my love for him, "may every beat of your heart be filled with peace, confidence, and freedom."

My magic swirled inside of me but did not leave me. I sat taller. Screwed my eyes shut. Concentrated. "May every beat of your heart be filled with peace, confidence, and freedom." Each time I repeated the words, they felt truer. My hands trembled like leaves fluttering in the wind. I pressed them against Papa's skin.

He flinched and inhaled sharply. I drew back at once, feeling the heady, exciting warmth drain from me.

Xavier took a step closer. "Are you all right, Mr. Lucas?"

"I'm fine," he said, his eyes squeezed shut. "Perhaps—perhaps it's just the strength of the spell." He took a few quick puffs of air and then nodded. "Once more."

I glanced back at Madam Ben Ammar. She nodded once, but kept her fingertips pressed to her lips. She was staring at my hands, eyes wide with fascination.

"You must tell me if I'm hurting you," I said to my father. Tears clung to my eyelashes. My chest felt like it had been knitted shut. "I couldn't bear it if I did."

He managed a smile even with his tired eyes. "When you

were little, you made me soups of wildflowers and spare ingredients from the kitchen. And I ate every bit of your 'magic potions.'"

"I probably made you ill."

"I'm here now, aren't I?" He grinned, his eyes and nose crinkling just like mine did. "To what else should I credit my long life and good health?"

I loved him so. Hearing his voice and realizing that I had lived nearly two decades knowing him, calling him *my father*, filled me up. I was warm and cozy, delight spreading through me like I'd drunk a cup of warm tea—ginger; our favorite.

I clung to that feeling, imagined it as a rope I could climb—up, up, up, into a better future.

Magic sang through my body, vibrating in my wrists and then buzzing in my fingertips. I exhaled, letting the thrill and the hope and all of it exist peacefully within me.

"May every beat of your heart be filled with peace, confidence, and freedom," I wished for him. I could see the two of us, as if I was standing above us, watching—I felt years and years older, looking down on us, feeling content and knowing that all was as it ought to be. That, yes, I would succeed, I had *already* succeeded in blessing him.

I touched my hands to his chest one more time.

He lurched back. I kept my hands still, as he'd asked. His eyes clenched tighter. His brow wrinkled. His face grew redder and redder. His jaw clamped shut.

You're hurting him. You're killing him. You're only made for destruction, my magic whispered.

My heart quivered in my ribs. My grip on the rope was slipping. I took a breath to center myself and said, "M—may every beat of your heart be filled with peace, confidence, and—"

He cried out. I stumbled back and fell onto the floor.

Two large pink welts glowed on his pale chest, in the shape of handprints. Tears beaded in the corners of his eyes as he coughed: an ugly, heavy sound. He pressed his fist against his mouth.

Madam Ben Ammar slammed her potion case onto the table and flipped it open, tearing the cork out of a bottle.

Papa drew his hand from his mouth. Three pink petals lay on his palm, covered in spit.

I didn't even have a second to apologize before she gave my father the potion he needed. Xavier darted into the kitchen and returned in moments with a bowl for Papa.

Nothing had changed. Just like the week before, he coughed up more flowers, moaned at the pain in his stomach, grew paler by the second. And judging by the marks on his chest, I'd just made him worse.

After several, agonizing minutes of expelling flowers, he lay back on the sofa. Madam Ben Ammar gave him a sleeping draught to help him rest and recover. As he drifted off to sleep, I covered him in the thin blanket, my gloves on once

161

more; where they would forever be, I vowed.

"Miss Lucas?"

I gaped up at Xavier, who offered his hand. He helped pull me to my feet and didn't let go. The gentleness and the sympathy in his dark eyes made me wish for the days when I could hug him tight and cry into his chest. But such a thing would be improper now that we were grown.

"Don't blame yourself," he said softly. "This was your first attempt."

"But I hurt him."

His lips pressed in a line. "You didn't mean to."

I gave a bitter laugh and stepped away from him and from Papa, who was fading away to sleep. "I'm not certain my intentions mean very much."

"Young man?"

Madam Ben Ammar stood by the front door. The Morwyns' shop lay beyond the open doorway.

"I think today has proven that your lessons with Miss Lucas are an exercise in futility," she said.

She spoke to Xavier—but I could not help but feel responsible. *I* was the difficult pupil. *I* was the failure.

Hopeless, my magic hissed. *Monster. Murderer.*

Xavier grabbed his potion case but didn't bolt through the door like I thought he would.

"I disagree," he said.

My mouth fell open.

Madam Ben Ammar's hand tightened on the doorknob. "Excuse me?"

He stood at my side and kept his head high. "I believe in Miss Lucas. She's already shown immense growth in a very short time. She's made a portal spell and grown a whole field of flowers—"

"It's not Miss Lucas I have doubts about," she hissed. She glanced back to Papa drifting asleep on the sofa, and then stepped closer to us, her sharp stare upon Xavier. "If you think I believe that nonsense about a vow of friendship . . . !"

My stomach sank clear through my feet. "Madam, I assure you—"

"Master Morwyn, explain this *now*," she whispered.

Xavier wrung his gloved hands together. "I—I can't."

"You can't or you won't?" She raised a black eyebrow. "Shall I write to your father?"

Panic flashed in his eyes. "No!"

I stepped in front of Xavier. "He's telling the truth, Madam. We hadn't seen each other in years. It—it was my idea."

She looked past me and watched Xavier, unblinking. "I'll ask one more time. Why did you choose Clara as your pupil?"

When his dark eyes met mine, my heart skipped, half out of fear, and half out of delight of just being *seen* by him.

"Miss Lucas needed help," he said, his voice soft and weak. "I'm not more qualified than anyone, I don't have much experience . . . but she needed me, so I was there."

Her jaw was clenched tight. She tipped her head towards the door. "Go home."

Xavier fished around in his pocket, procured a golden calling card, and passed it to me.

"Goodbye, Miss Lucas," he said, giving a little bow of his head before he ducked back into his shop.

Madam Ben Ammar snapped the door shut behind him and pressed herself against it. Her brown eyes sparkled with tears. Was she angry? Disappointed? Afraid? To think of her as anything other than fearless was chilling.

"I know you lied for him," she said. "Please, Clara, tell me—if you're being coerced—"

"I agreed to the vow," I said, each word hot and dry and painful in my throat. "I came up with it in the first place; I did it so that he'd help me hea—"

Suddenly, my tongue began to burn like I'd eaten a hot pepper. I gasped, pressing my hands to my mouth. "I'm sorry."

"So it's a vow of secrecy." She chewed on her lip thoughtfully. "Just tell me this. Is he asking you to do anything illegal on his behalf?"

"No," I said.

"Are you in danger?"

I didn't know. I didn't *think* so. Xavier's service as my teacher had come with a dangerous condition; a price that still pained me to think about. But he'd also *guaranteed* me that he would help me heal Papa. Perhaps I'd finally be strong enough the next time I attempted a blessing. Perhaps I'd finally be good enough.

I shook my head. "I'm safe. I promise you."

She sighed. Her eyes were shining and mournful. "Then you've made your bed, Miss Lucas, and I'll let you lie in it. I won't interfere with your lessons. At least not until I have proof that he's been irresponsible."

Madam Ben Ammar held her hand against my shoulder. "I'm going to fetch Robin and inform them of the situation. The two of us will continue to treat him."

"What . . . what about the next time?" I asked. "When I attempt to bless him again, what if I make him even worse?"

"It's possible, Clara. Your magic is . . . unusual. I cannot tell you if you'll succeed in healing your father, or if he will ever be healed."

My eyes stung with tears as I looked back at him, shivering, grimacing, *in pain*.

Her gloved hand against my cheek shocked me into looking at her again. "Because it was your strange, unique magic that caused this, you are the only one who can cure him," she said. "But you, little tempest, have a brave and noble spirit. I can see that you fight your magic every minute. Don't surrender to it. No teacher can create the strength that I already see in you."

The tears in my eyes made the lights in the room dance. "When I said the blessing, I could *feel* the magic in my hands. It felt as if I really was helping him."

"Perhaps you were. Perhaps you only need a little more time." She faced the door and wrapped her gloved fingers around the doorknob. "I'll be back in a minute."

As she stepped through her portal into a house on the outskirts of Queensborough, I sat on the floor beside Papa, my head propped against the arm of his sofa.

"Are you leaving for Xavier's on Monday?" he asked, his voice groggy with fatigue.

In the vase by the window, the peonies Xavier had given me glowed in the sunshine. "Yes," I said. "Did . . . did you feel any better at all, Papa, when I was saying that blessing?"

"I did . . . I felt this great, warm sense of hope spreading in my chest. This sense of elation. It felt like gold."

I turned back to him, my eyes narrowed to scrutinize him, to be entirely certain he wasn't lying just for my sake. He smiled, his hand against his chest. He looked . . . nostalgic. Thankful.

"Maybe it'll work next time," I whispered.

"I'm sure of it."

He dangled his hand off the edge of the sofa. I clung fast to it.

"Something's different," he said, his voice soft, distant, and dreamlike. "You seemed more confident. And hopeful."

He hummed a little laugh. "I think it's your teacher."

My blood chilled. I longed to tell him all I knew—and all I didn't—about Xavier. About the secret arrangement we had made.

And how I was wondering if I would regret trusting him.

12

With Robin by my side, I helped Papa feel better, bit by bit. His bedside table was filled with potions and cups of tea. But our Sunday was only an echo of what our time together used to be. He felt dizzy when reading, so I read aloud to him. He didn't stay awake for very long. We couldn't spend our evenings side by side cooking wild meals. He couldn't sing with me, because he'd start to cough up flowers. So Papa rested, and Robin and I debated what sort of soup we could give him that would still have the slightest bit of flavor. And I couldn't sleep soundly because I knew all of it was my fault.

On Monday, I didn't want to leave him—but at the same time, I worried that the longer I stayed, the sicker he would become. When I wished him farewell in the morning, he was too drowsy to even tease me about Xavier.

I burned Xavier's card and stepped into his shop, leaving

behind my guilt and worry. They wouldn't help me now. I needed to be entirely focused on training my magic.

Xavier was in the kitchen, hard at work on a potion even at this early hour.

"Good morning," I called to him.

He spun on his heel. His eyes lit up at the sight of me. "Oh! Welcome back. How's your father?"

I grimaced. "Fair. Robin helped me tend to him, but he is . . . in poor health, still. I can't say that my attempt at the blessing worsened his condition, but . . ."

Xavier grabbed a stack of books from the countertop and carried them over to the table in the entryway. "I'm entirely confident in your ability to bless him. I believe you'll succeed the next time you try."

I prayed that his hopes weren't misplaced. I wondered if *my* hopes were misplaced.

"About Saturday," I murmured, "with Madam Ben Ammar . . ."

By the blush on his cheeks, he remembered the encounter as vividly as I did.

"Yes. Thank you for defending me, by the way."

"She suspects something of us. Of you." I'd give him another chance. One more chance to let me into the past he'd locked me out of. "Are you ready to tell me why?"

Xavier winced. "I—I'm not. I can't. Not now."

Disappointment sat in my chest, cold and hard as a stone. I

169

wanted to know him. I wanted to *trust* him.

But there were more important things.

"Never mind, then," I murmured. "It's Papa that matters now, more than anything. What is it that you've been studying?"

"Well—you. Your magic, rather." He cleared his throat and fanned out the books. *Magical Anomalies*, read one. *The Training of Untamable Magic*, read another. I supposed he'd read the same books when his own magic gave him trouble. "Normal magic is fueled by emotions and then controlled by the magician. They order their magic about with their words and their intentions. One usually masters their magic after years of training, but *yours* . . . it does not work that way. When you made a potion, it overflowed. Instead of treating nausea, it took away my sense of taste altogether. When you asked your power to make one flower, it made thousands. When you tried to make a portal, it landed far away from its destination."

"You're listing my failures. We're well aware of them."

He held up a finger. His eyes were bloodshot and wild—he'd probably been studying all weekend—but there was hope sparkling in them. I gave him back the floor.

"I have a theory," he said, "that your magic is somehow doubly stronger than the average person's. It's not that it's stubborn, or that you're incapable, or anything like that. If the magic of a normal magician were a dog to be trained, yours would be like a bear. Or an elephant! It's as if we, your teachers, the Council, are trying to fit something house-sized into a snuffbox." His shoulders slackened. He caught his breath, and then smiled apologetically. "Does that make sense?"

I paused, letting the information settle in. "Then it's not a lack of competence?"

"No, not at all!"

It was risking a lot, placing so much faith in me. It was risking Papa's *life*. "How can you be so sure?"

"Because your spells *do* succeed. You asked your power to make you Carpet of Snow, and it did. You asked it to make a portal, and it did. It's too strong, not just for you, but for any person."

Perhaps it would be too strong for him, too, once he had taken it for himself. I thought of the band on my finger. A question lingered in my mind and pulsed like a headache—*Is he doing this research just to learn about the new powers he'll gain from me?*

"You have a *gift*, Clara," he continued. "If we can learn to manipulate it, you'll be able to make potions twice as easily, twice as fast. You could cast stronger spells with half the energy."

I leaned back against the counter. "Need I remind you that this gift of mine also led to my father's illness?"

He said nothing to this. When I lifted my head again,

I found him wringing his black cravat in his hands. "I'm sorry," he said.

I squeezed my eyes shut. "I fear . . ." *I fear my magic will kill him.* But I could not speak such a thing aloud. My magic might make it so. Instead, I breathed, slowly, steadily, calming myself and my magic. "I fear what could happen, should I attempt a blessing again."

He pressed his hand to his lips in thought. "Saturday, you were trying to bless him with the full strength of your magic—your inordinately strong magic. I wonder if that could have led to some adverse effects."

"O Great Master Morwyn," I said, "I enjoy academia as much as you, but *theory* is not going to help me free Papa from the bond of my magic. If my power is so strong, I need to know how I am supposed to master it." I gestured to myself. "I am not very formidable."

His brown eyes glimmered. His cheek dimpled as he smirked. "I'd like to put that to the test."

"What sort of test? Shall I be breaking any more porcelain animals?"

"No, no. This one will be very easy. You're going to make me a potion."

I laughed. "What will be different this time?"

"When you speak to your magic, I want you to imagine you are pouring half of it into the cauldron. I want you to tell it to exert itself very little. Just a bit of your power should work just as much as, say, all of my strength."

I crossed my arms tight around my middle and glanced to the large shelves, filled to bursting with potions of every kind. The worst scenario played out in my mind—my creation flooding the shop, spilling down the hill and then sweeping the nearest town away in a magical deluge.

I took a mop from the pantry and pressed it into Xavier's hands.

"Just in case," I said.

"I trust you."

Magic writhed in my chest, preventing me from even a second to bask in the compliment. *"Please."*

He conceded and sat down in a chair facing the store counter. He looked like a strange sort of prince, in a simple throne with a mop instead of a scepter.

You're going to hurt him, said my magic.

"It'll be all right," I whispered back.

Xavier raised a brow. "What was that?"

My face burned. "I was wondering what sort of potion I should try to make."

"Make whatever you'd like," he said. "This is purely experimental." He pointed to the shop sign in the window. "Actually, first try to spin that around. Tell your magic to move it. See it in your mind with complete confidence. But use as little strength as you can."

The simple task seemed impossible. I stood at his side,

holding both hands out towards the little rectangular sign in the window.

Turn, I told my magic. *Don't spin it. Just a gentle turn.*

I flicked my index finger.

The sign pirouetted once, twice, clattering against the glass, and then halted, the word *Open* facing us. Joy fizzled through me like sparks. I gasped delightedly.

"Very good," he said. "Now for the potion."

As I took a step back, my boot crushed something soft and pliable. Dozens of lilies of the valley had sprouted between the floorboards.

"Oh, dear," I mumbled.

"Ignore it. Just a by-product of your magic. An innocuous one at that." He smiled, sweeping a sprig of the little bell-shaped flowers off the floor. He twirled it back and forth. "You don't need to be ashamed of your power. You're happy. Let your magic celebrate with you."

I nodded and marched to the shelves containing ingredients in bottles. So many potion recipes were etched in my memory after years of training. I glanced to Xavier for inspiration. With a free hand, he rubbed his eyes again, then his neck.

A potion to alleviate headaches. It was simple, one of the first that every student learned.

Each of the patient's senses had to be addressed and balanced.

I filled the kettle with milk and set it on the stove. From the pantry, I procured a large tin of cocoa, the kind that doubled as a lovely morning treat and an excellent solution for menstrual pain. I combined the cocoa with scoops of coarse-grained sugar, which were often mixed with fine-smelling oils and prescribed to smoothen skin or alleviate joint pain.

In a mortar, I ground forget-me-nots into a bright blue paste. According to magicians of old, blue was the most soothing color to the eye. I added the paste to the sugar and cocoa, and then poured lavender oil over the mixture. With a mixing spoon, I worked the scent into the sugar, stirring in a smooth figure-eight motion. Out of the corner of my eye, Xavier shifted in his chair. I paused. I'd nearly forgotten he was there, and that he'd been watching me all the while. The thrill of combining a potion had had a hypnotic sort of pull—but so did looking at him.

He had his hands folded against his knee, the mop lying on the floor beside him. His eyes were dark and ringed with shadows, but they were attentive, even so. His black hair draped over one eye. I found myself longing to brush it back. He'd tucked my lily of the valley behind one ear.

He sat taller in the chair, lifting his brows. "Do you need me?"

I blushed. What was I in the middle of doing? "I, erm, I need to sing over this potion."

A grin spread across his face. "Shall I cover my ears?"

I laughed too loudly and then bowed my head to avoid his gaze. "I'm a wretched singer, so for your own safety, you probably ought to."

"I'm not here to judge you." When I opened my mouth to protest, he amended, "Well, not your singing, anyhow."

This was the man Madam Ben Ammar had warned me to be wary of? I kept my back to him, shaking my head. What a contradiction he was. Silly. Gentle. Open. *Severe. Reckless. Secretive.*

With my head down, I sang a soft reel to the ingredients. I lifted the kettle off the stove with a rag and poured the hot milk into the bowl. The more I stirred the thick periwinkle potion, the louder I sang. Mixing like this reminded me of making bread with Papa. Singing reminded me of how he said we both sang like cats, and how we sang all the louder for it. The beat of my heart quickened to match the rhythm of the song.

Magic and light rushed down my arms and into the bowl, faster and faster. Xavier remained in my periphery like a lighthouse on a dark, endless horizon. Well. If lighthouses dressed in all black.

Steady, I told myself and my power. *I only want a little bit. I don't need all of you. Half of your strength—and then half of that. And then only a pinch of that.*

I breathed in the sweet, calm scent and smiled.

Happiness rested warm in my heart as joyful memories

floated through my mind: Papa spinning me in a clumsy dance; beating Xavier in foot races as a child. Magic made my pulse jump—I thought of the stray dog that I always passed outside of Williamston, bouncing and wagging its tail, eager to play with me.

I see you, I told my magic. *I'll let you play a little. But you'll do as I tell you.*

The ideal spell for this was a palindrome—something involving thought; something balanced. Speaking clearly, calmly, coaxingly, I told my magic, "Verily, I speak peace of mind and tranquility and ease; ease and tranquility and mind of peace speak I, verily."

The little bowl quivered in my grasp, but not like the quaking of the earth—the simple buzzing of a bee. My eyes flew open, and I grinned at it. The thick, pale blue potion remained in the confines of the bowl.

"I—I think I've done it!"

Wide-eyed, Xavier rose, leaned his lanky form across the table and gazed into the bowl. He took a silver teaspoon and filled it up before taking a careful taste of the potion. But I bit my lip all the while—when Papa sampled my cakes, I didn't have to fear that he'd somehow drop dead because of a mistake.

His eyebrows rose. "It's perfect," he said.

"How does your head feel?"

He shrugged. "It doesn't hurt at all!"

"And—and there are no side effects?"

Xavier shook his head. "I feel fine."

I lifted my arms in the air, jumping and shrieking like I'd just won a prize.

"Congratulations," said Xavier. "This is quite an accomplishment. It's an excellent sign."

He held out his hand for mine to shake it, as if this were a business transaction. As if this were not the promise of a good and noble future for my magic. Of hope for my father.

I slid my gloved hand into his grasp, watching a flush creep up his neck as we touched. My heart fluttered. His warm, gentle eyes. The elegant slope of his nose. The dimple in his cheek. The soft pink of his lips. Did he find me as lovely as I found him handsome?

Please, I begged, *hold my hand just a little longer.*

It fit so nicely with his. My black glove looked beautiful against his moon-white skin—marred by the black bands on his ring finger and his thumb.

"What was your second vow?" I asked abruptly.

The color drained from his face. He withdrew his hand and slipped it back in his pocket. "It's nothing important," he said with a soft, forced laugh.

"Master," I said, "such secrets make me think ill of you."

"The truth would make you think worse."

My chest tightened. "I made you a vow." I curled my gloved hands into fists. "I deserve to know what you've done."

178

"You *do* deserve it." He sighed, gazing at the countertop, at my hands. "I wish it never happened. I wish I'd never been the person I used to be."

My fingers brushed his elbow. His eyes grew wide.

"Talking about it won't make you that person again," I said.

He stepped away from me, his hand against his arm, right where I'd touched him. The distance, as well as the sorrow sparkling in his eyes, made my heart ache. "I'm sorry," he said. "I can't."

13

Not long after my magic lesson, customers began filing in, and they didn't stop all day. I barely spoke with Xavier about anything outside of business. We were far too busy prescribing tonics for coughs, pills for minor transformations, teas that could alter the pitch of one's voice, lotions for rashes, even oils that would change the client's hair color.

Just as Xavier was telling an incensed customer that no, we did not carry allergy potions in any other flavors, the front door flew open with a loud *bang*.

A dark-haired man stood on the porch, his hands on the shoulders of a girl about my age. She was smiling, laughing, stumbling into the shop. When she swung her head in my direction, my heart fell.

Bright yellow dandelions were blooming on her right cheek.

Euphoria.

"Your Greatness," said the man behind her, "please, there's something wrong with my daughter!"

Wide-eyed, Xavier strode around the counter to address the other customers in the shop. "Everyone, I'm afraid I'll see no other patients today. Please come back tomorrow."

I shepherded the grumbling customers out the door and onto the porch, not even bothering to apologize—my eyes were fixed on the stranger and his daughter. Xavier carefully helped the girl into a nearby chair and spoke to her father in frantic, hushed tones.

I closed and locked the door behind the final exiting customer. When I whirled back around, I found that the girl had bounced to her feet, and was now humming to herself, gazing at the ceiling.

"Emily—Emily, sit down, darling," said her father, reaching for her wrist.

"She can't hear you," Xavier murmured.

The man whipped his head towards Xavier. "What—what do you mean? What's happening to her?"

"It's because of a potion. Euphoria." Xavier kept his head bowed, almost as if he was addressing the floor instead of the man. "It's a heart-altering potion. The kind that magicians aren't permitted to sell. As you can see, magic that manipulates emotions can lead to unanticipated results."

As Xavier spoke, Emily danced along to music none of us could hear. She lifted the hem of her gown with

181

dandelion-covered fingers and spun in place.

"An illegal potion?" asked her father. He approached Emily, trying to grab for her arm, but she slipped away, giggling and dancing.

"Yes," said Xavier, "it gives the user the feeling of being in a dream. They feel blissful, but they cannot see or hear anything around them, nothing but the dream—"

"Beautiful!" exclaimed Emily, her hands held high. She grinned and twirled around. "Beautiful, beautiful!"

Her father took hold of her arms, giving her a gentle shake. "Emily," he said, "Emily, *wake up*!"

But she wouldn't. She sang a strange, slurred song, and then started to laugh until her face turned red.

I raced to Xavier's side. "We have to do something."

He nodded frantically and then darted to the back of the shop. In a moment, he was back in the entryway, slamming a wooden potion case onto the nearby table. With trembling fingers, he unlatched it and chose a phial filled with midnight blue liquid. He turned to the man, grimacing. "Sir—Mister . . . ?"

"Kinley."

"Mr. Kinley," said Xavier, "I'll need you to restrain your daughter. Sit her down right there." His dark eyes met mine. "Help hold her down. The potion gives her nearly endless amounts of energy."

Anxious magic writhed in my chest as I looked at her. Her

182

father tried to hold her hands behind her back, but she wriggled and squealed like she was a little child playing a game.

The two of us taking an arm, we sat her down in a chair and held fast as she squirmed and pushed against us. Xavier tremulously tipped the contents of the blue potion into her mouth.

"What is that?" asked Mr. Kinley. "A cure?"

"Possibly." Already, Xavier was reaching for another phial. "I am in the process of trying to create an antidote for the effects of—"

"Create? You mean this is *experimental*?"

By the sound of Emily's laughter and the dazed smile on her face, the first potion had failed. So Xavier tried another.

"There isn't a cure, not yet," he explained, carefully cupping Emily's chin and pouring an orange potion into her mouth. "But perhaps one of these will—"

"What kind of wizard are you?" snapped Mr. Kinley. "You're supposed to help her!"

Emily thrashed beneath my grasp. She grinned at something I couldn't see. Tears and sweat matted the dandelions on her cheek.

"I—I can try another potion," said Xavier as he reached for his case.

"No." Mr. Kinley released his daughter's arm and knelt before her seat, taking her hands in his. "Sweetheart, please, *try* to wake up . . . I know you can break out of this."

Xavier shook his head. "Mr. Kinley, it's magic. Powerful magic. She can't—"

"My daughter is a good girl!" His voice shook with rage. Emily didn't notice—she just sang to herself, an empty, distant look in her eyes. "She wouldn't fool around with illegal potions!"

The shouting, the fear, the uncontrollable singing of the girl—it stirred the magic within me, humming like an angry swarm of bees. My chest was tight, my heart hammered, and it ached all the more as I looked at Xavier. At the anguish gripping him. He trembled, silent and pale, as the desperate man shouted at him.

It was too much for me. And my magic was a hair's breadth from unleashing its power onto all of us.

I acted without thinking. In a blink, I left the foyer and was standing in the shop, riffling through our potion cabinet. I found a box labeled *For Sleep*, grabbed a pill, and ran back into the entryway.

Mr. Kinley was berating Xavier for his incompetence when I said, "Sir?" The older man turned to me with a frown.

I held the pill out on my open palm. "Can I give this to her?" I asked over the sound of her laughter. "It'll just help her fall asleep. I don't want her to hurt herself—"

Mr. Kinley took the pill and popped it into Emily's mouth. Her laughter stopped in an instant. Her face fell. Her head drooped, and her posture started to sag. Both her father and I caught her before she could collapse to the floor.

"Come—come, there's a sofa in the salon. She can lie there," said Xavier.

The room adjacent to the shop was a small salon, with a fireplace and several chairs, as well as a sofa. The Morwyns used to entertain important guests in this room. It was also a place where, on a normal day, customers needing a consultation could wait and have a cup of tea before Xavier would attend to them.

Today, Mr. Kinley laid his daughter out on the crimson velvet of the sofa. The misery in his eyes as he set her down—I knew it so well. It was the same sort of hopelessness I felt as I watched Papa shake with coughing fits. It must have been even worse for Mr. Kinley, having no magic, being completely at the mercy of magicians . . . only to find that those magicians were helpless, too.

Xavier appeared in the doorway of the salon, carrying a new, larger potion case. "Sir," he said, "it will not address your daughter's mental state, but . . . if you'd like, I can remove the flowers on her skin. I have seen other patients, and the dandelions don't seem to grow back, since they're only superficial—"

"Just . . . don't hurt her." Mr. Kinley pulled up a chair beside his daughter and cradled her hand in his.

Xavier set his supplies upon the nearby tea table: a bottle of numbing ointment. Forceps. A jar of salve with the label

For Wounds, the same he'd used on my father. While he carefully applied the numbing ointment to her cheek and her arms, I moved a chair to sit beside Mr. Kinley.

"When did you notice that Emily was acting strangely, sir?" I asked.

Mr. Kinley pulled his gaze from his daughter. The whites of his eyes were turning red. His shoulders were slouched. His dark hair clung to his forehead with sweat. "She hadn't gotten out of bed for a while . . . and then my husband and I found her in her room in the middle of the night, dancing and smiling, laughing like a hyena. No matter what we said or did, she couldn't stop laughing. I suppose she couldn't hear or see us, like you said. . . . She was like that for hours. At first, we thought that it was just a game of hers. But it continued this morning—and there were the dandelions, too. That's when I knew it was connected to magic."

Xavier carefully snipped off the heads of the dandelions on her cheek. He pulled on the stems with his forceps—thankfully, they weren't attached deeply. He dropped the stems and their short, stubby roots into a glass jar beside him.

"I just don't understand," murmured Mr. Kinley. "She doesn't behave like this. She doesn't buy illegal potions." He squeezed her hand. "She—she won't get in trouble, will she?"

"No, Mr. Kinley," I said. "But . . . where could she have gotten this potion? Did she travel anywhere recently?"

"Not that I know of. She helps in the bakery, goes to the

library . . . nothing more."

As little dots of blood began to bloom on her skin, Xavier painted the yellowish salve onto her cheek and onto her arms, after he'd cleared them of flowers, too. Then, with the utmost care, he cleaned her face and wrists with a cloth, until her skin was smooth and clear.

"I'm afraid that's all I can do, Mr. Kinley," he said, his voice heavy with fatigue. "She will wake in a few hours. By my estimations, she is soon to enter the third stage of the effects of Euphoria. She'll be able to eat and drink and sleep, but she won't be as energetic as she is now. She'll be so enraptured by her dream that she won't want to leave her bed."

Mr. Kinley gripped his daughter's hand tight. Tears welled in his eyes.

"I don't want you to have to carry her all the way home," murmured Xavier. "If it would help, I can open a door directly there; to her bedroom, even."

Mr. Kinley's eyes grew wide. So did mine. The last time Xavier had made a portal, he'd fallen horribly ill. With a gentle hand, I touched his arm. "Xavier, I could—"

"It's no trouble," he said, drawing back.

"If . . . if you could," replied Mr. Kinley. "We couldn't even begin to repay you."

"I need nothing but your help." Xavier stood tall, cleaning his hands on a handkerchief. "Describe the room to me in precise detail. Leave nothing out."

Mr. Kinley closed his eyes. "The walls are brownish-gray with old white trim on the bottom. She has drawings framed on the walls. Sketches of flowers and trees," Mr. Kinley described tremulously. "It's a square room, with wooden floorboards . . . they're gray."

"The furniture?" Xavier asked.

The man's brow wrinkled. "A small bed, with white sheets. She has a quilt that my mother made—red and gold diamonds. A desk where she draws. Pencils and paper all strewn about. And there's a bookshelf next to the bed, a lamp . . ." He paused, his eyes sad and fond all at once. "There's a dent in the wall across from the bed. She read a book and didn't like the ending, so she threw it at the wall."

"That should be enough," Xavier said.

On the far end of the salon was a narrow back door that led to the little garden behind the Morwyns' house. Xavier approached the door, held the doorknob and shut his eyes.

He sang a strange melody in Albilan, broken by staccato whispers and rolled *r*'s. Then he inhaled deeply and jerked the door open. Through the entryway, where the garden ought to have been, was a simple bedroom. It was just as Mr. Kinley had described it: the drawing desk, the quilt, the indentation in one of the walls.

Mr. Kinley breathlessly thanked Xavier, shaking his hand so profusely that, already dizzy from the spell, he trembled like a willow branch in a windstorm. Xavier pressed his handkerchief to his nose again.

Mr. Kinley didn't notice as he passed through the doorway, laying his daughter on her bed. She stirred slightly, but just sighed and flopped on to her side, her breathing steady and loud.

Xavier lingered in the doorframe. "My search for a cure is ongoing," he said. "If I make any progress, if I finally find a solution . . . I promise I will be in contact, immediately."

I stood at Xavier's side, watching the little bedroom almost like it was the set of some strange, sad play.

"We live at the bakery in Iverton," said Mr. Kinley. He lifted his head, his dark eyes miserable and empty. "Please. Do not let her suffer this for long."

Xavier nodded. His hand trembled against the doorknob. "I will help her," he said. "I promise."

I took one last look at Mr. Kinley, holding his daughter's hand and crying. I wanted to take my magic and give it all to them; to let its warmth pass over them and heal them. But my magic rarely seemed to listen to the wishes of my heart.

Xavier slowly shut the door, and with that, the grieving father and his suffering daughter were gone. With his hand still clenching the doorknob, Xavier suddenly dropped to his knees.

My pulse leapt, and I fell to the floor beside him. "Xavier?!"

"I need a moment," he whispered.

"Do you need water?" I squeaked. "Tea? Some food—you

haven't eaten at all today—"

"I need to be alone," he rasped, "just for one minute."

"No," I said, "you cannot isolate yourself again, not like—"

"Please." His voice was desperate. Frayed at the edges. Beads of sweat clung to his brow. He was breathing like he had just run for miles.

Worry burrowed in my gut. His breath hitched, and he pressed a free hand to his face and began to cry. His weeping grew louder, and something scratched against my ankle. I leapt back.

A withered gray vine covered in thorns had burst from the floor. More vines circled around his feet, crawling up the door, winding around his wrist.

I threw myself at the door and ripped the vines away. Xavier gaped up at me, eyes sad and bloodshot. He staggered away from the door, torn and withering vines crumbling beneath his feet. For his magic, as weakened as it was, to express his emotions like this—he must have been in true anguish.

The vines wilted in my gloved hands. I looked into his eyes, desperate for answers, but he turned from me, shaking free of the weak, sickly brambles.

"Curse me twice. I'll tend to that later," he mumbled, making a fast exit towards the shop in the next room. Without even glancing back at me, he said, "That'll be all for today, Miss Lucas. I'll see you tomorrow."

Anger and heartbreak mingled within me. I tossed aside the vines, and they disintegrated to dust as I marched after him into the shop.

Already, he was at the shop counter, opening his notebook and dipping a pen in ink. He scratched out some words with one swift strike of the pen, and then scribbled something down. With a free hand, he hastily brushed away tears from his gaunt cheeks.

"You don't mean to keep working, do you?" I asked.

His eyes grew bright with fury. "I am not so depraved that I'd let my own emotions get in the way of making the cure—"

"It's not depraved," I insisted, crossing towards him. "Look at yourself! You're exhausted. You can't work like this."

After a final glance into his notebook, he shoved it into a drawer and then locked it with a key he'd pulled from his pocket. I frowned at the drawer—he'd been scribbling in that book the night I caught him brewing a Euphoria cure.

"She's our age," Xavier murmured. He set a bowl against the counter and ripped a dried sprig of lavender from where it hung on the window frame. "She's *our age*, and she got her hands on that horrible potion—how many more lives will be ruined? I cannot simply stop my research—"

"You've already done so much. You tried a cure on her,

and it didn't work. You'll find another way."

"But what if I don't? What if I've spent months for nothing; what if there's no hope for these people?"

I grabbed his arm. His eyes grew wide. "Listen to me," I said. "You'll do no good to anyone if you don't get some sleep. You have a brilliant mind. You're letting it waste away abusing yourself. If you want to help these patients, you need your rest."

His eyes softened to the warm, chocolatey color I liked the most.

"What would you do, if I was in your shoes?" I prompted.

"I'd have sent you to bed at once." A small, timid smile crossed his face. "Though I'm certain you would have fought tooth and nail to keep working, too."

I tugged him towards the staircase. "Go to bed. I'll clean the shop, and you and I, we can attempt to make another cure in the morning. Together."

He let me drag him all the way up the stairs and to his bedroom. He halted me just outside his door.

"I can take it from here," he assured me.

I raised an eyebrow. "*Can* you?"

His cheeks reddened. He tilted back against his door for support. "Yes, and I'll sleep, I swear it."

I sighed. "The way you've shut yourself off from the world, tortured yourself, it—it isn't good for you. You . . ." The thought I'd had was better advice for myself than for him, but he was waiting, watching with complete attention.

He always looked me in the eye when he was truly listening. "If you get too trapped in your own head, you'll start to think that there isn't a world at all outside of your own thoughts. The voice in your head telling you that you're rubbish . . . you'll think that it's right." My throat had gone dry as old parchment. There was a faint whisper in the back of my mind from my magic, but I focused on him. "And, well . . . I don't think you're rubbish. Not at all."

Xavier laughed his one-beat laugh. "I don't think you're rubbish, either."

Something fluttered in my middle and made my cheeks start to burn. Noticing how long his eyelashes were certainly didn't help. I pointed a threatening finger at him. "If I find you stayed up reading all night, or if I hear you clanging about with your potions downstairs . . ." But the warning tapered off. He and I both knew that I wouldn't do much besides yell at him.

He smiled at me. "I wish I was like you."

"Stubborn, you mean?"

"No." He rubbed his hand against the back of his neck. "Fearless."

I didn't know what to say. I bit my lip. He watched.

"Good night," I burst out at last. "I mean, I know it's still early—"

"Good night." He bowed his head, his hair flopping over his forehead, and then slipped into his bedroom, clicking the door shut behind him.

I touched my gloved fingertips to the striped grain of the oak door. I needed the truth from him. Whatever he was hiding from me, it left him like *this*. Isolated and desperate, wrapping himself in brambles and shame.

Whatever he was hiding from me . . . was in the notebook locked away in the kitchen.

I barreled down the spiral staircase. A tiny, sweeter voice in my head seemed to say, *He's keeping it private for a reason.*

But I knew him. He *never* asked for help, even when he seemed to be screaming inside. I had to find answers for myself. It was for his own good. If I learned whatever his secret was, I could help him. It would be worth it in the end. He didn't even need to know that I had pried at all.

Back in the kitchen, I stared down the locked drawer. He stored the till in there at the end of the day. So whatever was in that book, he saw it as equally valuable. And he had the key with him upstairs.

But I had magic.

I glanced at the green front door in the foyer. The door I had opened and knocked over.

Flexing my gloved fingers, I carefully held onto the drawer's handle.

"All right, magic," I whispered. "Let's be gentler this time."

First—embrace emotion.

I breathed deeply and kept him forefront in my mind. The way he made me feel. Happy. Safe. Welcome.

This affection for him, the sparkling feeling in my stomach when we stood side by side. The burning in my cheeks, the quickening of my heart.

Next, intention. I imagined opening the drawer smoothly, silently, effortlessly.

Lastly, tempering.

"Not too much," I whispered to my magic. "Just a gentle . . . little . . . pull . . ."

I tugged on the drawer, and it flew out of the workstation, punching against the boning of my corset with a loud *thump,* knocking the breath out of my lungs. All the coins inside the till jangled around, and I hoisted the drawer onto the floorboards, my heart hammering and my stomach throbbing with pain.

After such a racket, I stood perfectly still, watching the staircase. Surely Xavier had heard. Surely he'd suspect. I'd tell him it was an accident. That I was looking for quill ink. Or that my magic had acted on its own.

I waited. Then I stole a quick glance at the watch on my chatelaine and blew out a sigh of relief. Two minutes had passed and he hadn't come to investigate.

Kneeling beside the drawer, I pulled out the leatherbound notebook and flipped through the pages.

They were instructions for potion-making. All in Xavier's spidery handwriting. Lists of ingredients, flowers and seeds and roots and oils of different kinds. On the top right-hand corner of every page, a date was written, and then an X was marked in the corner. Some pages had the text scratched through with great gashes of ink, like a wound bleeding black.

I riffled through the recipes until I found the most recent one. Some of the amounts of ingredients were struck through, and on the top of the page, he'd written a note:

> *Tested on a young girl in the second stage of Euphoria's thrall.*
> *102, 103 ineffective.*

I sat back on my heels, my shoulders sinking. This wasn't a notebook where he kept his darkest secrets. It was simply a record of the Euphoria cures he'd attempted. Over a hundred of them.

My thumb brushed across the edge of the pages, making them rapidly flip by. The numbers at the top of the pages grew smaller and smaller—*81, 70, 64, 52, 25, 11*—

At the front were some unnumbered pages. More potions, labeled this time with descriptions and notes.

> *An attempt at an anti-nausea pill.*
> *Experiment—tonic to keep someone awake.*
> *A potion to relieve anxiety and melancholy.*

My pulse faltered.

A potion to tamper with the heart. A potion for melancholy. I thought of the man in the market, how he'd begged

Xavier for relief, for *Euphoria* . . .

I read on, my heart galloping in my ribs.

> *I have made contact with five willing participants for an initial trial.*
>
> *Filled cauldron with water from a sunlit spring.*
>
> *Added:*
>
> *Tipton weed—twelve blossoms, removed from stems, chopped finely. Reduces anxiety.*
>
> *Twenty-four sunflower seeds. Induces hopefulness.*
>
> *A small jar of finely chopped orange peel, dried, and melted dark chocolate, about enough to fill a teapot. For cheerfulness.*
>
> *For abundance, three small cuttings of wisteria.*
>
> *The bloom of an orange lily for fervor.*
>
> *Seeds from a yellow poppy—for success.*
>
> *At the same time: three petals of yellow tulips, delphinium, anthurium, lavender, and meadowsweet for happiness.*
>
> *Brewed stirring counterclockwise.*
>
> *I'll let this set for two hours and bottle. Will report back with initial results.*

The date in the top-right corner—three months ago.

Three months ago, when his family had left.

Three months ago, when he'd suddenly been given an impossible assignment from the Council.

Three months ago, when his magic was cut in half. Almost

like . . . almost like a *punishment*.

The words blurred and swam on the page before me through a film of tears. I slammed the book shut, buried it back in the drawer, and slid the drawer back into its spot.

I couldn't breathe. Black spots fizzled in the edges of my vision.

It was impossible. He couldn't have made Euphoria. He was too kind, too good.

But he was so secretive and so very ashamed. He had *wept* after seeing Emily. If he *had* made it, he was remorseful, surely.

Unless he was lying. As he'd already done. About everything. He'd kept this, kept everything from me. He had said he was afraid I'd see him differently if I knew the truth.

Slowly, I pulled myself to my feet. I would give him one last chance. I would ask him for his story, in his own words.

Magic burned in my heart and pulsed in my muscles. All of this anger and confusion and sorrow was fueling it.

In a few days, this magic would be his.

What did he plan to use it for?

14

Early the next morning, I flitted about the kitchen. The kettle whistled, and I filled up the pale pink teapot, fragrant with bergamot and lavender.

The floorboards creaked. I lifted my head, pressing the warm teapot against my fluttering heart.

As Xavier stepped into the kitchen, flooded with morning light, I was pleased to find that the dark circles under his eyes had faded significantly. He looked like the Xavier I'd known before I read that notebook. Kind and meek. Not the sort of person who would make a dangerous, illegal potion.

"Good morning," I exclaimed then cleared my throat, making a note to be a little less enthusiastic. "Did you sleep well?"

"Yes—best I've slept in months." Then he gaped at the kitchen table, which I had set better than a café. I'd baked lemon scones and set them out on little dishes with painted daisies. I'd found a nice tablecloth, pale yellow with matching cloth napkins, and the fine silverware marked with an M for Morwyn.

He lifted one of the scones from its tiny plate. "Did . . . did you make these?"

"Yes, though I'm certain they're not as good as the kind Papa makes." I placed the teapot on the table before him.

"What's the occasion?" he asked, holding out my chair for me.

"The occasion is that you've slept through the night," I said. I fluttered a napkin into my lap as he sat down across from me. "I *insist* you eat something. You look a little peaky."

He laughed softly and poured the tea, first into my cup and then into his. I watched his cup fill with deep brown tea.

After he'd done so, he lifted the teacup to his nose with a smile. "Bergamot. My favorite." He set down the cup, his brows pushing together. "Wait a moment."

My stomach clenched tight. He knew that this was an interrogation, not a tea party. Somehow he knew. "Yes?"

Xavier pointed over his shoulder. "We haven't checked the magic cupboard in a bit."

My shoulders fell with relief. "Oh! Of course. I'll go see."

I dashed to the cupboard, my heart pounding in my throat. What if he shouted at me? What if I'd misunderstood? And worst of all—what if his gentleness was all a lie?

Reaching up, I shakily pulled the handle of the little cupboard. Within, already on a plate to match the others, were two white meringues. They were palm-sized, and had little spikes like petals, like—like chrysanthemums.

For truthfulness.

I huffed through my nose. It was as if his grandmother's spirit was watching me through the magic cupboard.

The truth would be good for all of us.

I carried the plate of meringues back to Xavier. "It seems your grandmother knew we'd be having a tea party," I said, my voice cracking in my awful attempt to sound pleasant and cheery and normal.

"Lovely!" He lifted a meringue. The light in his eyes was so beautiful, like he was made up of sunshine itself. My pulse quickened. "Cheers."

"Cheers," I mumbled, tapping my meringue against his.

I barely noticed the sweet, light taste of the meringue—I was too focused on him. First, he was eating, and that was a marked victory. But more importantly, he needed to speak to me. He needed to be brave.

"Thank you for arranging this," he said.

My fingertips fluttered against the flowers painted on my teacup. "There's something I want to talk to you about."

He sat tall in his chair, a small, encouraging smile on his lips. "Of course. Anything."

Stop being wonderful, I begged him.

I took a slow, deep breath. "There've been some . . . things that I've noticed. Concerning things. I—I know I'm your pupil, so I just . . . want there to be transparency between us." Carefully, I reached my gloved hand across the table. His fingertips brushed mine. Flames jetted up my arm, and my heart knocked about in my ribs, and my head pulsed, and I wanted this strange, sunlit nightmare to end already. "You can speak frankly with me, Xavier. I just want to understand. I—I care for you."

His fingers wove with mine. His cheeks had gone bright pink as rose petals. "I'm sorry," he whispered. "I'm rubbish at hiding my feelings. I should have said something sooner. I—I care for you, too." Xavier laughed, a huff of quiet breath. "Since the very first day I met you. I have loved you for some time now."

In an instant, the fire in my blood turned to ice.

I certainly hadn't expected *that*. Deep down, I'd hoped for it; I'd wanted it even before I had words for it.

"Do you mean that?" I asked. All the breath seemed trapped in my lungs.

He clenched my hand tighter. "Sometimes, I feel like I'm just . . . flesh and bone and fear. But these past few days have reminded me how I used to feel. When I was with you. You make me feel brave."

Did I love him?

I cared for him, yes. And my heart skipped foolishly when

I looked at him too long. But I could say the same of several people I'd been fond of, growing up in Williamston. Xavier had been a friend I could rely on for almost twelve years, then a ghost, and now someone new altogether. Sometimes I saw glimpses of that boy I'd liked so much. His laughter. His self-lessness. His shyness. At the same time, he'd very clearly built a wall around himself, a mountain-high fortress of secrets. He loved me, he said, but he still wanted my magic.

Slowly, I drew my hand into my lap. Some of the light seemed to leave his eyes, and my heart thrummed with pain.

"I can't love someone I do not trust," I whispered. Tears burned my eyes. "Please, Xavier. Just . . . tell me why. Why did you make Euphoria?"

All the color drained from his face. "What?"

"I know it's the truth. I—I saw your recipe."

He leapt to his feet, striding into the kitchen. He made for the locked drawer and looked from it to me. "I locked it away. Did you break into my things?"

"You weren't speaking to me! I asked again and again, and you were *miserable*—"

"I—I wanted to tell you. I was going to tell you. In my own time, Clara—"

"Why?" My voice broke in two. "We both saw Emily yesterday. This potion is so horrid. So wicked. How could you have made something like that?"

Xavier stepped back into the foyer. His lovely eyes, dark

as mahogany, glistened. "Is that what this little tea party was for? To . . . to interrogate me?"

"Answer me." There was no bite to my words. I felt hollow and frail as a dried, discarded chrysalis.

"There was no cure for melancholy," he said. "My sister is afflicted by it; she needed help. I was prideful and foolish to think I could fix things by myself, but all I wanted to do was help."

"Are you distributing it?" I whispered.

"Curse me, no! I didn't mean for any of this," he said. "I tested it first; I gave it to a few willing patients, but the side effects were . . . dreadful. I told my father at once about what I'd done. He did what he had to. He informed the Council of what had happened."

"I . . . I don't understand. How did it spread, if you told your father about it?"

"Someone came to me claiming to be a test subject. I gave him a potion, and he gave me a false name. He was able to reproduce the potion and spread it. The Council still doesn't know who was truly responsible, but it doesn't matter now. Illicit covens have been distributing it all over. The Council wanted to punish me by taking away my powers. My father advocated for me, and they reached a compromise with a binding spell."

The pity I'd felt for his poor health turned to sickening disappointment. He was a criminal. His weakened powers were his punishment. "You said it was because you were like *me*! That your magic was too strong—"

"I—I only conceded that it gave me trouble."

"It gave *other* people trouble!" I snapped. "You were rightfully punished, and still you wanted my power?!"

"The Council said they'd return my powers to me by Midsummer, if I was the first to make the cure as promised. They kept my powers limited, fearful that I could create something dangerous again, even if it made finding the cure all the more difficult. And I feared I wouldn't succeed. I feared I'd lose my magic forever, and then I could help no one. The vow I made to you was a contingency plan. And you—it was clear your magic was ailing you. When the Council spoke of your wild power, I thought I could shoulder that burden instead. I could harness that power and . . . perhaps I could make up for what I'd done."

If I succeeded in healing my father, I'd lose my magic forever. I was starting to understand my power better. Starting to hate it less and less. *I* had the potential to use it for good; my dream had *always* been to help people. And Xavier had wanted to take this future from me.

"*You* broke the Council's laws," I hissed. "You earned that punishment. It is only by the mercy of the Council you have any magic at all." My heart was shattering, breaking into painful splinters inside of me. "How can I believe you? How can you say that you love me? Madam Ben Ammar was right, you just wanted to use me—"

"Clara—"

"Did you even care whether or not my father was healed?"

"Of course I care." Tears gleamed in his eyes.

Everyone had been right about him. The truth was finally coming forward. He had hidden so much from me already—what else was he hiding? What else could he be keeping from me "for my own sake"? "You're a *liar*, Xavier. To the Council, to the Kinleys, to me!"

His cheeks flushed, but he did not break eye contact. "I . . . I didn't want to lie. But you were one of the only people who didn't know about my crime. I didn't want you to think poorly of me."

"I would have liked the chance to have made up my mind for myself."

He breathed slow, heavy breaths. His eyes glistened in the sunlight. "And *I* would have liked the chance to tell you in my own time. I would have liked you to *trust* in me—"

"How long were you going to wait?" I asked. "Until you had my magic?"

His gaze met mine. "I—I think you should go."

My stomach sank. I hated this. I hated not knowing him. I hated that he had been responsible for this darkness, had kept it from me, had acted like everything was *normal*. Treated me like an outsider. Like a child.

And then he said that he loved me.

I marched to the front door. Clenched my hand tight against the handle.

I thought of old, groaning floorboards. Reading books by the hearth. The scent of Papa's cologne. The way the sofa would sink beneath my weight. Papa's arms around me. The smell of lavender in my windowsill. The blossoms overflowing in our garden. The sunflowers we'd planted together.

"Clara," said Xavier, "wait, I—"

I tugged on the handle and slipped through, slamming the door shut behind me. It dissolved into a pile of green ash, carried off by the wind.

When I turned, I was no longer standing in Xavier's entryway, nor on his porch, nor in my living room. I was on a grassy hill, turned an eerie yellow green in the morning light. At the bottom of the hill was the tall spire of the town hall. A cluster of little brown-roofed buildings, shoulder to shoulder. A well, surrounded by bustling people. Williamston.

I sighed. "Close, magic. Close enough."

I crossed through town with my head held high. Some people noticed me. Some skittered out of my path. Others pointed and whispered, *There's the girl with the wild magic*, but I did not care.

I didn't need Xavier. I'd heal my father and then we would move away, where the wizard couldn't find me. I'd keep my magic through sheer force of will. I would learn to heal people; learn how to manage my magic all on my own. I'd make the Council proud.

He said that he loved me.

Had he been a fool to make the bargain with me? Was he cruel? Or perhaps it was like he'd said. He was a coward. He'd only helped teach me to avoid facing a future without magic.

Anger thrummed in my temples like a drumbeat. My magic was willing and excited. *Use me,* it urged. *Fight to keep me.*

As I marched past the town hall, something flitted across my vision, like a little green bird. I halted, frowning—it was a maple leaf, zipping through the air, right towards me. Something pale blue was tied to it.

I reached out a hand and caught the leaf, the same sort of charm my teachers had used to send notes to Papa on my behalf. One of my hair ribbons was fastened around the stem—it was meant to find me specifically.

My heart thundered as I turned over the leaf. All the heady, thrilling confidence I'd felt a moment before cooled into ice.

CL: MR. L EMERGENCY. COME HOME. RS.

Papa was in trouble.

15

Fear gripped me in cold, piercing claws.

I raced along the pebble-strewn path home. Sparks flew around me, and spiky-leafed ferns grew in the little ovals of my footsteps.

Our small yellow cottage sat in its personal meadow, peaceful—as if it were any other day. As if my father weren't in danger. I darted across the lawn and shoved open the door, my heart pounding so fast that my head spun.

The sofa was empty. My stomach dropped inside of me, and the world seemed to shrink, but somewhere far away came a voice—"Miss Lucas? Is that you?"

Robin. It was Robin; they were in the house, and they needed me. I sprinted into Papa's tiny bedroom. My senses came back, bit by bit—he was lying on his bed, his face gray as cinders. Robin stood at his shoulder, holding a case of potions, their brow creased and covered in sweat. And

Madam Ben Ammar knelt beside my father, her hands aglow as she pressed them against his chest.

"May you live long," she repeated, louder and louder.

I took a step closer. Papa's eyes were shut. Azaleas overflowed from two spots to the left and right of his breastbone, dropping petals onto the floor.

Robin caught me just before I fell.

"Miss Lucas!" they cried. "Thank goodness you've come—"

I willed my trembling legs to push me forwards, closer to his bed. He'd been fine Monday morning, and now . . .

"Papa?" My voice was small, shrill and fractured.

Madam Ben Ammar took a heaving breath and stood back, mopping at her brow with her sleeve.

Papa's chest moved faintly, burdened by dozens of azaleas pouring out of his ribs and through his shirt and down onto the floor. His white, freckled skin was covered in sweat. His hand was draped on the floorboards. His eyes were shut in sleep, but his brow was furrowed, like he was in the middle of a bad dream.

"I sedated him to help with the pain," Madam Ben Ammar explained between labored breaths. "Robin just called me. He's getting worse and worse. . . ."

I stood beside the witch, noticing the precise places from which the flowers grew. My failed blessing had caused this. "You—you tried to get the flowers out?"

"More keep growing," she said. She gripped my shoulders tight. "Clara, I've been trying to give him a blessing of my own. I'm doing all I can. But the curse . . . it's overcoming his body. He doesn't have much time left."

I stared at her, waiting for her to finish the thought. Or say that this was all a dream.

I turned to him and pressed my gloved hands against his cheeks. "Papa," I said, a calm and direct command, "Papa, wake up."

Robin cleared their throat. "You should let him rest, Miss Lu—" They were cut off when Madam Ben Ammar raised a hand.

I patted Papa's cheek. "Wake up," I cooed. I remembered him at my bedside on mornings before school, kissing my forehead, urging me to wake up or he'd eat all the berries he'd picked for me.

His eyes, the same pale blue as mine, fluttered open. His chest seized with a muddled, strained breath.

"Clara," he whispered.

I brushed my gloved thumb against his gaunt cheek, right where my hand had left a mark before. I hardly knew what to say. We teased each other so easily—but today, it felt wrong. The beautiful, soft perfume of the flowers that infested him was a constant reminder that no matter how we might pretend, Papa was not well.

"Why aren't you . . . with your teacher?" His voice was

whispery and faint and lasted only a few words at a time before he had to take another painful gulp of air.

My lip quivered. My already bruised heart ached from another blow. I wished I could fall upon him, weeping, and tell him everything about Xavier. Our sunlit childhood. The stretch of silence between us. Our promise. Our friendship, a new flower blooming from an old plant. And now, the truth about what he'd done. Anger and regret churned inside my stomach.

"We had an argument, that's all," I told Papa. It wasn't a lie, but it felt as heavy in my chest as if it had been. I brushed a tear from his cheek. "I missed you so."

He frowned, leaning his head into my palm. "Don't be . . . angry with him for . . . for long, dear. You're a good pair." Despite everything, he smiled, his eyes squeezed shut. "A good wizard. A good witch."

I wished he could give me all the wisdom in the world. I wished he could speak forever and not grow tired. I wished I had more to say to him—but my brain was a cloudy, tangled mess.

Madam Ben Ammar placed a hand on my shoulder. Her eyes glimmered. "If you want to attempt another blessing, now is the time."

My heart skipped. I'd failed so spectacularly the last time. And I knew full well I could hurt him more, even as he was already in such pain.

His brow creased as his body thrashed with another cough. I had no choice.

My fingers trembled as I pulled the embroidered gloves off my hands, finger by finger. A beautiful gift from someone who'd cared for me. Someone I'd cared for. *Breathe. Just breathe,* said a voice in my head, a memory. Of Xavier. Of the lessons we'd had together.

And there, too, was the black band on my finger.

I squeezed my eyes shut tight.

Papa had taught me that people were complicated. I wished there was only one side to Xavier; a flat, paper doll, a drawing of my childhood friend, and nothing more. But that wasn't the truth. He was a prism, cracked and brilliant all at once. He'd hurt so many people. He'd even hurt me.

But hadn't I done the same? Hadn't I hurt the ones I loved, even when all I meant was to help them?

And despite all we'd been through . . . Xavier had helped me. He'd taught me to temper my magic in ways no one else had.

All the rage in me swirled like a storm inside my chest. Outside, on my magic's cue, thunder crashed like the sky was falling down. The whole house trembled.

Breathe.

Throwing porcelain off a cliffside; screaming until our voices went hoarse. We did not tamp down our anger, but saw it for what it was, and released it. Used it.

My hands hovered over Papa's chest. My stomach burned and my throat was tied in a knot. I was a leaf quivering in the storm raging outside; tossed about by sadness and regret and anger and fear.

But like that day on the cliff, I let those feelings stay. They could push me about in the storm, but I would not be carried away in the wind.

I thought back to our lessons together and wondered how I could miss Xavier so much and loathe him all at the same time.

The first step of a blessing required intention—Papa *would* be healed. Then, I thought of my love for him—curse me twice, I loved him to bursting.

Papa wiping tears from my eyes. Tying my shoelaces. Consoling me when Xavier had stopped writing. Sending pressed flowers to me at each new apprenticeship. Letting me stay at the Morwyns' to play, even when he had grown tired. Singing me just one more lullaby.

It had only been Papa all these years, but I hadn't needed anyone else. He'd provided for me and protected me and raised me better than my mother ever could have. We'd thrived without her. He'd raised me to prosper.

I placed my hands against his chest. He gasped like I'd dumped cold water on him, and I clenched my teeth to keep from pulling back, from giving up or weeping.

"Papa," I said, "may every beat of your heart be filled with peace, confidence, and freedom." My arms shook. Sweat beaded on my skin. I waited for the familiar burn of magic to flow through me. Instead, it rested weak as an ember in my ribs.

"May every beat of your heart be filled with peace, confidence, and freedom."

My vision blurred. The world was nothing but dots of pink azaleas. My father coughed, loud and painful.

"Clara." Madam Ben Ammar's voice was soft as a breeze and miles away.

I pushed my fingers hard against his ribs. "Magic," I growled at it, tensing my chest, tightening my shoulders, "*heal him!*"

This beast inside of me, powerful and terrifying as it was, was *mine* to control. I had grown a field of flowers. I had succeeded in making potions and portals. This curse of mine had taken too much from me already. It would not rule my life. It would not kill my father. And I was *not* my magic.

My cheeks burned. I gritted my teeth and squeezed my eyes shut, red spots blooming behind my eyelids. Hatred thrummed through me, scalding like molten metal. Magic squirmed in my hands, fizzling and sparkling; a living fire. But I was stronger than it. I'd survived it for years; survived all the pain and mischief it had caused me.

This was where it ended.

"You will heal him!" I screamed.

There was a shriek, followed by a loud *crash*. I fell to the floor, covering my head. Madam Ben Ammar wrapped her arms around me to shield me.

When I lifted my head, peeking out from over her shoulder, I found the dark wood of the floorboards littered with fine bits of glass and azalea petals. The windows, hollow except for a few jagged shards remaining, allowed in strong, whistling gusts of wind. My wretched magic, causing chaos wherever it went.

Glancing up from Madam Ben Ammar, I looked to Papa, terrified that he'd been hurt by the debris.

But he was sitting upright, his blue eyes clear and alert. His cheeks had a healthy, rosy glow. His hand pressed against his breastbone, where no flowers bloomed.

Papa turned to me, pushing himself off the bed. Robin cried out, "Sir!"

But Papa didn't listen; didn't even wince as he reached down and grabbed me off the floor, squeezing me in a tight embrace. My ear against his chest, I could hear the loud, healthy, enthusiastic thrum of his heartbeat.

"Clara," he whispered in my ear, his voice hoarse and yet bursting with light, "my brilliant girl!"

I clung to him, my eyes shut tight, waiting for the first of many more coughs—but he breathed easily. How strange it was to be so tearful and grateful for a simple breath! A steady heartbeat! I threw my arms around his middle and fell into a mess of delighted, relieved tears.

At last, I'd conquered my magic. It had listened to me. The control and understanding that Xavier had taught me, it meant something; it meant I wasn't a failure. It meant I could keep my father.

For the first time in my life, I thought, *Thank you, magic*.

My magic didn't reply.

16

As Madam Ben Ammar effortlessly coaxed the windows into repairing themselves, Papa decided he would make us all lunch. He dragged Robin and me into the kitchen and forced us into the little wooden chairs. The blessing had only been performed a minute before, but here he was, racing about the kitchen, gathering spices and pots and pans, grinning from ear to ear.

Madam Ben Ammar entered the room, her eyes widening at the sight of my exuberant father. "Mr. Lucas! Are you certain you should stress yourself like this, in light of having been on bed rest for so long?"

The metal skillet resounded like a gong as he slammed it against the wooden countertop, his brow wrinkled, and his mouth pursed in an exaggerated fashion. "First of all, after all we've been through, please, call me Albert. As for my health? I could run ten miles. I could climb a mountain." He strode up to me, pulled on my hand, and flicked his wrist, twirling me in a sudden pirouette. "I could dance for nights on end!"

I gripped the countertop for balance, the whole world at a tilt. Papa, undeterred, waltzed back to the cutting board, finely chopping a bright orange carrot.

Robin procured a leather-bound notebook and a pen and quickly began to scribble. Madam Ben Ammar kept her gaze unwaveringly upon me—like I'd forgotten something. Like something was amiss.

"Does your father usually have bursts of energy like this?" Robin asked, their head bowed over their notes.

The steady thumping of the knife against the wooden board ceased. Papa attempted to glower at Robin, but his lips turned up at the corners. "It's not polite to speak about me as if I'm not right here!"

Robin let out a little nervous laugh. "Forgive me, er, Albert."

I folded my arms, watching over him, like a cloud hovering overhead. "This is perfectly normal," I said. My voice trembled. This was the Papa I'd loved all my life. The Papa I'd been terrified to lose. The voice in my head had reminded me daily of his imminent death . . .

But that voice said nothing now. After all that the spell had put us through, I must have truly exhausted my magic this time.

"Clara, dear, could you light the stove?"

219

I glanced up from my muddy boots, the kitchen briefly dancing in my vision as I came down from the cloud my head had been in.

Papa grinned at me. "Who were you thinking about?"

Robin failed at stifling a giggle. Madam Ben Ammar's solemn look didn't fade. Her brows drew together. My cheeks flared with sudden heat.

I sighed and shook my head. "No one, Papa." I marched past him and crouched before the large boxy stove. It had always been easy for me to unintentionally conjure fire, in the past. Something Papa found astonishing rather than dangerous.

Drawing back the little cast-iron door, I reached in a finger, waiting for a flame to come on its own accord.

It didn't obey.

Frowning, I thought back to what Xavier had once taught me. The goal was not to subdue one's anger or shame, but rather to embrace it. Control was not the objective; freedom was.

It was not difficult to find an angry memory to latch onto.

The blush on Xavier's cheeks. The lies pouring from his lips. And the truth, the ugly truth. Admitting he loved me. Admitting he *needed* my magic for himself. The possibility that he had been using me.

A chill ran through me fast as a rushing wind. Drawing my bare hand back from the unlit stove, the feeling turned sharp. Apart from freckles, my hand bore no marks. The black band, the seal of Xavier's vow—it had vanished.

My heartbeat thundered in my ears.

What had the conditions of the vow been?

If I healed Papa—and I *had* healed Papa . . .

I whirled around, jerking open a drawer and pulling out a matchbox. My fingers shook as I struck the first match, failed, and then finally set a lit match into the stove. When I stood, I watched Papa closely—had he noticed? My magic was so boisterous. Could he tell I'd changed? I could imagine him falling to his knees, weeping over the foolish daughter who'd sacrificed her gift for his sake.

But he smiled and said, "Thank you, dear," his attention still on chopping carrots.

With my unmarked hand firmly in my pocket, I approached Madam Ben Ammar. I needed her. I dared not tell her about the vow; I couldn't see the anger and disappointment in her eyes after learning what I'd done. But I needed to know if my choice was putting others in danger.

"Madam Ben Ammar?" I asked, my voice squeaking like a poorly played violin. "Could I speak to you privately? Please?"

She stood, and Robin did, too, reflexively. Now on their feet, they promptly decided to help Papa prepare our meal, while Madam Ben Ammar took me by the arm and into the sitting room.

I dropped onto the sofa, now bent in the middle from where Papa had been lying for days and days. In my pocket, I rubbed my fingers against the part of my skin that had once been marked black.

Madam Ben Ammar lighted on the sofa, her hip against mine, her forehead puckered. "Are you going to tell me why the mark of your vow is gone?"

My eyes blew wide. "I—you saw?"

"Yes," she said, holding out her hand. I reluctantly removed mine from my pocket and laid my palm against hers. "It vanished when you healed your father."

The beat of my heart crashed loudly in my ears. If she knew the conditions of the vow . . . she'd think I was such a fool. And she might even seek punishment for Xavier for making such bargains behind the Council's back. *Further* punishment.

"I—I made him promise me," I murmured. "I made him promise that he'd help me heal Papa. That's all. I wanted him to know how serious I was. The vow seemed like a good idea."

Her brows were still furrowed; she was calculating, deciphering where the lie was hidden within my words.

After all I'd learned about Xavier, after his own deceitfulness, I didn't blame her for being so cautious about this vow between us.

My shoulders sagged, heavy with the weight of his

confession and our argument, only an hour ago. I brushed my thumb against my ring finger where the black band had once been.

"This morning, he told me everything," I murmured. "Xavier."

Even his name made my stomach turn. I licked my dry lips. With my power now in his possession . . . what other potions would he make? "I need to know . . . I need to know more about him. His heart. I just don't . . ." I shook my head, unable to catch up to the carnival of my thoughts. "I trusted him; I looked up to him . . . and yet it's true. He made Euphoria. And he hid that from me. What else could he have lied about? Did I ever really know him at all?"

Madam Ben Ammar's brown hands covered mine. "It's not easy, losing your faith in a friend," she said.

I blinked back tears and wondered if I was even speaking to her at all or only to myself. The more I said, the more I understood his motivations. "He told me he hated himself for what he'd done. That he didn't anticipate his potion would hurt people the way it did. And, and he's worked so tirelessly to find the cure; he hardly sleeps. . . ."

She rested her hand against my shoulder, anchoring me. The world slowed down from the whirlwind it had been before. Was this a sort of spell?

"The Council very generously gave Master Morwyn a chance to address his wrongdoings," she said. "Three months to atone for creating such a disaster."

Disaster. My insides churned. Emily Kinley's laughter echoed in my head.

"He said he doesn't make or distribute it." I pinched my apron in my hands. "Do you know who does?"

She puffed out a breath, long and weary, but didn't answer.

My second question came softer. "Is it my mother?"

She pressed her lips. "I suspect she's part of it. She's made potions like these before. But whoever it is, they're uniquely skilled at evading the Council's attention." Madam Ben Ammar rubbed her fingertips against her temple. "The Council will continue our efforts to create a cure for its effects. If we can't stop it spreading, we can at least help its victims."

I thought of Emily again. Of Xavier's desperate attempts to help her. To help all those his potion had hurt. "What . . . what will Xavier's punishment look like?" I murmured. "If he cannot make a cure by Midsummer?"

"The Council will lay hands on him and take away his powers. And he will lose his title, of course."

I undid my braid and started it up again, my fingers working fast. I brushed my hand down the plait, instinctively feeling for any loose leaves or flowers—but of course, that was no longer a possibility.

It wouldn't just be his power he'd lose.

He'd lose mine, as well.

But that's what I'd wanted, wasn't it? Almost two weeks ago, I had resigned myself to being a regular girl. And in exchange for Papa—laughing, dancing, joking Papa—it was worth it.

I hadn't realized I wouldn't be *myself* without my magic. My chest remained hollow and cold. An empty geode, filled with plain, dusty rock.

Xavier was the same way. When he'd first discovered his power as a child, he whooped and hollered and ran around his house. We'd had so much hope, dreaming of how magic would be a shining part of our futures together. That love of magic was still a part of him. You could see it in the kindness towards his customers. In the thorns that sprang up around him when he'd failed Emily. Even the twinkle in his eyes as he regarded the shelves, stocked with potions he'd made himself.

Would I even recognize him without magic, were he to fail? Were he to lose his and my magic forever?

Madam Ben Ammar patted my arm. "You don't need to concern yourself with Master Morwyn's punishment, Clara. You can gather your things, and when Robin graduates in a few days' time, I'll take you on as my apprentice again. After that blessing you performed, I'm sure I could make a case for you to study with me in Queensborough."

I could have had that life. I could have had another year of training my magic, of finally tempering it, if I hadn't given it up.

Madam Ben Ammar beamed at me, pride still glimmering in her eyes. "With your father back in good health, you'll be able to tend to your studies without worrying, and surely you'll be ready to be certified—"

"It's not too late," I piped up. "Xavier could make the cure. He could keep his powers."

The smile faded from Madam Ben Ammar's lips. She gathered the black satin of her dress in her fists. "Yes. Yes, he could."

She gave my shoulder a firm pat. "When you *are* ready to continue your education, just let me know. You've only just gotten your father back—take all the time you need."

Then she drew close, pulling me into a tight hug. My heart ached.

"I am so very proud of you," she whispered.

I hated myself. I hated that I'd given away my gift, that she suspected nothing.

"I know how hard you've been fighting your magic," she continued. "It's wonderful to see it finally listening to you."

She wasn't the one I longed to hear this praise from. I pictured Xavier's bright smile, how proud tears would spring into his eyes. He would demand to hear every single detail of the blessing I'd cast.

"I'd have been hopeless without Xavier's help." I whispered.

Madam Ben Ammar laughed, sharp and one-beat, pulling

back from me. "Oh, no, dear. You didn't need his teaching, or that vow. You've had this strength all along."

She rose and swept back into the kitchen, her head held high. The door swung shut behind her. I only had a few moments to myself before Papa would grow suspicious.

I hunched over, my eyes screwed shut as I waited for the familiar burning of my power.

"Magic?" I whispered. "If you're still there, you must give me a sign. Break something if you wish. Just answer me."

I waited. There was no voice in my head, no churning in my stomach, no tingling in my fingertips or sweat on my palms. I gazed at the lines on my hands and hoped for flames to burst forth or flowers to start blooming from the sleeves of my blouse. But there were no more miracles.

There never would be. That dream of mine, along with the wish to work side by side with Xavier—to be *Morwyn and Lucas*—was dead.

17

I was supposed to be happy.

So why couldn't I pull myself out of bed?

I hated myself for it, but every part of me ached. Pain pulsed behind my eyes, and when I tossed and turned in my little bed, I thought of how I ought to be waking up in the Morwyns' tower.

The silence my magic had left behind chilled me. I tugged my quilt over my head, leaving my stockinged feet uncovered.

The door to my bedroom clicked, and I heard the familiar padding of Papa's feet on the floorboards. His fingertips brushed against the inch of my head not swallowed up by my quilt.

"Where's my early riser?" he cooed.

I didn't speak. Any complaint I had felt like a betrayal of him. We had fought so hard for him to be happy and healthy.

It should have been enough. It should have been all I ever needed. I was selfish and foolish for wanting anything else; especially for wanting my magic, which had hurt and pestered me for so many years, to come back.

The part of the mattress beside my head tilted slightly as Papa sat next to me. He peeled back the quilt, making my vision go white from the sunshine spilling from my window. I glared, both at him and the light, until I could finally focus on his face.

His freckled brow was crumpled with pity.

I'd cried all night. My eyes were probably as puffy and unsightly as I'd imagined them to be.

"What's wrong, blossom?"

I lifted my head and dropped it in his lap. He petted my hair as I stared at the wall.

"Madam Ben Ammar told me how complicated blessings were," he said, his voice low, tempting me to fall asleep again. "She said it was perfectly normal for you to feel under the weather after casting one."

I nudged my head up and down in a slight nod. That certainly explained the aches and the fatigue. But I didn't suppose exhaustion from casting a blessing would lead me to sob as I had.

"I'm not as smart as she is," said Papa, "but I have a feeling that there's something more that's troubling you."

How did he *do* that?!

I pulled the quilt up, draping it over me, past my nose. "It's nothing."

"Clara Lucas, you have a great many talents, but lying is not one of them."

"I'm not lying!" My words bit sharply, and I instantly hated the venom with which I'd spoken them. I feared Papa would leave me, or that my magic would strike him again with some affliction due to my carelessness.

No. That was no longer a danger.

I wrapped an arm around his middle. A tear rolled down my nose onto the dark gray fabric of his trousers.

His thumb brushed back and forth against my cheek, where the tear had been. "Why haven't you gone home?"

My voice came out hoarse. "I *am* home."

"No. Why haven't you gone back to Xavier?"

I clenched my fists against the soft fabric of the quilt, smelling of dust and lavender.

"You said you had an argument?"

"Yes," I murmured, and decided that was all I would say on the matter.

I couldn't tell him the sort of quarrel we'd had. What I'd learned. What I'd done—what I'd given away. I'd made the right choice, but Papa would never forgive me if he found out.

Papa sighed. "You can't avoid him forever."

I didn't want to. I desperately wanted to see him, to know how he wielded my power; if he'd found a cure; if he'd saved

Emily. If he'd meant it when he had said he loved me.

Once more, I pulled the quilt over myself like a hood.

"Clara." His voice took on an uncharacteristic edge.

"Just let me sleep," I grumbled.

"Don't be unreasonable."

I tugged down the blanket, all of the rage inside of me tinged with the pain of the tears stinging my eyes. "Is it unreasonable for a daughter to wish to stay at home with her father when just yesterday she thought she'd lose him forever?"

His scowl faded away. He squeezed my shoulder. "I'm sorry," he said.

He was always the first to apologize, even when he'd done nothing wrong. I wanted to disappear or to stay here in bed forever, wrapped tight like a moth in a cocoon.

"You know I hate to hold you back, Clara," said Papa. "But I'm well now. I can take care of myself." With my head beside his stomach, I could feel the push and pull of his breath as he sighed. "I'll let you stay here one more day. But then you must go back to the Morwyns'. You have potions to make. People to help." He had no idea how his words, meant to comfort, only plunged an invisible knife further into my gut. "That work fulfills you. It would be a shame for you to give that up over a quarrel with your friend."

It fulfills you. I winced. I had been filled with such hope seeing my potions succeed and knowing that they could change a person's life for the better. Without magic, what would I

231

do? Be a gardener? A seamstress? I couldn't fathom having as much passion for darning socks as I did for healing.

Papa shifted on the bed, lifting me into a sitting position. My cheek throbbed from where I'd been pressed up against him, and my hair stuck to the tear tracks on my face.

He fingers wove between mine. "See? And you've grown so much already. I can hold your hands and it doesn't hurt at all. You've won. You deserve to share your magic with those who need it."

I managed a small, false smile for him.

"For now," said Papa, "if you're going to be at home, you're going to at least come to town with me for the festival." He stood and put his hands on his hips like this was a lecture. I'd never received one from him, but I imagined that's what they'd look like.

My heart skipped. A festival. One I'd loved as a child, with sweet food and air filled with music and the perfume of flowers. I held a hand to my chest. "The first day of the Midsummer festival?"

He frowned. "Yes . . . Midsummer's tomorrow, love. Do you have a rendezvous I should know about?"

Xavier had one day left to save his magic. My magic. Our magic. One day to right his wrongs.

"No, no." I pulled my hair from my face, surveying Papa up and down.

How lovely it was to see color in his cheeks, and even to

see him standing again. His ginger hair was combed back nicely. He'd finally been able to shave away the stubble from his chin, and the pale blue of his cotton shirt made his eyes look like pieces of turquoise.

"Is this for the festival?" I asked, waving my hand at his ensemble.

"Yes. Everyone's dressed up." He tweaked my nose. "As should you be. It's nearly noon."

Midsummer. Xavier. Euphoria. The words cycled through my head over and over, annoying and repetitive as a bird singing the same song for hours. I shut my eyes and sighed. It was time. Time to forget all of this magic and wickedness and pain.

The only dresses I had left at home were ones I wasn't fond of. I donned the bodice and skirt which offended me the least. They were primrose pink, but the sleeves and the skirt were too short, displaying my freckled arms and my bright yellow stockings. I felt a right fool, no matter how many times Papa insisted how pretty I looked.

Outside, the air was thick and hot. Sweat gathered under my arms and under the collar of my blouse. Around our little yellow house, the garden I'd thought was beautiful yesterday was now full of dry, dying flowers. Papa had not been well enough to care for them for many days.

But he didn't let me tarry; he pulled me by the hand down

the dusty road and towards the town.

As we approached the Williamston town square, I was flooded with memories. People carried and shared large sweet bouquets of flowers; flowers that Papa and I had delivered when I was very little. The Midsummer festival was once how we'd earned a great deal of money.

But they'd managed to find flowers without Papa this year. They'd probably bought from another gardener. We'd lost a lot of customers, a lot of security, because of the magic that had left him bedridden.

Around the little fountain in the middle of the square, strangers and townspeople had set up small tents and were selling their wares.

The square was wild, teeming with people chattering and talking to one another. The milkman played his fiddle from the steps of the schoolhouse. The town cobbler and her wife stood near a stand that sold bright pink drinks. They entwined their arms and tipped the round glasses of wine into each other's mouths.

My stomach fluttered. There'd been another part of this festival I'd once adored as a girl. It was a festival to celebrate romantic love. Listening to the splashing of the fountain, I remembered sitting on its edge and watching as young people kissed one another unabashedly, out in the open, even without chaperones.

Xavier and I, we'd played a game once. We'd pretended

it was the Midsummer festival, and he had given me a violet, and I had given him a clover, and I'd kissed him on the cheek. Being seven years old at the time, he'd gagged and wiped his face like I'd covered it in mud.

Papa grabbed my hand, an anchor keeping me from drifting away too far. I kept my eyes on him and concentrated on the roughness of his calluses against my palm.

He took us to the stand the baker had set up, displaying the white-and-red cherry tarts we adored. The baker—Mrs. Burwell, a muscular woman with dark brown skin and beautiful black eyes—gaped at us.

"Albert!" she exclaimed. "Why, I thought I'd never see you again!"

Papa grinned and patted my hand. "Our little witch cast the blessing that healed me."

She blinked furiously. "You—you did?"

I nodded slowly, pressing myself closer to Papa.

"Well, thank goodness," said Mrs. Burwell with a soft, nervous laugh.

"She's doing great work with Master Morwyn," said Papa. "Blessings are extremely difficult to perform. Only advanced magicians can do them." He grinned down at me. The sun was hidden behind a mass of clouds at the moment, but my face burned even so. "I bet it won't be long now until Clara is officially made a witch!"

I gritted my teeth in an ugly smile and widened my eyes,

pinching my hand tight against Papa's arm.

"Let's not keep Mrs. Burwell," I whispered, pulling on his sleeve.

Papa handed the baker some coins, and she passed us two cherry tarts wrapped in squares of paper. Papa said goodbye for the both of us and shepherded us away from the little stand.

He did everything he could to get me to smile. He let me thumb through a table of old books; he offered to buy me one, but I saw an old, worn copy of *Waverly's* and lost my appetite for reading. He bought me a crown of daisies for my hair, and though I thanked him for it, I couldn't help but think of how daisies meant *I have a secret*.

The fiddle and a guitar and a flute and a singer all started up a song, and the swirling chaos of the town square changed into four rows of people.

"Let's dance," Papa urged. I dragged my feet.

The closer I got to the others, the more people began to stare at me. There'd be no more wild magic; no more sudden storms or broken glass; no more flowers bursting from my footsteps. But they didn't know that.

Papa stood at the end of one of the rows of dancers and placed me in the row across from him. A pretty girl in a pale green dress took a step away from me, glaring out of the corner of her eye.

I didn't have long to wallow over this fact.

The song picked up, and the people around me leapt

forwards, taking their partner's hands. Papa swung me in a circle like the others did, and then released me. I followed the line of dancers in front of me, weaving through Papa's line, grabbing hands and skipping and laughing. Faces blurred together. Eyes widened. Sweaty hands grabbed my own. I reached for someone, but they didn't grab back, and I lost track of the rhythm. I took two wrong steps and twisted in place, falling into the dirt.

A young man who'd married one of my childhood classmates threw me a quick look over his shoulder but continued the dance.

I swallowed my shame and pulled myself to my feet, dusting off my knees. *This is normal*, I told myself. *With time, they'll know that you're no longer a witch. That you're no longer wicked. One day you'll feel like one of them.*

I took a step closer to the crowd, determined to try again, but in the sunshine, I caught sight of what looked like little flecks of yellow paint drifting through the air. My pulse began to race as I recognized them as dandelion petals.

Midsummer. Xavier. Euphoria.

A peal of high-pitched, discordant laughter soared over the townspeople. But the crowd was filled with joyful sounds—though the laugh was sharp and strange, it was not out of place here.

The scream that followed, however, *definitely* did not belong.

18

I whipped around towards the sound of shrieking. People backed away from the center of the circle of dancers, from whatever was so horrifying.

From a young man, dancing, though the music had stopped playing.

When he turned his face in my direction, his eyes were unseeing—and yellow dandelions were growing amid the freckles on his face.

A young woman ran up to him, grasping his arms. "Daniel," she asked, "Daniel, darling, what's happening to you?"

I knew that name. He had been in primary school with me; he was just a little older than I was. Daniel drifted away from her, staring blankly at the bright sky above and humming along to a song we could not hear.

The girl grabbed him again, tears rolling down her cheeks. I recognized her now—Annie Booker—she'd also been one of my schoolmates. "Daniel, please, *look* at me!"

My heart ached. It was just like watching Emily with her father. As Xavier had said, it was as if they were trapped in a dream—as if all that made them *them* was gone. Replaced by the unending bliss of this potion.

Papa jogged to my side, red-faced. "What's going on?" he asked me.

"It's Daniel Watters," I murmured. "He's under the thrall of a potion. Euphoria."

My father's brow wrinkled. "A potion . . . ?"

"He . . . his mind is trapped in a dream," I explained. "A beautiful dream." My heart was fracturing; I could see Xavier, vines wrapping around his arms, tears falling down his face, and his final confession to me. The ugly truth—that he was the root of all of this.

Papa nodded, as though he understood perfectly, and approached Annie as she followed after Daniel. "Don't worry," my father said. He gestured to me. "Clara can heal him."

Heat sapped away from my face and gathered in my middle. I wished more than anything for the flame of magic to return inside me; for its voice to hurl curses at me. Instead, I stood frozen, gaping at the crowd, at the couple, at Papa.

Annie raced up to me, clutching at my sleeve. "Please," she said, her voice choked with tears, "he acted so strange last night, and I couldn't find him this morning, and now he's like this . . . !"

Midsummer. Xavier. Euphoria.

This potion of his, this blight of his, it was *here* now. Who'd sold it?

"There must be something you can do," Annie said, shaking my arm.

Daniel staggered about in the center of the crowd. Papa tried to get his attention, to call his name, to bring him back—but Daniel was gone. Pulled under by the tide of Euphoria.

I thought of Xavier. How hard he was fighting to end this. How he was even willing to take my magic from me so that he could right this wrong.

Their futures were in his hands, now.

"Take him to Master Morwyn," I told her, my voice thin and quivering. "I—I can't help." I spun around and ran home as fast as I could, wind and tears stinging my eyes.

Our little house trembled as Papa slammed the front door shut. The sound of it was so odd. My father didn't know the meaning of the word "angry." I hid my head underneath my pillow.

"Clara!" he shouted.

As his footsteps rumbled towards my room, I flicked my hand, willing the door to close—but without my powers, nothing happened.

Papa's shoes thumped against the floorboards of my bedroom. "Something is wrong, and you need to tell me what it is, right now."

I lifted my head from my pillow, saw the concern in his eyes, and hated that I had caused him so much anxiety.

"Please," he said, bending slowly to kneel on the floor in front of me. "I can see it on your face. I only want to help."

"There's nothing you can do." I sat up in the little bed, drawing my pillow to my chest. I chewed my lip to try to help myself speak without being interrupted by sobs. "It's— it's my m-m-magic."

His cheek dimpled with a hopeful smile. "It's all right if it's a bit unruly. It's been through so much. And you were able to help me, weren't you?" He sighed, shaking his head. "I was wrong to demand that you help that boy—"

"It's gone," I blurted, and with that, more tears came.

Papa grabbed my hand between his. "What's gone, dear? What's gone?"

"My magic." I buried my face in my hands. "I gave it to Xavier."

He said nothing. I listened to my own off-tempo breathing, waiting. He didn't speak until I looked at him through the gaps between my fingers.

There was a pained crease in the middle of his forehead. He held his hand against his mouth, horrified, and when I saw his eyes glimmering with tears, my stomach dropped.

"I—I don't understand," he said. "Is that possible? You . . . *gave* it to him?"

I nodded.

"Why?"

The word, so small and simple, cut at me. I crushed the pillow against my heart.

"He said if he could teach me to make a blessing, if I succeeded . . . that I could pay him back with my magic. That's what our vow was for. My magic was so wild, and it had hurt you. I wanted to be rid of it."

His eyes squeezed shut. "Oh, Clara. You did this for me?"

"You were going to die," I whispered.

He bowed his head, his hand curling against the top of my quilt. When he looked up, his eyes were bright, hopeful— but shining with tears, still. "You should go to him. Ask for your power back. Demand it back!"

"He needs it." I pressed myself against the wall and glanced sidelong out the window at the countryside, bright green in the afternoon sunshine. Xavier and I used to chase each other, rolling down hills like that and turning our clothes all green. "He has a chance to prove that he really is a good man. He has an important assignment due for the Council, and I believe he can finish it before tomorrow, with the help of my magic."

Amid the soft birdsong outside, I could almost hear their laughter, their desperation. Emily's. And now Daniel's.

"Xavier was the one who first made that potion, Papa. It wasn't supposed to make people react like that. It was supposed to help them. He wants to set things right again." I wiped my eyes with my sleeve and continued to stare out the window. The glaring light was easier to bear than Papa's tears.

"He told me he loved me, Papa, and yet he made a bargain to take my magic from me. Perhaps . . . perhaps he thought he was doing me a kindness." I shook my head, pressing my hand to my eyes. "He *is* kind, though. He lets me be silly; he lets me cry; he's taught me more than any of my other teachers . . . and he cares so deeply about his customers. I think perhaps he could truly do some good with my power."

"You need to talk to him. Maybe after—after this assignment of his . . . could he give you your power back then?"

Xavier had said he hoped to work with me as his partner. He'd wanted me. As a friend. As a partner. As anything, as long as we were together.

"I suppose," I murmured. "He needs to prove himself. He needs to show me that he's not what everyone says he is."

"Do you love him?"

Thinking of him, his blushing cheeks, his hands gently cupping mine, how he stood at my side and shouted over that cliffside and held the umbrella over me and celebrated my victories—he reminded me so much of that boy he'd once been. The boy I had loved.

I had loved.

I still loved.

"Yes," I whispered.

Papa's hand rested atop mine. "If your heart does not align with his on what is right and wrong, you must know now. Before you break your heart trying to change him." He

243

sighed, bending his head. A lock of ginger hair curled over his brow. "I truly loved your mother. But she and I—we did not see the world the same way. I've not told you much about her. It's an old wound, and I regret not telling you more. But she disagreed with the Council in a great many ways. She made potions that hurt people and twisted their hearts. She had the power to do great things. The problem was, she believed what she was doing *was* good."

He closed his eyes, remembering. His forehead wrinkled deeply in thought. "She said that her magic was a gift, that *she* was a gift, and that it was not her job to keep her magic from people who needed it. She believed her customers had the right to take their futures into their own hands, for good or for evil. She said the consequences didn't matter. . . . I disagreed.

"We can love someone with all our might, but we cannot force them to change. That's up to them. Does that make sense?"

It did—but something about his words made something shift inside my head, clicking like a key slipping into a lock.

Madam Ben Ammar had been leading an investigation into who was selling Euphoria. If my mother was selling heart-bending potions, surely Euphoria was among them. Perhaps Imogen even knew of some sort of antidote to Euphoria. Perhaps I could report her location to the Council; they could arrest her and force the answers from her like

244

they'd always wanted. Perhaps that could help forgive some of Xavier's wrongs.

I slid off the bed, scrubbing my face with my hands and lifting a ribbon from where it had been tied around the bedpost. I shook my hair loose and hastily bound it into a braid again, my fingers working as fast as machinery. "I need to talk to her."

He sat back, blinking as I zipped across the room. "Your—your mother, you mean?"

"Yes." I paced back and forth in front of him, lacing up my boots as I tried to think of a way to reach her. I'd never cared until today. "I can't use my own magic," I muttered, "and Madam Ben Ammar—"

"I have something," said Papa.

I halted, frowning at him.

He lifted himself from the chair, wide-eyed. "I'll be right back."

He returned moments later and pressed a long rectangular box into my hands. It was made of pale wood, with a jagged C carved into the top. It had been months since I'd seen it. Months since it had shown up on our doorstep for my birthday.

I gaped up at him. "But—but I threw that away!"

"I didn't want you to regret doing that one day," he said. He rubbed his hand up and down my arm. "She hurt us both. But I loved her dearly. And you . . . you deserve the opportunity to speak with her if you wish. To ask her things. To say goodbye."

With shaking hands, I removed the lid and found the gift she'd sent for my birthday, untouched.

First, a folded-up note: *Happy birthday, Clara. You will soon be a witch, and I hope you follow your heart in all that you do. Eat plenty of cake and have a beautiful life. If you wish to pay me a visit, just burn this charm. —Imogen*

Then, tucked beneath the note was the charm. It was unlike most of the magic I'd been trained to use. It was not a calling card or a powder or a bottle of beautiful, jewel-colored liquid. It was a bundle of bright green leaves, now dried with time. *Oregano, to find one's way.* The bundle was wrapped around a tube of paper and pierced through the middle by a needle. Instead of twine holding it together, there was a long lock of ginger hair. *Her* hair.

I didn't remember her at all. I'd never cared to. After the hurt she'd caused us, she deserved no place in my life. By burning this, by seeing her, I knew I would be opening a door that I could not close again.

My chest tightened as I set down the box on the floor and shifted the charm back and forth in the sunlight.

What would she be like? Would she like me? Would she make me doubt myself, doubt all that I'd learned with Xavier? Would she twist the way I saw the world?

I flinched as Papa touched my shoulder.

246

"You don't have to go," he said.

I had no magic. Nothing more I could give Xavier to help him or help the people affected by Euphoria. It ached more, to think that I should be helpless all my life, than the thought of seeing my mother.

"I *must* go," I told him.

He pressed his lips together in a smile, regretful and proud all at once, and held me in a tight embrace. "Remember: we can't force anyone to change. And she can't change who you are, Clara. No matter what she tells you, only you can decide who you are and what's right and wrong."

If she was selling Euphoria and other magic that manipulated the lives of others, I knew already that she was not a good person. I'd hold fast to this truth.

Even so, I was terrified.

Slowly, I parted from him and lifted a match from the matchbox on my bedside table. Papa stood back, his hands over his heart in some sort of prayer.

Igniting the match, I touched it to the charm with a quivering hand.

At once, I was enveloped in bright light. When I blinked, my vision returned. Black smoke, fragrant from the oregano, spouted from the charm like an industrial chimney, engulfing me. Torrents of wind whistled in my ear. The smoke didn't burn my eyes, but it fogged up my vision.

I batted away the smoke, and once it cleared, I gasped.

Papa was gone—no, my whole bedroom, all pale wood and soft colors, had vanished.

I was in a new room, filled with amber light, brightly colored drapes, and large oval mirrors. Various crystals and gems hung down from above like suspended raindrops. Several golden weathervanes suspended from the ceiling pointed towards me. There was a sort of organized chaos to it all; little tables here and there, or old traveling trunks covered in jars, pots, and glasses. What looked like pickled frog's legs floated in one jar, and another was full of sugar.

Most curious was the sheer number of smells in such a little space. Warm tea, lemon, cardamom, lilacs, freshly cut grass, and even the smell of rainfall, somehow. To the left was a staircase surrounded in railing like a cage. At the top was a red beaded curtain.

A bell tinkled over my head.

From somewhere behind the curtain, a voice called out, "I'll be right there!"

My heart lodged in my throat.

My mother's voice.

19

My mother would appear any moment.

To distract myself, I strolled through the section of the house that served as a shop. There were tall shelves lining nearly every wall in the back half of the room. From a first glance, they carried goods similar to the ones Xavier and other magicians offered. A small green potion claimed to have a solution for hair growth. A little jar had a label reading, *For Poison Oak*. Then, not too far away, was a square red bottle. The white label on the front read, *Causes Influenza*.

I frowned, picking up the phial with two fingers. It was heavy as a stone, but a thick-sounding liquid sloshed inside.

Disease in a bottle.

Grimacing, I set it back on its shelf, wiping my hand on my pink skirts.

There was a soft rustling from the top of the staircase, followed by the clip of heeled boots against groaning wooden stairs. My heart plummeted to my feet. I pulled on the hem of my skirt, smoothed down my hair, pushed back my shoulders—and then felt utterly ridiculous. A small, silly voice within me insisted, *I hope she likes me.*

She hopped off the final step, striding into the shop. Her smile dropped; her freckled, pale pink skin turned paler still.

I pressed a hand against the shelf to support me as I gaped at her. All at once, I wanted her to love me, and I wanted her to never look at me again.

We looked so much alike.

Her hair was orange as a flame, more vibrant than mine or Papa's, but just as curly as mine. Her eyes were dark, wide, and watchful, like a doe's. She had my small, round nose, and the same dimples in her cheeks. She was short and full-figured like I was, even with her heeled boots. She wore a loose, peacock-green blouse, and a wine-red skirt without a bustle, sweeping naturally to the floor like a waterfall. She was beautiful, a wildflower. Would she have flourished in the garden of my life?

She hadn't given us a chance.

Imogen blinked and touched her hand to her chest. "Curse me twice," she muttered. "I really didn't expect you." She gestured to me, up and down. "You . . . you really take after your father, Clara."

I didn't know what to say. Where to begin.

She cleared her throat and clasped her hands together.

"What brings you, then?" she asked softly. "Is—is everything all right? Or did your father hide that charm from you? I'd hoped you'd come here when you turned sixteen—"

"Why would Papa hide it from me?"

She huffed a sigh through her nose. "Albert always feared I'd be a bad influence on you."

"Then I trust him in that." I folded my arms, glaring back at her, even though there was nothing about her, on the surface, that should have drawn my hatred. She was small. Kind-eyed. She let me speak, and I could tell she was truly listening to me. I loathed the very idea of her, but I scarcely knew her well enough to make a judgment of any kind.

This thought deeply unsettled me.

Scuffing my boot back and forth against her wooden floors, I said, "Why did you want me to come see you when I turned sixteen?"

"There was something I wanted to tell you before you officially became a witch." She shrugged. "I suppose it's a little late for that, though, isn't it? You'll enter their ranks tomorrow night, won't you?"

My heart skipped. I touched my chest, wincing at the lack of the familiar pain of my magic. Did she know that I no longer had any power?

She walked past me, waving a hand in my direction. "Though you'll have to get used to their dreary uniforms. I've not seen a witch dressed in pink before."

The tightness in my shoulders melted away. She didn't know. "I—I'm not a witch yet. I'm not going to be inaugurated."

Back in her kitchen, amid the countertops overflowing with jars and boxes, she looked up from a tall red bottle, her brows raised. "No? Why not? Who is your teacher?"

Shame burned my face. "I've had many. But, er, Xavier Morwyn is my teacher now." In a softer voice, more to myself, I murmured, "Or *was*, I suppose."

Imogen's eyes grew wide. She leaned across the counter as much as she could, through the forest of multicolored bottles. "A *Morwyn*? The Council's favorite family. And one that is certainly not very fond of me . . . Why did they deign to take *you* on, then?"

Because he was my friend. Because he was desperate. Because *I* was desperate. Because no one else could help me.

"Extenuating circumstances," I said.

Imogen poured herself a glass of the amber-colored liquid and clucked her tongue. "You're as tight-lipped as your papa. Though I suppose I can't blame you. Given our own *extenuating circumstances*." She held the bottle towards me, as though I were only a few paces away instead of hiding by the potion shelves. "Do you want some?"

"What is it?" I peeped.

"Sherry."

I thought of Madam Ben Ammar, who had warned me

when I was young not to accept food or drink from magicians I did not know. Imogen was my mother. But I didn't know her. I shook my head.

With a shrug, Imogen replaced the cork in the bottle. She carried her glass with her as she strode up to me.

She propped herself on the arm of the sofa in the sitting room of her shop. "Wait a minute—Xavier. He's their son— the one about your age?"

"Yes."

Recognition lit up her brown eyes. "Ah. Rumor has it, he's the one who made Euphoria." She cocked her head to one side. "I heard the Council took away his powers for making it. Is that true?"

A rush of ice sluiced through my veins. "They intend to."

Still clinging to her glass of sherry, she pointed to me. "That's what I wished to discuss with you. I want you to know that, when the time comes, you don't have to obey the Council."

I furrowed my brow. Even if I had my magic, the only way I could practice was if I was licensed a witch by the Council. If I followed their laws. "I don't understand."

"There is another path. The Council's way is all rules and roadblocks, fencing in magic and trying to control it. Magic isn't good or bad, right or wrong. It just *is*." She sipped her drink and muttered, "Unfortunately, not everyone sees things this way."

My insides twisted. "Is that why you left us?" I asked. "Because Papa doesn't see magic like you do?"

The intensity and confidence that made her eyes gleam faded away like a painting under too much sun. "I . . . I wanted to practice magic that your father didn't approve of. He didn't like that it could get us all in trouble."

"What sort of magic could possibly be worth more to you than your own child?"

Setting aside her drink, she got up from the arm of the sofa, walking past me to run a hand along one of the shelves filled with a rainbow of potion bottles. "It's not that simple, Clara."

"Is it not?" I joined her beside the shelf, lifting a red bottle. *For Telling Lies*, it said. When I glanced to her, her eyes shone with fear, until I set the bottle back upon its shelf. As though I was holding a newborn improperly. Had she ever worried about me like that?

"I bring love back where there was none," she said, lighting her fingertips against a pink bottle. "I bring happiness where it was lost. I have even brought a man back from the dead. Those are good things, beautiful things, and it is in our power to make such miracles happen. How can the Council call such work evil?"

I bring happiness.

"Do you sell Euphoria?" I asked her.

She nodded casually as she plucked a phial off the shelf.

"It's very popular. Do you need some?"

My heart was a galloping horse in my chest as I accepted the phial. So small and simple, filled with violet-colored liquid.

For a moment, I wondered what it would be like to live in a dream. To no longer feel sorrow, or the shame of having lost my power. The fear of the years ahead of me; years without hope, without magic, without any prospect for a career for myself.

I shut my eyes and imagined it. A perfect place. My cottage, among sunlit flowers. Papa tending the garden, healthy and happy. And Xavier—to see him at all would be a dream.

But in my mind, I could also see Emily Kinley, laughing until she was red in the face, even while her father wept and begged her to stop.

Tears seared my eyes. The slight weight of the potion belied all the destruction it had brought. To Daniel. To Emily. To so many others.

All at Xavier's hands.

"Do you sell a cure as well?" I asked.

Imogen folded her arms. "No one's made one yet. But when people buy from me, I tell them what to expect. I warn them of the madness, of the unparalleled pleasure. They make the choice to buy. I am not like the Council. I would not take my customers' freedom away. They accept the potion's consequences."

Rage rose, hot and acidic as bile in my throat. I brandished the potion in her face. "You're taking their minds away! I've seen *children* lose themselves because of this potion." I imagined Xavier, tears in his eyes, thorns wrapping around him. The anguish in his eyes. How desperately he'd tried to help the Kinleys. "Do you feel no remorse?"

"I don't hold myself responsible for the choices of my customers."

"Then you're heartless," I said.

She stepped closer to me, her eyes flashing. "It's heartless to hoard magic and keep it from those who are *begging* for help. The Council won't even try to make treatments for people suffering from melancholy, or mania, or nerves, since they're too afraid to address any issues of the heart—"

"It's not safe to bend hearts," I said, my voice growing softer, because I was less certain now. I knew heartache well. I knew loneliness well. If that pain could be made *bearable* . . . wouldn't I want someone to make it so?

"It is not safe to let people suffer, either."

She was right.

Silence lay heavily between us.

"The Council isn't always just," said Imogen. "That's why I sought help elsewhere. My coven and I, we don't let these arbitrary rules keep us from helping people—"

"Your coven," I said. "They sell Euphoria, too?"

"Yes, but—"

"And poison?" I moved one step nearer to her, our eyes locked. "You offer that, as well."

She said nothing.

"You aren't as noble as you make yourself out to be," I said. I thought of Madam Ben Ammar, a woman I'd easily call a hero, and how she was searching so desperately for these criminals. These people like my mother. "Who are these people in your coven? Where are they?"

Imogen shook her head at me again, her arms wrapped tight around herself like a vice. "I'll not talk about that."

"You've not talked to me for fifteen years!" I snapped. "People are *suffering*, Mother, and if you could put a stop to it—"

A word I didn't understand echoed in my ears, as sharp and discordant as nails on glass. I fell to my knees at the shock of the sound, and in my surprise, dropped the phial of Euphoria. It plinked softly against the floorboards and rolled away from me.

Dots danced around my vision. My neck burned and strained as I lifted my head towards Imogen. Her finger was raised. Her eyes were soft and sad.

"Listen to me," she said. "If I tell you too much, the Council will be able to draw the truth from you. If they do that, they'll hunt down my coven, who'll come for you, even if you are my own blood. Do you understand? If you do anything that interferes with their work, if you tell the Council, they will find you and kill you."

The room tilted back and forth like a bobbing ship. "You—you enchanted me—"

"I'm sorry. I just needed you to listen."

Would she have treated me like this, had she stayed in our house? Would she have punished me with curses for bad behavior?

Crawling on my hands and knees, I propped myself against the shelf of potions. All along my line of vision was phial upon phial of purple potion, rows of Euphoria standing shoulder to shoulder.

Proof of Xavier's shame. Proof of pain that he and others had caused—which Mother was sharing so carelessly.

I threw my weight forwards, sweeping my arm across the shelf, casting all the bottles of Euphoria onto the floor. They shattered, spilling a pool of purple across her floorboards.

Imogen yelped and grabbed both my wrists. I pushed against her, my hatred of her ringing in my head like a battle cry. Heat rose in my face, and some animalistic part of me wanted to scream at her, wanted to hurt her, wanted to let her know how I loathed her for all she'd done and hadn't done for me these many years.

But I wasn't like her.

I pulled out of her grasp, staggering to my feet. The longer I looked at her, the more anger boiled within me.

With a flick of her hand, she cast the shards of glass into a nearby dustbin. Her brown eyes were cold and sad. "Clara," she said, her voice firm and, I supposed, motherly. "All I mean to say is that you can use your magic to do great things. Things beyond what the Council allows—"

"I cannot use my magic at all," I spat.

Her face went lily white. Seeing her so horrified gave me the strangest sort of thrill. "What?"

Anger was heady and addictive. I wanted to blame her for everything. To use my own pain as a weapon against her.

"That's right," I said. "Your daughter can never be a witch because she gave her power away."

She held a hand to her forehead, like the very thought of this was making her ill. "You gave it away? To whom?!"

"You've kept your secrets from me. I'll keep their name secret, too."

The witch shook her head vehemently. "No, no—I don't care who has it." She averted her gaze, running a hand through her curls. "When you were a child, I blessed your magic so that it would grow strong, like a weed."

Like a weed. All of Xavier's theories about me, that my magic was different, disobedient, too powerful—he'd been right.

"You cursed me?"

"No, I *blessed* you."

A blessing required intention, and strength, and most importantly, *love.* This startled me, unsettled me—but the fear in her eyes, even more so.

Sweat glistened along her hairline. "Listen to me. I also

259

blessed your magic in this way: if someone took that power from you, it would be so wild that it would kill them."

My heart plummeted into my toes. I gripped the shelf for support. "What?!"

"I did it to protect you," she said, her voice low and steady, like I was a wild horse.

And I felt like one, then. I strode to her, grabbing the front of her blouse, looking at her eye-to-eye, tears rising.

"You have to stop it," I hissed.

Her eyes were so wide I could see the entire circle of her irises. She shakily held up her hands. "There's nothing I can do. If they're dead, you could bring them to me—"

"He's not dead." The idea made no sense; an unfathomable equation, imagining a color that didn't exist. Xavier Morwyn was not dead.

"Make me a portal," I said. The more I talked, the less I was able to breathe. My chest was collapsing in on itself. The world was shrinking. My heart beat so fast it was humming. "I'll describe his house to you."

She nodded but held up a finger. "For my safety and yours, I must put a silencing spell on you. You'll not be able to tell anyone about me, this shop, anything we've said today, no matter what enchantment the Council places on you."

I thought of the Euphoria victims for one second, and then let all hope of vindication fade away.

Xavier's life was in danger.

"Do it," I said.

I lowered my still-trembling hands to my sides. Tears and sweat gathered on my cheeks. Every second pained me. Was Xavier dying? Was he already dead? What had my cruel magic done now?

Imogen placed two fingers against my lips. She spoke an enchantment I didn't understand, whispers that made my head grow foggy and my ears ache. When she finished, when her lips closed around the final syllable, my mouth burned like she had struck it with a hot poker. I gasped, touching my tongue. When I drew back my hand, though, I saw no blood on my fingertips.

"There," she said. She hooked her hand around my arm, lightly tugging me towards the door, tall, skinny, and black as night. "Now, describe his house to me."

Imogen touched her hand to the brass doorknob, intricately carved with vines.

I shut my eyes and remembered. The rush of excitement, bouncing on the porch, waiting for Madam Morwyn to open the door and let me in to play with her children. The salty smell of *tortilla albilana* in the kitchen, mixed with the heavy, floral scent of potions.

"When you open the door," I said, "you see polished floors, deep brown like chocolate. The walls are covered in pale green wallpaper, with fleurs-de-lis."

"Good," murmured Imogen. "Keep going."

"There are cast-iron lamps on either side, and a round table and two small chairs on the left, like a bistro."

The tea we'd had together. The way I'd shouted at him. Curse me sevenfold; would our final argument be our last words?

My voice trembled as I continued. "Across from you is a mahogany counter with a stone top. There are cabinets all around it, and pots and pans hanging from the ceiling, and drying plants along the top of the walls. One cupboard is white, the others are dark wood. And the whole place smells of tea and flowers. It's—it's peaceful there."

Something clicked softly, followed by a sharp creak. I opened my eyes, watching as Imogen drew back the door.

Xavier's shop lay beyond, dark and empty.

I was too frightened to move.

"Be careful, Clara," murmured Imogen. "Don't let my coven see you as a threat. People are always watching."

Nothing could threaten me now. There was only one thought in my head, an anthem echoing in my heart, repetitive and desperate: *Save him, save him, save him.*

I stepped over the threshold and did not look back.

20

The door slammed behind me, severing the only way back to my mother. I did not care; I jogged through the sunlit entryway. I craned my neck and called out in a hoarse, broken voice, "Xavier?"

I looked over the back of the sofa in the sitting room, behind the counter in the shop, and then as I darted into the next hallway, my thoughts plagued me with the image I feared the most. His body, cold and still, strangled by my own magic or choking on flowers.

My breath was noisy in my ears as I searched the first floor. The spare room was empty, save for rolls of bandages and a little bed in case a patient needed to lie down.

My boots clacked against the stone steps as I raced up to the second floor. "Xavier!" I shouted. "Xavier, please, are you there?"

I threw open door after door to each of the bedrooms.

One of the doors to the library was ajar. I ran in, crying his name, but he wasn't there either.

A desk chair was edged out slightly. On the desk was a small sprig of yarrow, about the length of my forefinger. The red blooms were beautiful, but slightly damp.

Yarrow for love. For healing. For courage.

As I stared at the flower, the smell of smoke began to curl around me. I frowned, turning backwards, and indeed a great white cloud was blooming up from the plush rug. But I couldn't see any flames—only the shadow of a figure, a woman, slowly coming into focus. Madam Ben Ammar stepped through the fog, holding a charm of some sort—leaves and string wrapped around what appeared to be my hairbrush. Just like the charm I'd used to find my mother, it too vanished in a puff of smoke.

"Clara?"

I raced around the desk towards her, gaping. "Madam? How have you come here? And—and have you seen Xavier? Do you know if he's alive?"

She reached out, her hands cradling mine. After two weeks, I'd almost forgotten what it felt like to hold a person's hand and not fear hurting them. But my magic was still out there, harming someone else.

"He's alive," she said. "Though he's not well. He came to us ranting and raving, saying that he has your magic. . . ." She looked down at our hands and narrowed her eyes. "Was this a condition of your vow?"

I couldn't answer; couldn't think. My mind was racing, providing me with images of his body contorted and maimed by my own magic. I resisted the maelstrom of my own worries—I needed facts, not my imagination. "What do you mean, he's not well?"

"Clara," she said, her voice firm but heavy with grief. She met my gaze. "Did you give your magic to him?"

"Yes." Tears spilled down my cheeks. "It was the vow, but please, I—I fear my power may kill him—"

"So do we." She held up a finger. "When this is over, you'll have to explain yourself to the Council. Trading magic away, and to someone considered a criminal, no less . . . it is not behavior the Council approves of—"

"I don't care," I whispered. "Please, please, just let me see him!"

Madam Ben Ammar nodded, waving me towards the library door. She closed it and placed her hand upon the curved handle. Before she started the enchantment, she glanced over her shoulder at me. "I need you to prepare yourself. His condition is . . . disturbing."

I'd seen my father spit up flowers. I'd seen the hysterical, uncontrollable laughter, the dancing, the delirium caused by Euphoria. Magic could be a wild, cruel beast. But I would face anything if it meant saving his life.

Madam Ben Ammar pressed her forehead to the door and whispered to it. Her arm trembled and her voice grew in volume, echoing through the room and through my mind. The acrid scent of smoke snaked through the air, and somewhere far away, I could hear magicians murmuring to one another.

The door swung open, and a hallway unfurled before us, pale as the moon and never-ending. Madam Ben Ammar stepped through, and I followed close behind. The sconces along the walls were made of thin black stone, the candlelight filtering through almost gray. I shivered.

Gradually, the flat, marble walls curved, like a stream directing us onward. My heart thrummed faster with every step.

The faint smell of smoke gave way to a suffocating floral scent: roses and freesias and freshly cut herbs. My eyes watered. I gripped Madam Ben Ammar's sleeve as she guided me through the corridor.

A loud cry echoed through the hall, deep and pained like a wounded animal. I stopped where I stood, my stomach plummeting.

The cry came again. It was my name.

"Clara!"

My heart pounded against my breastbone. *Xavier.*

Leaving Madam Ben Ammar behind me, I raced down the hall towards the horrible noise. The corridor opened into a large, rectangular chamber.

The courtroom had soaring, white ceilings like a castle might, crowned with a massive black chandelier bearing orbs of golden light. Gold mosaics lined the walls, showing magicians of centuries past performing wonders and laying hands on the ill and the desperate.

On three sides of the room were rows of chairs, enough to fit the whole queendom's worth of Councilmembers. And in the center of the room stood at least twenty magicians. With a sickening lurch of my stomach, I realized that Master O'Brian and the silver-haired wizard from my previous Council meeting were among them all, their bodies acting as a wall around something I could not see.

Around Xavier.

As I darted forwards, a wizard with long, pale blond hair caught sight of me and held out a hand. At once, I was stopped in place, falling to my knees. I let out a cry of surprise as I hit the hard marble and found myself unable to move.

In the center of the circle of magicians was the back of a tall chair. It wobbled back and forth. "No," growled a voice, twisted and pained and hauntingly familiar, "No, Clara, Clara, Clara!"

"Please let me pass," I begged the wizard, pushing as hard as I could against the spell that had glued my hands to the marble. The more effort I put into it, the more the magic seared against my palms. "It's me he wants. I'm Clara Lucas."

The blond wizard raised his eyebrows and then pulled back his hand, as if he were tugging on a string. As I scrambled to my feet, Madam Ben Ammar called from behind me,

"Keep watch over her. Don't let it lay a hand on her, do you understand?"

The wizard's heels clicked as he crossed the marble floor, helping me get my balance once more. "My apologies, Miss Lucas."

I strode past him and knelt before Xavier's seat.

His wrists and ankles were clamped tight to the chair with iron manacles. He was missing a shoe, and leaves fluttered from his right pant leg into a little pile beside his socked foot. Xavier's white shirt was torn along the arms, where long thorns had burst through his pale skin. New bruises bloomed around his eyes and along his left cheek, deep purple and black. Blood had left a dark trail beneath his nose. Large red tulips were nestled within his long, black hair. *Red tulips—for true love.*

For a moment, his eyes shone like stars, and a small, relieved smile flickered upon his lips. "Clara," he whispered—and then his head whipped to the side, slamming against the wooden chair. When he looked at me again, his irises were matte black. "Monster," he growled in a different voice entirely. "Fool!"

I knew this voice all too well.

"You gave me away," my magic spat: an accusation. "You were never strong enough!"

Xavier opened his mouth to speak again, then suddenly clamped his jaw shut. He wrenched his eyes closed and curled up his fists. Gasping for air, Xavier whispered, "I'm sorry, I can't . . ." Blood stained his teeth. He'd bitten his tongue trying to silence my magic.

I reached out to him, touching his hand, but immediately drew back at the sharp, searing pain. My fingertips were scalded, like I'd passed them through a flame. Xavier—no, the magic taking hold of him—twisted his mouth in a satisfied grin.

Madam Ben Ammar gripped my arm, her brow furrowed with concern. "Miss Lucas, stand back—there's no telling what your magic will do, even with our bonds in place."

"It could hurt *him*, too," I said, prying myself out of her grasp. "This is my magic. I'm responsible for it."

She opened her mouth to protest, but to my right, my magic spoke again in its low, whispering tones.

"Yes," it hissed. "This is between the two of us."

Xavier's forefinger flicked out, and at once, a long green vine shot up from the floor and snaked around my wrist, chaining me in place. I staggered and pulled on the vine, but it was as thick as a braided rope. The manacles around Xavier's wrists and ankles glowed bright white for just a second, and Xavier—or the magic inside of him—hissed at the pain.

"Clara!"

I looked over my shoulder to where Madam Ben Ammar was—to where she *had* been, along with the other Councilmembers—but more dark, spiky vines had sprouted from the fissure in the marble. They grew fast and tall, creating a thorny wall that blocked off Xavier and me from the other, elder wizards.

The barrier rose as high as Madam Ben Ammar's shoulders. She reached out to me through the mass of thorns but cried out in pain.

"Don't!" I called, tugging at the vine with my free hand. "I'll get to you as soon as I can!"

The brambles surged up to the ceiling like the bars of a cage, completely obscuring the other magicians from my view.

I heard Madam Ben Ammar grunt, and a flare of bright light glowed from behind the tangle of thorns. The vines began to catch fire, and smoke rose into the air in thin ribbons. I grinned with pride, but from behind me, my magic gave a dramatic sigh.

"Must we?" it said.

Then, once more, it flicked Xavier's finger, this time towards the domed ceiling. From nowhere, black clouds gathered. Buckets of rain poured down, dousing the fire. The breach in the vines that Madam Ben Ammar had created was mended at once with more thorns, even larger than before. Blood-red roses began to bloom among the brambles, as large as wagon wheels.

Xavier cried out again as the manacles flared with bright light, stinging him once more.

"Stop!" I shouted. "You're hurting him!"

I clawed uselessly at the vine around my wrist. Xavier's face contorted in a strange, wrong smile as he watched my efforts. Seeing my magic twist him to its will, as it had tried for so long to bend me, I became filled with hot anger. I pulled harder on the vine. "Magic, let him go; you have no right to do this to him!"

Xavier's chin lifted defiantly. His head bent to the side, and he leaned over the arm of the chair, opened his mouth, and spat up scarlet yarrow branches. After a moment of coughing, he sat tall again, his night-dark eyes upon me.

"I have every right to," it said. "You were too weak for me. You gave up. You surrendered me to him." Its eyes narrowed and its lips curled at the edges. "And this is what he wanted, too. I can read his heart. He only wanted this power. He never wanted you. You are a fool. Trusting others recklessly, wanting so desperately to be loved that you would even give away your own magic! And now look at you." Its eyes gleamed. "You still want me. You know you're nothing without me."

"I'm here because I love him!" I snapped, so loud and so fierce that even my magic leaned back. "That is not weakness."

"Your love is misplaced."

"Clara!" I heard Madam Ben Ammar cry again over the roaring rain. "Clara, are you all right?!"

The chamber lit up with a bright flash of lightning, making the whole room shake. I stumbled and grabbed onto the chair for support.

My magic chuckled in satisfaction, even when the manacles flashed back to life. "The Council wants to punish

Xavier, and for good reason. He's a coward, just like you."

When my magic had been a part of me, it had revealed in loud colors the true feelings of my heart. It had bloomed bluebells when I remembered our childhood, and lilies of the valley when I'd been joyful.

And now red tulips, symbols of true love, grew in Xavier's hair.

The voice of my magic had always been wicked. Had told me the worst parts of myself, demeaned me, discouraged me, brought me low.

I could not trust anything that came from its lips. Only the flowers it grew spoke the truth—spoke Xavier's true heart.

"You're a liar," I said, stepping closer.

Its eyes widened. It growled and pushed against the iron restraints around its wrists, but still it couldn't move. "There is cruelty in you, Clara Lucas. You want power. You want glory. Just like your mother."

But I'd met my mother. I'd seen how she was willing to hurt others. To hurt me. She had chosen her own way above anyone else. Even above her family.

I wasn't like her.

"You say whatever you think will make me weak!" I spat. In my mind, I could see Papa, the light returning to his eyes as I blessed him at last. I had done that; I had wrestled my magic into submission and had saved his life. And I could do it again.

I reached out and clung to Xavier's wrist, even though

it burned, even though everything within me begged me to let go.

"I only say what I know. And I know you," my magic said. "You think I hurt your father all on my own? That desire was already in you. You have *hatred* within you. For him and his foolishness. For your mother—"

"Quiet," I said, straining against the vine until I could clasp Xavier's other hand in mine. Both ached. Tears beaded in my eyes and my arms quaked at the pain, and I fell to my knees before the seat, looking up into the eyes of my magic.

Behind the wall of thorns, Councilmembers beat against the barrier. Wind howled; metal clanged; lightning crashed, and Xavier's bonds shone with that horrible light. The barrier remained. My magic was capable of such destruction.

But I was stronger than this magic.

"You're wrong about me," I said to my magic, more certain than ever. "I've made mistakes. I've hurt people. But I'm not a monster. I'm good and I'm kind and I'm strong. I want to help people. And I have endured you thus far. I have tamed you before. I made portals. I healed people. I blessed Papa."

It opened his mouth, but I cut it off, saying, "I am the one who controls you."

My magic looked out at me through Xavier's eyes, waiting, watching, assessing, like a snake about to strike.

One of Xavier's books on blessings had said that to bless someone, a magician must be in complete control of their magic. And I had succeeded in this. I was its mistress.

"Magic," I said. It leaned forwards against the bindings restraining it, its hungry eyes flashing at me. "As long as you are bound to Xavier, the Council will take you away. They'll destroy you. Is that what you want?"

It said nothing, only writhed about, trying to escape my hold.

"I will offer you a home." I touched one stinging palm against my breastbone. "I will accept you as you are. I will allow you to unleash your power." At the eager smile spreading across its lips, I held up a hand. "But I make the rules. You shall harm no one. And if you do, I will go to the Council and ask them to take you away for good. Do you understand?"

It curled his lip. "You stifled me." Tilting its head towards the rainstorm and the thorns, it said, "Look at the wonders we could perform together. If you'd *use* me—"

"I'm not afraid of you," I snapped, and it leaned back, its eyes blown wide in surprise. And it was true. I'd endured the worst pain of my life; I'd nearly lost my father to my own magic. But I had conquered it.

"I will use you to perform wonders of my own," I said. "But now you must choose. Either you exist within me, or not at all."

A loud crash of thunder boomed over my shoulder. I turned back and saw that lightning had struck a large, targeted hole in the barrier, scorched at the edges. Already it was mending itself, but Madam Ben Ammar ducked through and stood tall, her hands crackling with electricity.

"Don't let her destroy me," whispered my magic. When I faced it once more, there was fear gleaming in its black eyes. "Take me back, please, take me back!" My magic unfurled Xavier's hand, now marred by a faint pink mark on his palm from when we'd made the vow, as well as one black band around his thumb.

I looked into the eyes of the beast and fit my hand in its own. "I control you," I said. "Now come back to me."

My hand burned as if a thousand flames licked at my skin. Sharp little teeth pricked at my palms and my fingertips, and then, like a dam bursting, the fire swept through my arm, and landed in my heart like a burning coal.

I staggered backwards from the shock of it, my hands pressed hard against my chest. With a *snap*, the vine around my wrist broke. The room filled with glorious light as the clouds above vanished completely, along with the rain. The wall of thorns and roses collapsed to the floor in a great heap. The Councilmembers stood beyond, every one of them drenched. Water pooled on the white floor in large, stagnant puddles full of petals and leaves.

"Oh, Clara!" Madam Ben Ammar's voice was hoarse and weak as she raced up to me, wrapping me in a tight embrace. "Thank goodness you're safe." She drew back, her hand soft against my cheek. "Did you take your magic back?"

I nodded, cold and dripping and shaken after all that had happened.

You are nothing without me, said the familiar voice. It was softer now, only a weak little whine of a thing.

But looking at Xavier, his bleeding mouth, his tired eyes, the iron cuffs around his wrists, I paid no mind to my magic.

I pulled away from Madam Ben Ammar and turned back to Xavier. With a weary, grateful smile, I knelt before him, pressing his palm to my cheek. The thorns on his arms clattered to the floor, leaving bloody gashes behind. The tulips, too, fell, whispering against the marble as they landed. The spark had returned to his eyes; they were warm and brown again. Tears clung to his lashes.

"I'm so sorry," he whispered. "I was selfish and cruel and—and I'd do anything to make things better for you. I wish—" He paused, his breath hitching. "I wish I could help you endure this—"

I hushed him, touching my lips to the heel of his hand. His face flushed, and my stomach turned.

"I *am* strong enough to endure it," I told him.

He nodded. "I know you are."

Despite everything, despite the tears in his eyes, he beamed down at me. My heart swelled.

"Miss Lucas?"

Reluctantly, I looked back at Madam Ben Ammar and the other magicians now standing at her side. Some were creating small gusts of wind or little flames to help dry one another off—and they were laughing, both at themselves, and out of relief that the danger had finally passed.

"Miss Lucas," said Madam Ben Ammar, "I'm afraid that

despite our circumstances, we must proceed with his trial."

I rose, standing in front of Xavier, my stinging hand still holding his. Imogen's voice echoed in my mind. According to her, these people had no true authority. They chose right and wrong based on their own whims. To deprive someone of their magic, when they were repentant and wished only to do good—surely that could not be right. They'd planned to remove my magic too, when all I had needed was the right teacher and some more time.

"Wait," I said, my mind racing, my heart bounding. "This is too early. Midsummer isn't until tomorrow!"

"Tomorrow is only a few hours away," she said. "And in light of the revelation that Master Morwyn tried to use your magic to subvert the Council's punishment, I think justice is long overdue."

No. They were wrong about him; he wasn't a criminal, he wasn't a monster. They had to see that.

"He is not a cruel man," I said, my voice breaking. "He's done nothing but try to help people. Even with half his power, he worked tirelessly to find the cure to Euphoria. He has done his penance; he has served his community even when he barely had the strength to—"

"Clara." Xavier squeezed my hand. I turned back to him, and despite the blood on his chin and the wounds along his arms, he smiled. "I accept their punishment."

21

The words chilled me. And so did this: my hand against his, his skin against mine, and neither of us burning or hurting. His thumb brushed back and forth against the top of my hand, and my heart swooped.

The blond Councilmember stepped to my side, touching my elbow. "You'll need to leave while we proceed with the trial," he said.

I pulled away from the wizard trying to keep me back. Now that I had touched Xavier's hand once, I didn't want to let go; I clasped his hand tighter and looked down at him in his chair, my heart twinging at the sight of him. Bruised. Bloody. Afraid.

"This is *wrong*," I said. "He doesn't deserve to be punished. Xavier, did you mean to cause any harm by creating Euphoria?"

He shut his eyes, his brow lining, like the memory

physically pained him. "No. I just wanted to help treat melancholy. To help people like my sister."

I turned back to the Councilmembers. "You see?" I could not forget the hopelessness of the man in the market; the desperation that would drive people, young people like Emily and Daniel, to seek such dangerous relief. And my mother's words—that the Council simply refused to create any potion that could treat issues of the heart.

"We cannot leave our patients without hope," I pled. "This emptiness that they feel . . . I know it well. Master Morwyn should not be punished for trying to help those in need—"

"Miss Lucas, cease this outburst," said Master O'Brian, frowning. "The Council has made its decision about Master Morwyn. And as Madam Ben Ammar said, *new* transgressions have been brought to light—he accepted your magic from you for his own gain, all while knowing full well that we would disapprove."

A witch with scarlet hair raised an eyebrow at me. "Am I to understand you *gave* your power to Master Morwyn?"

"She didn't know about my punishment," said Xavier. "I was the one who asked for her magic in the first place."

Looking the Councilmembers in the eyes, he sat tall despite the irons on his ankles and wrists. "She has done nothing but help others. Therefore, while I still have the authority to do so," he said, "I hereby propose to you that Miss Clara

Lucas should join our ranks as an official witch."

My heart leapt into my throat. I gaped down at him. "Really?"

You don't deserve this honor. You and he are both wicked, whispered my magic, writhing in my chest, creeping up my throat, making me want to vomit. I held fast to Xavier's hand like an anchor. The voice was a liar.

Madam Ben Ammar stepped forwards, her long black skirts sweeping across the marble.

"I second the motion to inaugurate Miss Lucas," she said. My heart skipped at the sound of her voice and the pride in her eyes. "She has proven herself a fierce advocate of all the Council stands for, and she has fought hard to learn and to train her power. She even successfully performed a blessing, something many trained magicians cannot accomplish. Any fears the Council once had about the volatility of her magic should be laid to rest. We know the control that she exhibits. We would consider ourselves lucky to call her Madam Lucas."

After years of failure, after wrestling and losing against my magic, I would finally, *finally* be a witch. But my joy was short-lived: as Xavier beamed at me, only pride in his tired, bruised eyes, my stomach twinged. He would be powerless.

"It's not fair," I whispered to him.

"It's more than fair. You've worked for years to earn this," he said. "You will do greater things than I could have ever dreamed. You will help so many people, I know it."

There was still much work to do. I looked back to the vast group of Councilmembers, raising my voice, though there was a quiver in it: "What will be done about the Euphoria patients? What will be done for them next—for their melancholy?"

Master O'Brian frowned. "You know the opinion of the Council on such matters. We do not interfere with issues of the heart. If you cannot abide by that, you cannot practice magic."

The words stung—the thought that I could lose everything, lose my dream, because I wanted to help people. Wasn't that what magicians were supposed to do? Heal those who were suffering?

My mother would have agreed with that. My mother would have told me to do as she did; to leave the Council and their rules behind.

Xavier's thumb swept against my hand, and once again, I remembered where I was. What mattered. The fondness and the pride glittering in his eyes.

"It's clear that Miss Lucas has great compassion for her patients," said Madam Ben Ammar, looking me in the eyes, her gaze unwavering. *Listen close,* she seemed to say. *This matter is not finished.* "Will you then obey the rules of the Council, Clara? Will you do whatever it takes to heal those in need, and never use magic with ill intent?"

Whatever it takes. Even if it meant breaking their rules.

"Yes," I said, leveling her with the same firm gaze. *I will not let anyone suffer, no matter the laws.*

The other Councilmembers looked at one another and murmured their assent. Master O'Brian nodded. "Very well—tomorrow, at the Midsummer ceremony, Miss Clara Lucas can be made Madam Lucas."

"That brings us to an important question," said the silver-haired wizard. "Master Morwyn, once you have lost your title, there will no longer be a magician treating the patients of your jurisdiction—"

"That choice should belong to my parents," he said. "Please send for them. It's their shop, after all. And . . . I have not seen them in a very long time."

Madam Ben Ammar smiled at him. "I will call on them by maple leaf before the night is done."

"Thank you."

She folded her hands in front of her, her lovely, deep brown eyes solemn and sad. "It's time, young man."

The Councilmembers tightened their circle around us.

Xavier's hand pulsed against mine, and our eyes met. Just soft enough for me to hear, but with formidable certainty, he said, "Clara Lucas, may your days be long and safe. May you live long and be safe."

My brow furrowed. "What are you doing?"

"May you live long and be safe," he repeated, louder and

louder. His brow was pursed in concentration. His blood-stained arm trembled, and my hand ached in his grasp. The manacles gleamed with a light so bright it stung my eyes. "May you live long and be safe!"

His voice crescendoed, echoing off the soaring walls of the chamber and thundering in my bones. A shock of electricity zipped up my arm from where he touched my hand; I flinched and drew back. Flecks of gold shimmered against the skin of my palm. My pulse hammered in my ear, and I was aware of my every breath: calm and beautiful and clear. I was alive, I was thriving, and something new was coursing in me, golden and bright.

Xavier drooped in his chair, red-faced and panting, his long hair stuck to his forehead.

The blond wizard marched towards Xavier. I shielded him with my arm.

"What did he just do?" demanded the wizard.

Madam Ben Ammar's heels clicked against the marble, her black skirt fluttering like a butterfly's wing with each confident step. "He blessed her," she said, her eyes wide. "A very noble way to use one's magic for the last time, I suppose." She touched my shoulder. "Do you feel all right, dear?"

I nodded, pressing my trembling hands to my heart. Xavier's chest rose and fell in an almost exaggerated way. A drop of blood dribbled from his nose, and my heart ached. Even with his power painfully confined, and the pain of the irons he wore, he'd managed to perform a *blessing*. For me.

"You didn't have to do that," I said, my voice thick with tears.

Despite his exhaustion, the blood and the bruises, he smiled. "Of course I did."

The other magicians circled around us. My breath caught in my lungs.

You're to blame for him being in this state, said my power, but its words didn't matter. I clutched Madam Ben Ammar's sleeve.

"Please," I whispered, "is there nothing we can do to stop this?"

"The time for that has passed," she replied, her hand light on the space between my shoulders. "But I know what it means for him to have been able to bless you so."

Something fluttered in my stomach, sweeter and kinder than magic. I recalled what Xavier had taught me about blessings.

The caster needed to feel pure, true love for the person they blessed.

I blushed.

Madam Ben Ammar lowered her head to look me in the eyes. "He has a debt to pay, Clara."

Xavier leaned his head against the back of the chair, his eyes shut, and I thought, *He so dearly needs rest.*

"It's all right," said Xavier, his tired eyes upon me. "If you can endure your magic, surely I can endure this."

He still wished to comfort me—as if *I* were the one about to be punished.

I bit my lip. "Will it hurt him?"

"No, dear."

She laid a hand against his arm. The red-haired witch touched his shoulder. Master O'Brian touched his hand; each magician had a hand placed on him. Standing around the chair in a circle, I could no longer see an inch of him, and this alone was enough for my stomach to twist inside of me. I pressed my hand hard against my trembling heart.

They spoke in one voice, all different tones, but each syllable spoken in unison: "Xavier Morwyn, you have broken your vows against our Most Esteemed Council. Therefore, you forfeit the gift of your ancestors, your magic. You forfeit your title. You may no longer be called 'Wizard.' We sever you from your power and from your title, forever."

There was no fanfare, no crashing of thunder, no bright light. The crowd of magicians stepped back, and the bonds around Xavier's wrists and ankles unclasped with a *click*. His arms shook as he lifted himself from the chair.

I pushed aside the blond wizard blocking my path to Xavier, and I swiftly draped his arm over my shoulder to support him. His head drooped atop mine.

"Miss Lucas," said a wizard wearing glasses, "we shall see you tomorrow for the ceremony."

I did not acknowledge any of them as I pulled Xavier along, my arm fast around his middle. The blood on his arm dripped against the bright pink of my dress. At the end of the rectangular chamber was a set of double doors.

"I'm going to make us a portal," I whispered to him. "With any luck, we won't land too far from your house."

"You'll do wonderfully," he breathed. "As long as we don't end up in a void, you can take me wherever you'd like."

When I glanced at him, he was grinning down at me.

"You're ridiculous." Looking at him, earnest and adoring, I agreed with the skipping of my heart.

You love him, said my magic. An accusation. A fact.

Yes, I thought. *I really do.*

Before us was the same door that had once been a portal into my sitting room, for a long-ago visit. It had a large, golden doorknob with a sun carved in the middle, like those magicians wore. I held it so tight I imagined it branding the symbol into my palm. With Xavier still pressed to my side, I touched my forehead to the door and shut my eyes.

Magic was emotion. For me, too much. But I was strong; strong enough to withstand even the wildest of my own moods. I felt a thousand things, even then. Warm, bubbly delight as his hip pressed up against mine. Sorrow, having seen him in such a state, knowing that the magic he adored was no longer inside him. Anger at the Council for bringing so harsh a punishment upon him. Regret for not helping more, for not being able to.

And they were all a part of me. All of these feelings were taking up residence in me, living in me, but not controlling me. I controlled them. I controlled the magic inside me.

I thought of journey. Arrival. Completion. Success. I pictured Xavier and myself, back at his manor, safe at last.

"Take us home," I whispered.

I twisted the doorknob and pushed. The door swung open, revealing a sunlit room. Stacks of books on a wooden floor. A lamp on a nightstand. A painting of a family, serious but united. A four-poster bed.

Xavier's bedroom. He blinked rapidly, his cheeks reddening.

"That'll do, magic," I declared, and pushed us across the stoop.

22

"You've brought me the whole shop," he said.

I'd carried up a basin of water, some washcloths and bandages, and his potion case. I rolled my eyes and waved at him, making him shift aside in the bed. I sat down beside him, dipping a cloth into the basin. Silently, I tended to the wounds the manacles had left behind on his ankles and wrists—raw, red burns that wrapped around them like bracelets.

Disinfectant. Salve to numb the pain. Gauze, to keep the wounds clean.

When I looked back at him, my heart faltered. In the midst of my work, I'd forgotten how badly my magic had bruised him.

I didn't know what to say. With one hand I cradled his face, and with the other, I brushed the dried blood from his lips and nose.

"Do you remember when we were little?" he murmured. "You always made me the patient then, too."

I smirked. "I sound like quite the tyrant, from your tales."

"You played a tyrant once. I was one of your servants."

Tipping his face, I sighed, catching sight of the ugly, blue-and-purple bruise that covered the skin from his temple to his jaw. "I'm so sorry my magic did this to you. You were right about it. It's stronger than normal. My mother bless—"

All of a sudden, my tongue pinched with pain. I touched my lips, wincing.

Xavier sat up taller, frowning. "Your mother blessed you?"

As I opened my mouth to explain that I'd visited her, and tell all that I'd seen, a searing pain sliced along my tongue like a blade. I gasped, tears springing into my eyes.

Xavier touched my wrist. "You can't speak of it?"

I shook my head.

His forehead wrinkled with thought. He watched my lips—and my heart fluttered.

"It must be a seal of some sort," he murmured. Xavier's dark eyes brightened with an idea. "Was it your own mother who placed it on you?"

When I attempted to nod, my neck grew stiff and ached like I had been hunched over for hours. I said nothing, only watched him, my lip caught between my teeth.

He leaned back into the pillows and pursed his lips. "Your

mother blessed you . . . with strong magic." He looked to the ceiling, his eyes tracking back and forth as if he were reading one of his magical textbooks. "That would explain why it was so volatile. And why it reacted so poorly to me, perhaps. But how would you know this? Did you meet with your mother?"

I could say nothing. My neck and shoulders were as unmoving as if I were a stone bust. There was so much I wanted to tell him. That she sold Euphoria. That she had a coven, and they, too, were distributing Euphoria, heedless of the consequences.

His eyes met mine again, and he blushed. "Sorry," he said. "I don't want to risk hurting you again by badgering you with questions. I suppose I'll just have to live with my curiosity."

I unlatched the potion case resting on his nightstand and chose the yellow bottle labeled *For Bruises*. "I wish I could tell you."

Using my forefinger, I painted the pollen-yellow lotion across his cheek. His eyelids shut as my fingertip brushed against his skin.

"I'm just glad you're safe," I said. Despite myself, my voice broke. I swallowed the knot tying itself in my throat and hastily turned back to the potion case.

He touched my sleeve. I whirled back, my cheeks aflame.

"Have I thanked you?" he asked. "For saving my life?"

I laughed, high and nervous and weary. "I can't remember."

"Well—thank you." Sadness flickered in his dark eyes like moonlight on water. "And I'm sorry, too. It was horrid to think that I was doing you a favor by taking your magic. Your circumstances were dire; you were desperate, and I should have given you my help for nothing at all. I'm truly sorry."

"Yes, you should have."

After wiping my sticky fingers against my apron, I took the damp cloth and tended to the wounds on his arms.

"Your father," said Xavier. "He's better, then? I know the blessing was completed, but after that . . ."

Contentment glowed warm as sunshine in my chest. "Papa's back to his old self. And I couldn't have cured him or tamed my magic without you."

He laughed. "No, Clara. I was no match for your magic. My power only ever whispered to me, and I could push it aside, but yours . . . it's so relentless. Yet you fought it all on your own. I cannot *fathom* how you bear it."

You can't, growled my magic. *One day, I will break you.*

You speak in lies, I reminded it.

He frowned at me. "It's talking to you now, isn't it?"

I nodded. "It says it'll break me someday."

Xavier exhaled deeply, his thumb brushing against my sleeve. I shivered. "It cannot break you," he murmured. "Not when you've mastered it."

"I'm in control." I looked at him instead of focusing on the loud voice of my magic. I *was* in control. It still writhed and whispered, but I was the one who commanded the spells. The attention Xavier gave me, the way he looked at me so watchfully, like a knight holding vigil, made me grin. "It's . . . nice, in a way. You, knowing how it feels to carry my magic."

His hand rested beside mine, palm up. Now each of us bore a faint pink scar along the lines of our hands. Where I had held his hand and first made the vow. And when I had held to him as my magic took hold of him and burned me.

"I respect you all the more," Xavier said. "You have fought it so bravely. But if there's something I can do to help you fight it, please, tell me. You shouldn't battle it alone."

He was right. I fit my hand in his, a glimmering, excited hum running from my fingers to my middle. "Thank you," I whispered.

My magic shouted at me, telling me that I didn't deserve love. *You broke into his things, violated his trust*, it reminded me.

It was right this time. "I owe you an apology, too," I said. My magic screamed its assent, hurling accusations at me, but I concentrated on the task at hand. "I invaded your privacy. I read your journal and stole away your chance to tell me the truth in your own time. I'm sorry."

"It wasn't too soon. I had just been too much of a coward to say something before."

"No, Xavier. It wasn't right. I shouldn't have done that."

His eyes crinkled in the corners, gentle and kind. "I forgive you."

I leaned close, pressing a kiss to his brow. When I sat back, I found his cheeks deeply flushed. He averted his gaze.

"Miss Lucas," he said—how I hated the formality!—"You have a brilliant future ahead of you as a witch. You could go anywhere, do anything . . . I want you to know that you should not feel hindered by me in any aspect."

I scowled. "Why would I be hindered by you?"

"I—I just mean that, if you wanted to work independently as a witch without any distractions, or if you didn't want me to trouble you with all of my . . . with all of *me*, then—I dunno, I'd go to Álbila or—"

"Xavier Morwyn, what are you talking about?"

He burrowed himself back into the mountain of pillows behind him. Now his whole face was turning red, even the bruised bits. "Well, you're a young witch about to start your career, and I'm a disgraced ex-wizard with nothing to offer, and I went and—and made a declaration of my love. . . . I'd wish to escape that, if I were you."

It was as if he was speaking a foreign language. I narrowed my eyes at him. "Do you mean to say I cannot be a witch and love you at the same time?"

His eyes grew round. "No, no! I just thought that you— that you wouldn't . . ." He shut his mouth and then opened it again. He was bright red; I beamed, knowing I could cause such a reaction in him. "Perhaps I shouldn't have said any-thing."

I pressed the washcloth to his face, wiping away the honey-colored salve. His skin beneath was smooth and unin-jured, but stained yellow temporarily. When my knuckle grazed his cheekbone, it was warm to the touch.

Setting aside the potions and the cloths, I balanced myself above him, one hand pressed to the bed on either side of him. His eyebrows shot up.

"You know," I murmured, "I *will* be an excellent witch. But whatever I am, wherever in this world I end up, I'd like most of all to be with you."

His eyes glimmered like polished ebony. "You . . . I . . . we?"

I drew his hand close, tilting my head to kiss his palm. "If you'd like me to put it plainly, I will." I brushed my lips against his cheek, which was soft and tasted of honey from the balm. My hand pressed against the open collar of his shirt, and I could feel his heart pounding.

"I love you," I said, and my magic sang in agreement, unable to deny it. It squirmed and fizzled through my blood, begging to be set free.

His face grew pink as cherry blossoms as he lifted a hand, resting it softly against my jaw.

"Can I kiss you?" I asked.

He nodded, his gaze upon my lips. "Please."

I leaned closer till my braid tickled his cheekbone. We did not touch, not yet, remaining an inch apart. His breath was broken and off-tempo. His hair smelled of cloves and wild-flowers. When I touched his face, the rushing sound of his breathing cut off altogether.

He pressed his lips to mine; warm, giving, kind. The beautiful, champagne-fizzing joy I'd felt, kissing the boys and girls I'd fancied in school—it was hardly as sweet as this.

Yearning and fear and delight and stomach-dipping anxiety and contentment and want—coloring my mind as vivid as a sunrise, as hot as a wildfire. My magic was so blissful, so free.

Yes, I thought, *do what you will, magic; I'm quite occupied for now.*

The moment was like a bubble threatening to burst; a glittering, thread-thin spider silk ready to snap at any instant. And when it did, my heart, too, would fall apart at the seams. I curled my fingers around the hair at the nape of his neck. I anchored my hand fast against the collar of his shirt.

Somewhere downstairs, a door creaked.

I pulled back just an inch, enough that his nose still rested beside mine.

His hand cradled the side of my face as tenderly as if I were made of glass. "What's wrong?"

"I heard a noise."

I drew back from him, sliding off the bed. My face

instantly burned as I looked at what had become of the room in a few short moments: the deep green carpet now served as a meadow for hundreds of flowers.

Purple gloxinia. Red chrysanthemums. Stark white gardenia. Arbutus blooms, pink as blush. Ivy. Fragrant orange blossoms. Golden orchids. Myrtle. Red roses. Dozens of garish blooms declared my love in a dozen different ways.

"Oh, dear," I murmured.

"Xavier!" A high voice came from the ground floor, bouncing through the house. "Xavier, are you there?"

He sat bolt upright in bed, his hair sticking up in the back like black feathers. He scrambled off the bed, spared one quick, confused glance for the flowers around us, and then took my hand.

"It's my family," he said, a brilliant smile setting his face aglow.

With astounding energy, he tugged me out of his bedroom, down the winding staircase, and onto the ground floor.

A gaggle of tall, dark-haired people stood in the shop. A woman with a red shawl was rearranging potion bottles on the counter, and she jumped when one of the girls at her side cried out, "It's him!"

He'd only taken one step towards the shop when the three girls stampeded into the corridor and threw their arms around him. The smallest pressed her face into his stomach and shook with tears. It was Inés. His sweet, shy, youngest sister. The one he said he'd blessed with courage. As the others jabbered away with questions, he placed his hand against her short, curly black hair and murmured to her.

"Have you been all right without me?" he asked, his tone light and soft.

She drew back, wiping her eyes and smiling. "Yes—yes, I've been so brave. I go to the market all by myself every day. I even made a new friend. It's nice, but . . ." Her face crumpled and she ducked her face back against his shirt. "I missed you so much."

He kissed the top of her head, holding her tight. "I missed you, too. I'm so, so sorry."

The tallest sister, with her long hair pulled back with a red scarf, scowled and poked him hard on the shoulder. "You should be," she snapped. "You were a right arse, staying here and working yourself to death without hardly sending us notes! Mamá was distraught."

He shook his head. "I'm so sorry. I wanted to write—I should have written, I . . ." Xavier reached out an arm. "Come here."

Leonor ducked close, joining the embrace with Inés.

The third sister, who was wearing a lovely, olive-green gown and had her hair pinned up like a noblewoman, regarded me with a smile. She darted towards me, kissing me on both cheeks.

"Clara Lucas, I'd recognize you anywhere!" She tugged on the curl lying on my forehead. "Even though your hair isn't as wild as I remember."

Looking at her, at the little freckle above her painted-red lip, I remembered her at once. She used to drag me away from Xavier so we could have tea parties together.

"Dalia, how are you?" I asked, hugging her tight. "It's been ages!"

Leonor, the tallest sister, left Xavier and marched over to my side, her hands on her hips. "Why didn't you ever come to visit us?"

My stomach sank. They didn't know. I'd lost them as much as I'd lost Xavier.

"Your brother never wrote to me," I said meekly. "I thought that he was cross with me about something, so I didn't want to bother him."

She rolled her eyes and wrapped an arm around my shoulders, as if all the years hadn't passed, as if we were still friends, as close as we were in childhood. "Well, you should have bothered *us*."

"Don't fool yourself, Leo. You know Xavier was always her favorite."

Xavier glanced back at Dalia, a blush coloring his cheeks.

Suddenly, Inés yelped. "Xavier, you're hurt!"

His mother swept across the kitchen in her long black dress, holding his hands and frowning at the bandages on his wrists and the yellow stains along his forearms. "What happened to you, mijo?"

"It's a long story, Mamá, but I promise I'll tell you all of it. For now, though, you don't need to worry." He smiled back at me. "Miss Lucas did an excellent job of caring for me."

His mother reached over to me, squeezing my hand. "Thank you, dear. Madam Ben Ammar mentioned your father in her letter—he's in good health, then?"

I thought fondly of how she always paid Papa too much for the flowers and herbs we brought them, and always had a mug of cider to offer him. "Yes, madam. He's doing much better, thank you."

Footsteps thudded as Master Morwyn the Elder crossed into the corridor, his hands behind his back. Xavier's father looked much like his son, if all the softness had been stripped away. His face was sharp and angular, with a pronounced forehead and low, dark brows over his black eyes. "Good evening, Miss Lucas," he said with a bow.

My heart clattered against my breastbone. Xavier's father had once decided that I, a child, was a threat to his son. That he shouldn't communicate with me. Shouldn't be friends with me. It was thanks to him that for five long years, I'd been without my dearest friend.

Xavier stepped between his father and me, shielding me with his shoulder. I gripped his hand tight, skin against skin.

The older man's eyes widened just a fraction. "Son," he said, a greeting by the loosest definition.

Without his cravat, the swell of Xavier's throat bobbed prominently as he swallowed. "Father." His hand pulsed against mine. "There's something I'd like to propose to you."

He curved his hand against my shoulder, his arm across my back. "Miss Lucas has the utmost control over her magic. I nominated her to be a witch for a reason." The silence around us was thick and tense, but the passion in his eyes, the way he spoke about me, *defended* me—it made my heart skip. Xavier held his head high. "And I think she should work here in the shop with you and Mamá."

My heart jumped in my chest. I gaped up at Xavier—I'd always hoped to work here. But with him at my side.

His father cleared his throat and glanced sidelong at me. "Xavier, we ought to continue this conversation in private."

"No," said Xavier, his voice trembling, "this directly involves Miss Lucas. She has every right to work in the shop if she'd like—"

"She has none at all," said Master Morwyn, folding his arms. "In the first place, this is my home, *my* shop, and secondly, she has no title yet, and you have none at all. It is not your place to decide." He rolled back his shoulders, his eyes like flint as he stared at his son. "Furthermore, Morwyns have worked alongside their children for more than six hundred years; you *know* that. Even if Miss Lucas's reputation was not sullied by her mother's *activities*, she is not a Morwyn—"

"She has nothing to do with her mother!" said Xavier, taking a step forwards. "She's her own person, and a bloody fantastic witch. She saved her father's life. She cast a blessing! And she saved *my* life. Why should it matter what her name is?"

"You know very well the importance of a name. Or you once did." Master Morwyn huffed. "Madam Ben Ammar wrote to say that it's over and done with. You've lost your power."

"I should have lost it months ago."

I pressed myself against his side, wishing him courage with all my might. *Remember how brave you are.*

Master Morwyn ground his teeth and glanced at his wife over his shoulder. "Take the girls to their rooms, please, Montserrat," he murmured.

Madam Morwyn slipped past, her hand lighting on her son's shoulder for just a moment before she escorted Leonor, Dalia, and Inés up the stairs. I could hear them grumbling and whispering as they left.

Xavier's father strode closer, looking down his nose at his son. "I worked hard to get you the time to restore our reputation."

"Our reputation is why I made Euphoria to begin with," Xavier said. "I would rather someone, *anyone*, cure this mess I've made than receive the credit for it! Father, *that* is why

Clara deserves a place in this shop as much as any Morwyn—"

"The decision is mine alone, and I refuse!" He whipped his head towards me, his black eyes glinting. He was just as frightening and severe as I'd remembered him to be. "Miss Lucas, I think you should go. Whatever brought you here, I certainly didn't approve of it."

Magic flared in my middle—and so did the lamps in the room. Master Morwyn glanced around him, scowling. Xavier took another step between his father and me.

"Enough, Father," he said. "You owe Miss Lucas an apology."

I gasped.

Master Morwyn's brow furrowed, and blood rushed into his cheeks. "I beg your pardon?"

"You forbade me from writing to her. You judged her to be a bad influence on me, simply because of who her mother was." He laughed, soft and humorless. "And look at me. I made a proper mess of myself all on my own."

"You're being a child."

Xavier flinched. I stepped closer to him, and he breathed again.

"If this is me being a child, then I don't care. I didn't defend Miss Lucas before. I feared you too much then. She deserves as much respect as any other magician, and if you won't grant it to her, we can go elsewhere."

"So be it," snapped Master Morwyn. "You've no magic;

no title. You'll not ride on the coattails of our family anymore. That's what you want, isn't it? So go."

The wizard marched past, not giving his son a second glance.

Xavier looked to me and back at his father. His eyes shimmered.

Master Morwyn had been so wrong. Xavier had been terrible on his own. He hadn't thrived as a Morwyn. He'd been a bird trapped in a too-small cage. This shop, this mansion, this place that I'd loved—it had been his prison for three long months.

We didn't need this house.

An idea flew into my mind, fast and ridiculous and utterly perfect. Over my shoulder, I could see his father stomping towards the staircase. I swept up Xavier's hands in mine, looked him in the eyes, and said loud enough for his father to hear, "Xavier Morwyn, will you open a shop with me?"

He blinked. "What?"

Out of the corner of my eye, I saw Master Morwyn halt at the foot of the stairs.

"You don't have to," I said, "but if you'd like, you could come stay with Papa and me. We'd set up shop in my house! My father would grow our ingredients, and you could help me with customers, and I could cast the spells, and you could help me learn new magic, too!" My voice quickened; magic was a warm, sunshiny flood in my cheeks and down my arms as I thought of the possibilities. His expertise, my magic—together, we could help so many people.

"We could find a cure for Euphoria," I said. "We could work as hard as possible, and we—we'd make a great team."

One last look. Xavier's father had left.

Xavier squeezed my hands, and I looked into his eyes again. Warm, forest-dark, and dripping with tears.

"Do you mean it?" he whispered.

"Of course I do," I said, and I couldn't help it; I laughed. "We can get started on the cure first thing in the morning. If—if you want. If you'll work with me. We promised each other, remember? We'll be 'Morwyn and Lucas.'"

A beautiful, sincere smile spread across his face. "Yes," he breathed, and then held my face in his hands, kissing me gratefully, unabashedly.

23

When I showed up on my doorstep with my luggage and Xavier Morwyn in tow, Papa was surprised—but pleasantly so. I didn't even have to explain the situation; Papa just declared he would sleep on the couch that night and that Xavier could use his bedroom until I figured out a spell to make him his own.

That next morning was the start of the longest day of the year. Midsummer. In the evening, I'd graduate from my studies and become a witch.

But first, even though dawn had barely broken, I crept into the kitchen, hoping to start on the Euphoria cure.

Xavier was already there, standing by a bubbling cauldron on the stove, his notebook in hand.

"I'd hoped you would sleep some more," I said.

He snapped the notebook shut and looked at me with wide eyes. "Clara! Good morning; I wasn't expecting you so early."

I crossed towards him, fixing my arms about his middle and smiling up at him. As I'd hoped, he turned even redder.

"What are you brewing this time?" I asked.

He swallowed, snaking his arm out from under me to hold up his notebook. "Another possible cure. The potion hasn't been imbued with any magic, of course. I just thought . . . Well, I have a great deal of knowledge about Euphoria and how to counter it. All of my potential recipes are written down here. As—as you've seen." He lowered his hand, showing me the notebook. "Perhaps these could give you some idea as to how to make the cure."

I withdrew my arms and accepted the black leather notebook. My stomach tightened with guilt. I opened my mouth to apologize, but he had begun to smirk at me.

"You know," he said, "I'm impressed that you unlocked the drawer without breaking it. Your lockpicking skills have greatly improved since the time you kicked down my door."

I glared at him, fighting back a smile. "You think you're *so* funny, don't you?"

He pointed at me. "Is that a pity laugh, then?"

I rolled my eyes and settled at his side, my hip touching his, his hand against my shoulder. When I turned back to the beginning of the book and found the instructions for Euphoria, I could feel his chest tense as he held his breath.

So much destruction, all from such a small potion.

And yet . . .

"This recipe," I murmured. "I think you have the beginnings of something here. Something that could help a lot of people."

He pressed his lips together until they went pale. "You can't be serious."

I frowned. "I am. Melancholy is a very real problem, and the magical community seems hesitant to tend to those suffering from it—you were only trying to help."

"My *intentions* didn't do them any good."

I snapped the book shut and held it close to my heart. "What I'm trying to say is that the need to cure this ailment is far greater than you, or me, or the Council and their laws. There are people who are hurting, people who are *dying* from this, and they don't care *who* makes a treatment, as long as one exists."

Leafing through the pages, I stared at the recipe for Euphoria, rapt in thought.

"Wisteria," I read. "For abundance, yes, but also for obsession. I can only imagine what that did to the effects . . . and orange lilies? They also mean passion." My finger dragged down the words on the page. "All these flowers for happiness—it isn't happiness they need. Not exactly." I thought back to my own darkness. Of yesterday. When the world felt so bleak, when it seemed that without my magic, without Xavier, I had *nothing*. No future.

"They need hope," I said. "They need strength—not a

potion that will change who they are, but something that will give them the power to be themselves again."

A smile started to dawn on his face. "You definitely make it sound more feasible, when you describe it like that . . . but what about the Council?"

"I'll work on a recipe and seek the guidance of others—of people like Madam Ben Ammar," I said. "Surely there must be some magicians in the country who would be on our side. Then I'll petition the Council and make certain the treatment I create is safe before testing begins."

He didn't say anything. I narrowed my eyes at him, trying to decipher the strange, almost sad look in his eyes.

"You're not optimistic," I said.

His brows rose. "No, no! Not that. I'm proud of you. But what if . . . what if the Council says no? After all that work?"

I shrugged. "We aren't there yet." I spun in a circle, gesturing at the cauldron, the ingredients, everything laid out in our makeshift potion shop. "First, we're going to cure the symptoms of Euphoria, then tonight, I'll become a witch, and tomorrow, we'll get to work creating a proper treatment for melancholy. Simple as that!"

He laughed. "Simple."

I settled by his side, letting him peer into the notebook. "So let's begin. Tell me about the other Euphoria cures you've tried."

"I've written down possibilities, but I haven't tested all

of them—I've tried to brew three a night for the past three months."

As I turned through the pages—dozens of them; dozens of recipes—dread pooled in my stomach like icy water. "How would you know if they worked?"

"I stayed in contact with the families of the first few people I gave Euphoria to. I usually spent Sundays giving them my attempts at making a cure." He slowly pushed back another page, marked, like all the others, with a black X in the corner. "I hate building their hopes up every time, only to disappoint. I don't know what's missing. I don't know what I'm doing wrong."

I stilled his hand. "You're *trying*," I said. "Tell me about these attempts. How do they work? What symptoms are you trying to address?"

He sighed through his nose. "Ideally, I want a potion that will calm the patient. That will do exactly the opposite of what Euphoria does—it turns a patient's mind frantic." He gestured to a jar full of long sprigs of goldenrod, fresh from our garden. "So I want ingredients that will inspire concentration and calm and balance. That is also why I've been adding every ingredient in equal portions."

At the counter, he pulled a cutting board filled with peppermint leaves before him and began chopping them into little squares. "Let's try to make potions number one hundred and six through one hundred and eleven."

Over a hundred variants. A hundred attempts to undo the wrong he'd done a season ago. I bit my lip and opened to the proper page. I read aloud:

> *"Entry one hundred and six:*
>
> *"To counter mania: calm—chamomile and lavender. Sing a lullaby; whisper over the potion.*
>
> *"To counter restlessness: contentedness—pink roses. Profess something you're grateful for.*
>
> *"To counter a lack of control: focus—forget-me-nots to prompt memory, and peppermint for concentration.*
>
> *"To counter delusion: clarity—white chrysanthemums. Add pure water. Add ice to cool anger. Imagine peacefulness.*
>
> *"To counter imbalance: all ingredients should be in equal parts.*
>
> *"To counter a lack of fulfillment: include all parts of ingredients."*

I lifted my head. Xavier was scouring our pantry for ingredients, plucking jars and boxes off of shelves and adding them to the cluttered table before us.

"I don't understand why this hasn't worked," I said. "This recipe seems perfectly viable."

He sighed. "I'm glad you think so. Most of those are variations on that same recipe. I've added ingredients, substituted them, changed the order in which they're added . . .

sometimes I try to cast in Albilan to see if that will make a difference."

I set down the book and twisted open the jar of chamomile. "We'll find a way."

"We'll need a spoonful of each ingredient," he said, using the blade of his knife to sweep aside the shavings of peppermint leaves, stems, and roots.

He looked at me when I touched his arm.

"We *will* find a way," I said.

He pressed his lips together.

"You have to be confident," I insisted. "That's what you've told me all along. About blessings, about enchantments . . . we have to *believe* that we can fix this."

His hair flopped against his cheek as he nodded. He straightened his back. "You're right. We'll find a solution. We'll make it *today*."

The tea kettle whistled. I hummed in harmony with it and poured it out over the infuser he filled with chamomile and lavender.

"Our latest patient, Miss Kinley," I said softly. "Was there nothing more to be done for her, aside from giving her a sedative?"

He shook his head, plucking pink roses from their stems and chopping their petals into fine ribbons. "Not until we find the cure."

I aided him in cutting up the stems and thorns.

"If possible," I said, "I want to test these next potions on her."

The knife hesitated mid-chop. "I am reluctant to give the Kinleys hope if there's none to be found."

"But you *could* be giving them a solution."

His hand touched mine. "*You* could."

My stomach pinched. The two days I'd been without my magic, I'd felt small and helpless and scared. Now Xavier would feel that way for the rest of his life. "This is your recipe," I reminded him softly. "If we make a cure—*when* we make it—you're just as responsible for it as I am."

"The credit doesn't matter to me." He turned back to the cauldron, adding a spoon's worth of the ice he'd brought in from the ice box. As he did so, fragrant, silvery steam like fog rose from the cauldron. "Father may still care about our family name. But I can't bear to think of anyone having to live with this burden. I want them to be free from the bonds of Euphoria. I don't care how."

I thought, too, of Daniel Watters at the Midsummer festival. He was *our* age. And had become so tormented by this potion.

"There's a boy here in town who's taken Euphoria, too," I said. "Can we make certain that he gets the cure? When we make it?"

"Yes. I'll see to it that the Council knows who to treat." Xavier glanced at me over his shoulder. "I need you to cast over this, please. First, profess something you're grateful for, to instill contentment in the patient."

That was simple. I stood before the cauldron, breathing in the calming, grassy air. I had so much to be thankful for. But two words came to mind first.

"Xavier Morwyn," I whispered, the name hissing and echoing against the cast-iron walls of the cauldron.

He squeezed my hand tight. "Thank you," he murmured. "Next . . . next, wish peace and comfort and calm upon the patient who drinks it."

Magic squirmed under my skin and tugged on my muscles, begging to be released. Shutting my eyes, I concentrated on the ideas I wanted to imbue into the potion.

Control: the thrilling feeling of my magic finally listening to me. Patience: Xavier and I the night before, forgiving one another, loving one another, despite our many, many mistakes. Peace: feeling my skin tingle at being so close to him, standing in a quiet, sunny kitchen with a hopeful future before us.

And above all: confidence.

This potion will fail, growled my magic.

"Now's not the time," I whispered. After all I'd learned, after all I'd done to control my power, I knew that I had the strength to be able to create something *good*. That this potion could be the one to save lives.

I held out my hand over the cauldron, little drops of steam clinging to my palm. Concentrating on the images of control, patience, peace, and confidence, I murmured to my magic as sweetly as if I was telling it a bedtime story. "You don't need to overexert yourself. I only need a bit of you. Just enough to help settle a patient. There's so much strength to you, magic. Save some of it for later."

As Xavier had instructed, I sang the words over the potion, soft as a lullaby, "Control, patience, peace, confidence, control, patience, peace, confidence . . ." The last word came out as a hiss, and I felt a surge of magic rush through my body and down my fingertips, coming out not as a waterfall but like gentle rainfall. The cauldron clanged as magic jostled it back and forth, but it soon grew still again.

My chest heaved like I'd just summited a mountain. The potion gurgled contentedly, bright green and whispering with magic.

I'd done it. I couldn't explain it, but I knew, marrow-deep, that *this* potion was the one we needed.

Behind us, the door to the kitchen creaked open. Papa was wearing his old red dressing gown, rubbing his eyes almost theatrically. "Something smells delicious. I don't suppose it's breakfast?"

Xavier paled. "Oh, er, no, Mr. Lucas, but I'd be happy to make you something, if you'd like—"

"He's teasing," I translated, giving his arm a squeeze. I grinned back at Papa, who watched our little interaction with a smug look on his freckled face. "We're hard at work,

Papa. Is it all right if we use the kitchen for potions?"

Papa chuckled and held up his hands in surrender. "By all means. Carry on, Your Greatness."

He slipped out the door, and I beamed. Tonight, that title would be mine at last.

Xavier's finger traced my cheekbone as he brushed a stray curl behind my ear. I caught his hand, smiling. "This potion is the one," I said to him.

He paused. "What?"

"We need to deliver this one," I said.

"I—are you certain? What if we show up and it doesn't—"

"Confidence, Xavier. That's what the strength of this potion relies upon." I pointed at the cauldron. "I have no doubt. This will work." I squeezed his hand. "It's different this time. The two of us together. My hope, your hope—"

"My hope doesn't make a difference. I don't have magic," he whispered—as if I'd forgotten.

I drew his hands to my lips, kissing his knuckles. "I think it makes all the difference."

His brown eyes shone like amber in the sunlight; shone with a sort of optimism that was so rare for him.

He had faith in us.

"Let's go," he said.

So that we would not have to portal unceremoniously into Emily's bedroom, we decided on a more traditional means of transportation. Within minutes, we hired a hansom cab and were on the road to Iverton, my potions case on my lap. Xavier reached for my hand, and I didn't let it go until we arrived.

The Kinleys' house, they'd said, was the one adjacent to the town bakery. We found it in no time—a quaint little brick building next to a shop with beautiful pastries on display in the window. I knocked on the front door, waiting so intently I did not even breathe.

To my right, Xavier had gone as white as chalk.

"It's going to be all right," I promised him.

He nodded frantically, locks of his long black hair falling against his face. "I know, I—it's hard, that's all. I caused all of this."

I reached out, weaving my fingers with his. "We'll set things right. I know it."

The door swung open. Mr. Kinley stood before us, his apron dotted with chocolate and berry juice and his hands dusted with flour. Like the both of us, there were circles around his eyes.

"Your Greatness," he murmured. "How—how can I help you?"

I took a step forwards and shook Mr. Kinley's hand. "Good morning, sir. We're sorry to bother you. It's about your daughter and her condition—we would like to test a possible cure on her."

Mr. Kinley stepped aside with wide eyes, his hand against

his heart. "Yes, yes, of course!"

Xavier grimaced at the hope beginning to dawn on Mr. Kinley's rosy face. "We must be clear, this is experimental."

Mr. Kinley's lips pursed. "Well . . . I suppose it's worth a try, anyhow. Will it hurt her?"

I shook my head. The potion's ingredients were all made to soothe. Even if the potion failed, there wouldn't be any negative side effects. "No, sir."

The baker nodded and stepped aside, allowing us into his home.

It was sunny and warm, with colorful quilts thrown over rustic, wooden furniture, and the smell of fresh bread wafting over from the shop next door.

"How has she been?" Xavier asked softly.

"Asleep, nearly constantly. We wake her to give her food, and she's keeping it down, thankfully, but . . . she's so hollow. It's like . . . it's like she's gone." Tears beaded in the corners of Mr. Kinley's eyes.

Xavier bowed his head. "I am so sorry, sir."

We stepped through the sitting room into the small corner bedroom we'd so recently visited from Xavier's shop. The drawing desk, the quilt on the bed, the dent in the wall—a room once filled with life, with color. But today, it was dim and quiet.

Sitting beside the bed was a small man with deep brown skin. Emily lay under the covers, her eyes shut. Her hands rested limply atop her cream-colored sheets, and she scarcely

317

moved as the man spooned broth into her mouth. As Xavier had promised, none of the dandelions on her skin had grown back—to an outsider, she was just a young girl, fast asleep.

Mr. Kinley laid a hand on the man's shoulder. "Your Greatness, this is my husband, Adam. Adam, this is Master Morwyn and his assistant."

Xavier held up a hand, his face tinged with a blush. "It's actually the opposite. I'm assisting Miss—Madam Lucas." We exchanged a look—I hadn't been initiated yet, but I supposed such technicalities would have to be ignored. "She's the one who brewed the potion we hope will cure Emily."

Adam turned in his seat, his eyes widening. "A cure? Truly?"

I set down the potion case on a wooden chair, throwing open the latches with two soft clicks. Along with a few other potions—antiseptic, sedatives, anti-nausea medicine, just in case—was the cure I'd brewed this morning, in a small, square bottle.

"This is it?" asked Adam. His voice broke with tears, but a hopeful smile was spreading across his face. "It's over? She'll—she'll be back to us?"

"This will be the very first time we're testing this potion," said Xavier in a meek voice, "but—"

"This will work," I promised, showing them the brew, the bright green of a crisp apple. "May I give it to her?"

The two men exchanged a quick, concerned glance.

"What do you think, Julian?" asked Adam.

Mr. Kinley nodded, squeezing his husband's shoulders. "If this could help her . . . we have to take that chance."

Xavier stood by, his hands folded tight, his eyes upon the potion. I slowly twisted off the stopper and then knelt by Emily's bedside.

Her brown eyes were cloudy and distant. She stared blankly at the opposite wall. Every so often, her eyelids would droop shut, as if she were seconds away from falling asleep again. She couldn't hear me, couldn't see me—but still, I was cautious as I cradled her face, parting her lips.

"Emily, this will wake you up," I whispered. I touched the glass lip of the phial to her mouth, and under my breath, as I poured the drink, I recited the incantation again for good measure: "Control, patience, peace, confidence . . ."

My heart pounded as my magic screamed at me.

You will fail. You'll destroy her. You're a monster.

You're a liar, I replied.

Emily swallowed, and her shoulders went slack. My blood felt as cold as the potion.

She blinked, and she looked at me—she *saw* me. Then she turned, catching sight of her fathers. "Papa? Father?"

Julian and Adam exclaimed, reaching across the bed to sweep their daughter in a hug.

Xavier's hand clung to mine. I couldn't tear my eyes from the scene. "It worked?" I breathed.

"I think so." His voice was soft and trembled with tears. His thumb brushed against my skin. "You've done it. It's over."

I could scarcely believe it. Joy, and fear of losing that joy, warred within me—after mistrusting my magic for so long, could it truly be that it had obeyed me now, as it had when I'd blessed Papa?

While Emily's parents covered her head in kisses, she grumbled, "What's going on? And who are those two?"

"You—you took a potion, and you acted so strange," said Adam. "You were laughing and dancing and then you got very still and were just dreaming all day . . ."

A small part of me remembered my training—remembered my role, not as a spectator, but as a healer. I withdrew a stethoscope from my case and draped it over my head.

"Miss Kinley," I said, "I'm Miss—Madam Lucas, and Mr. Morwyn is assisting me today." He bowed in greeting, even though the title seemed to fit him so oddly. "I'm a witch; I'm here to heal you. Like your father said, you've been under the effects of a disorienting potion for the past few days. Might I examine you and ask you a few questions?"

She nodded and let me feel her forehead (no fever), then check her breathing with the stethoscope and her heart rate with the watch on my chatelaine. She was perfectly, blessedly normal. Even this news was enough to make Julian Kinley burst into thankful tears.

As Xavier passed him a handkerchief, I turned to Emily, pulling a chair close to her.

"Now then," I said, "do you remember taking Euphoria? Do you remember when you acquired it?"

Emily paused, glancing at each of her fathers. Her golden-brown fingers bunched up in the fabric of her quilt. "Have I done something bad?"

"No," I said. "You aren't going to be in any trouble. But I need to know the truth. There are other people who've been taking this potion, and they need help, too. Euphoria puts patients into a deep, dreaming sleep. And you are the first one we've been able to heal."

She stared at the diamond pattern of her quilt. Her eyes were alert, bright—but sad. "We were at the market . . . I wandered on my own. A man approached me. I—I can't remember what he looked like; I just remember that he gave me a card, and said, 'They can help.'"

"Who, love?" asked Adam.

Emily parted her lips, but in an instant, her mouth slammed shut. Her eyes blew wide, and she touched her tongue, like she'd burned it.

I knew that kind of pain. The same sort of seal my mother had put on me.

"She's been enchanted," I said. "She can't tell us who she met with, even if she wants to."

Worry knitted her brow. "I, I'm sorry—I burned the card and then—*ow*!" Once more, she touched her fingertips to her mouth—this time, a small drop of blood began to bead on her lip. Her fathers gasped and fussed over her, dabbing at her lips with Xavier's handkerchief.

I latched my potion case shut and looked to Xavier as the

two men tended to their daughter.

"I suppose I'll tell Madam Ben Ammar what we *do* know," I mumbled.

"Magical seals are difficult to break—but not impossible," Xavier said. "I'm certain she'll think of something."

Lifting the potion case off the table, I stood by, letting the family have another moment of togetherness.

"Emily," said Julian, "what kind of help were you looking for? From that wizard in the market?"

Her cheeks reddened. She averted her gaze, and then squeezed her eyes shut. "I'm just so . . . tired. My heart can feel so heavy, and I don't know why. I just want to feel *normal*."

It was just as I'd thought. If the Council didn't create some sort of safe treatment for melancholy, patients—even children—would seek out other means of help.

"You shouldn't have to feel that way," I murmured. "You deserve to feel like yourself. And we'll find a way to help you—I promise."

A small, cautious smile crossed the girl's lips. Her fathers grasped her hands and hugged her tight and promised to be there for her.

Xavier laced his fingers with mine. "Miss Kinley," he said, "if anyone can find a way to help you, it's Madam Lucas."

And I believed him.

24

Even late in the evening, the sun glowed bright as a light-house beacon through my bedroom window. I was dressed in my palest green gown, and when I stood in the sunshine just right, I could imagine that it was white, like it was supposed to be. If I'd been nominated to be a witch sooner, a year ago, even months ago, I would have spent all of my savings and commissioned a gorgeous white ballgown for my initiation ceremony.

I sighed as I looked at the gown in the mirror. It was a beautiful birthday gift from last year, showing my freckly shoulders and making my hair look even redder against the soft green fabric. Still, every apprentice looked forward to the day when they'd celebrate their certification as a magician, and their white clothes would turn black in a final grand gesture.

It wasn't the same—but at least I was being included in the ceremony.

I slipped on the white, elbow-length gloves that Papa had bought me years ago in the hopes that I'd have this ceremony one day. The dress would have been too much of an investment, but these gloves—they were proof that he'd always believed I could be called a witch. He'd always known I could control my magic.

I stepped out of my bedroom and into the living room, where Papa sat in his favorite chair, reading a novel. He was still wearing the same dirt-stained trousers as he had that morning.

"Papa," I said, my voice light and teasing, "if I'm late for the ceremony because you got distracted by a book . . ."

He set aside the novel and bounced to his feet, grinning at me. "Clara, you look beautiful!"

I tipped my head, proudly showing him the pearl earrings he'd given me. "I'm so glad I finally have an initiate ceremony to wear them to."

Papa kissed my forehead. "I always knew you would."

The tears in his eyes, his tall posture, and his confident, healthy smile. Even the mark my magic had left on his cheek had started to fade. And his heart was healed. *I* had done that. Maybe I *did* deserve this title I was about to get.

But I scowled at my father. "You're as excited about tonight as I am, so why aren't you dressed yet?"

"Well . . . as much as I'd like to go . . . I think that you should take young Mr. Morwyn as your guest instead."

The image was a pleasant one—Xavier, tall and handsome at my side in his finest suit—but it wasn't right. "All these years, it's been you and me. Every exam, every potion, whenever I did something right, I imagined *you* as my guest at the initiation. You've supported me every step of my journey." I gave his hand a firm squeeze. "There is no one I'd rather have at the party with me. We're going to dance and then we're going to eat pastries until we get sick."

"A splendid night indeed. But there's a very nice young man outside who has a surprise for you. Perhaps you'd prefer to dance with him once you see it."

"When I see what?"

Papa grinned mischievously and pointed towards the front door. I rolled my eyes and carefully lifted the hem of my long skirts, stepping out into the evening air.

A ladder was propped up against our little cottage. A box of tools had been left open on the grass beside it. With a frown, I stepped onto the lawn.

Xavier was perched on a high rung, affixing some sort of metal attachment over the door. He wore no jacket; only a simple, pale shirt with the sleeves rolled back, his hair tied in a short little queue. I gaped.

"Xavier Morwyn?" I asked. "Is that you?"

In his alarm, he dropped something onto the grass—a screwdriver. "Oh, curse me—ah, Clara! I didn't see you! This was supposed to be a surprise, but, er . . . one moment, one moment." He picked something off of the roof and slipped it onto the small metal pole he'd been attaching. It was a wooden sign, which read, in neat, painted letters, *Lucas's Magical Goods and Services.*

"I thought you could use this, since we start work tomorrow," he said, climbing down the ladder and hopping onto the grass. He stood at my side, observing his handiwork. "I think I've hung it a bit crooked, but I'll get better at working with my hands one of these days."

I stared up at the sign that declared me a witch.

My dream.

My dream.

"I—I figured that since I couldn't add on to my own house, I may as well add to yours. But, er." He scratched his head. "Do you like it?"

I nodded, tears spilling down my cheeks. I sniffed noisily.

You love him, my magic said.

Xavier wrenched a handkerchief from his breast pocket and passed it to me. I gratefully pressed it to my eyes.

"I'm so sorry, I didn't mean to make you cry—"

"It's lovely." I curled against him, my cheek against his heart. "After so long, I doubted I'd ever work in a shop, let alone *own* one!"

He gently tucked a ginger curl back into place in my elaborate coiffure. "I always knew you'd be a witch, ever since we were young."

326

I pressed closer to him, caring very little for how it would disturb my hair. "But it's not fair," I whispered. "How—how do you feel? I felt so *wrong* when my magic had left me. So empty."

His lips touched the top of my head. "It will take some getting used to. But . . . what scared me the most about losing my magic was the thought that I could no longer help anyone. Working alongside you today and giving that cure to Miss Kinley . . . I felt just as grateful and proud as I did when I had it."

Leaning back, my arms still around him, I beamed at him. "Then I think we should add your name to the sign, too. We'll be '*Morwyn and Lucas*,' just like we always said."

Xavier smiled. He rested his chin atop my head and inspected the sign. "I think my name would have to be in very, very small letters."

"As long as it's the two of us."

I stood on the toes of my dancing shoes to kiss him . . . when a loud *slam* sounded, like a door being shut somewhere on the hills around us.

To our left, a few paces down the gravel road, four figures stood beside an isolated emerald door. In a moment, it evanesced into green dust. With the door gone, the four women ran fast towards us through the sunlight. Xavier gasped.

His mother. His sisters.

"Xavier!" cried Inés, throwing her arms around him in

a hug. Leonor and Dalia were quick to join her, and even pulled me into their embrace, jabbering about how he *really* needed a haircut and about how brave he'd been, standing up to their father.

Their father—who wasn't there.

"Mamá," said Xavier in a small voice. "I—I thought you and Father wanted to leave me on my own."

The lovely, dark-haired woman stepped closer, holding a bundle of black and white fabric against her chest. "Vitus has his own troubles to sort through. We've spent too long being away from you. It's foolish of him to be so cold." She reached out to her boy, brushing a lock of black hair behind his ear. "This independence suits you." Her hand cradled his cheek. "Loneliness did not."

"Yes," declared Dalia, sweeping up my hand in hers. "That's why we've decided we are going to come visit you all the time."

"Yes!" echoed Inés.

Leonor squeezed her brother's arm. "Can I help at the shop, too? Please?"

Xavier laughed, gesturing to me. "I believe you'll have to ask my employer."

I beamed at the title. "Well, the shop opens first thing tomorrow, so I suppose we could use all the help we can get!"

"Excellent! Then for my first task as your second assistant, I came here—we all came here—to make a very special delivery!" Leonor approached her mother and accepted the bundle of cloth from her. "Inés checked the magic cupboard earlier and found *these* inside."

"And we knew they weren't for any of us," Inés added.

Dalia let out a prolonged sigh. "The dress was too big for me, anyway."

My brow furrowed. "Dress?"

"Here," said Leonor. The bundle she carried, it seemed, was actually several garments neatly folded. The first was white and glowing like moonlight, and she handed it to me.

I carefully lifted up the strange cloth, and suddenly it cascaded down into a stunning, pure white gown with little crystal beads sewn in it and embroidered with white flowers and vines. It was a dream. The most beautiful gown I'd ever seen. The perfect gown for an initiate.

"This—this can't be for me," I whispered.

"I believe it *is* meant for you, Clara," said Madam Morwyn with a little laugh. "That cupboard always knows what we need, just when we need it. And it came up with something for Xavier, too."

Like a well-oiled machine, the girls unfolded the rest of the clothing, slipping a jacket onto Xavier, and draping a black bow tie around his neck. He blushed and stammered and said, "Thank you, girls, but Miss Lucas is taking her father to the ball—"

"And *I* am taking *you*, young man," said his mother. She

smoothed his collar and brushed the hair out of his eyes. "You deserve to have a beautiful night, too, after all the sorrow we have endured."

The front door opened, and Papa stuck his head out. "Oh!" he said. "I thought I heard company." He stepped onto the lawn, bowing to the Morwyns. "Good evening, ladies."

"Hello, Mr. Lucas," said Madam Morwyn warmly. "So sorry to disturb you."

"No, no—please, won't you come in? I baked some scones earlier, if you'd like to try them."

"Yes!" cried Leonor, barreling into the house.

"I want to see your room, Clara," announced Inés before she tugged Dalia indoors.

"I'll be right there," said Xavier. "If I may, I'd like just one moment with Miss Lucas."

His mother and my father exchanged an unreadable look, then Madam Morwyn smirked and delicately lifted the gown out of my hold. "When you're ready, we'll help you with this," she told me. She lightly pressed a kiss to my cheek. Softly, she whispered, "Thank you for loving my son."

And with that, she and Papa slipped back into the house.

Xavier held my hands in his.

"Is there something you wanted to tell me?" I asked, unable to tamp down my eager smile.

"Firstly," he said, about to give one of his famous lectures, I was certain, "you look absolutely breathtaking."

The reverence in his voice startled me. I glanced down at myself, at my green dress. "Really? You haven't even seen me in that other gown—"

He interrupted me with a kiss to my forehead. His finger caressed my chin. "You are beautiful every single day."

I wanted to speak; I wanted to joke, to brush aside his compliment. But he meant it. Xavier looked at me the way people looked at the most extraordinary, most beautiful bouquets.

"Thank you," I whispered.

Xavier's hand settled against my cheek. "All the best moments of my life, you've been there. You've dried my tears and you've made me laugh and you've called me an arse when I've been one, and you—you're a marvel, Clara. I mean it; we've known all along that you could control this magic of yours. And your heart is beautiful; beautiful and good. For you to share it with me is a gift that I do not take for granted. I meant what I said before. I love you. I've always loved you."

I bit hard on the inside of my lip to keep from crying more and to keep from interrupting him.

He gave his lopsided smile and sighed. "That's all I had to say."

I didn't need to say a thing.

I threw my arms around his neck and kissed him.

The Council's ceremonial hall was filled with people from all over the queendom. Every magician and their initiate was there, milling about in the light of the Midsummer sun as it blazed down through a round skylight.

Among the pews, older magicians and other guests made small talk with one another, their laughter bouncing off the soaring stone pillars.

I stood in a wing to the side of the ceremonial hall with a group of other apprentices about to be inducted into the Council. There was a cacophony of different accents among our idle chattering. We all looked so different from one another, though our dress was alike: a tall witch-to-be with rose-pink hair, a wizard with a white top hat, his eyes enchanted to be bright green.

As I whispered to initiates hailing from all over the country, I was interrupted by a tap on my shoulder. When I spun around, Madam Ben Ammar was behind me, dressed in a glamorous black gown that sparkled like starlit water.

"I wanted to say hello one last time before you officially become Madam Lucas," she said, and without a second's thought, I wrapped her in a hug.

"Oh, I was hoping I'd see you!" I said. "I have something for you."

When we pulled apart, I led her by the hand into a small alcove in the large, noisy hall—the tiniest bit of privacy we could afford. I reached into the reticule affixed to the hip of my white gown. From within, I pulled out a small envelope and placed it in her hands.

"This morning, we tested a cure for the effects of Euphoria, and it worked. The young lady we gave it to is back to herself again." I tapped my finger on the envelope. "The directions for the potion are inside."

She tore open the envelope and read the copy of Xavier's recipe. As she read, her smile grew more and more.

"I can't believe it," she whispered. Then she swept me in another hug. "Oh, Clara, you've done it!"

"It—it wasn't just me," I said, muffled against her shoulder. "I mean, I enchanted the potion, I added my confidence, and I controlled my magic, but Xavier came up with the recipe in the first place—" Drawing back, I gripped her arm as a thrilling idea flew into my head. "He made it before this ceremony! Surely that means he could have his magic back!"

The joy in her eyes quickly faded away. "No, love," she said. "What's done cannot be undone." Her gloved hand squeezed mine. "I am grateful to him for his invention. With both of your efforts, we'll be able to distribute this cure. But justice has already been served."

It did not feel just. And according to my mother, this was in character for the Council. Following their own draconian rules. Giving themselves the authority to take away a wizard's power. They had even wanted to bind mine.

But they *had* helped people. They made healing potions every day, and taught more people how to heal. They were saving lives, just as Xavier and I had tried so hard to do.

Now I was about to join their ranks. It was what I'd dreamed of—and even so, there was a seed of doubt growing in my heart. Perhaps I could not trust the Council completely. But I could trust Madam Ben Ammar. And I could trust myself.

"After we free people from Euphoria," I said, "there's . . . there's more work to do."

She was quiet—she understood. She nodded and touched my arm.

"You are why we put such hope in the next generation," she whispered. "You will use your gift for great things. And I will support you as best as I can, I promise."

My heart lifted. She'd never lost confidence in me, not even when it would risk her reputation, not even when I seemed truly hopeless.

But her brow furrowed.

"Clara," she said, quiet enough so as not to be heard, "there is one thing you've done that I just cannot understand. Why did you give your power to that boy?"

The disappointment in her tone twisted my insides even more. It had been a rash decision. But I did not regret it.

"I did it for Papa," I said. "I knew what I was doing. And I'd do it again. I'd give my life to save my father."

Madam Ben Ammar touched a hand to her heart. Pride, pride that I'd longed for, shimmered in her dark eyes. "That, Miss Lucas, is why you will make a most excellent witch." She smiled at me and held my hands tight. "And as for young Mr. Morwyn . . . if he ever hurts you, I'll turn him into a toad."

He would never. But knowing that she cared for me so, that I was worthy of being loved by so many people—it warmed my heart and grounded me. *Yes,* I told myself. *This is real. You've earned this.*

She blew me a kiss farewell and joined a queue of other certified magicians dressed in elegant black gowns and suits.

Just as I rejoined the group of other initiates, a loud bell rang through the building. Single file, we students walked into the ceremonial hall. I gazed at the chessboard floor to help keep my steps measured. Every time I peeked towards the soaring arcs of the ceiling, I got dizzy again. Then, when the line had come to a stop, we turned and took our seats before a black-and-white sea of magicians and apprentices who'd come to see us.

Three magicians stood at the front of the hall atop a wooden stage, bathed in golden sunlight.

A man with long silver hair spoke, his words amplified by the same kinds of potions my teachers sometimes used to advertise their wares at loud marketplaces.

"Welcome, initiates, guests, and members of the Most Esteemed Council of Magicians. Initiates, you are about to enter a noble and ancient order. You will go into the world and act as representatives of our Council. You will heal those who come to you for help. All of you have been given a powerful gift, and with it, you will go forth and bless the citizens of the world."

He took a step back, and a short woman in a pointed black hat stepped forwards. "As future magicians, you will not only heal people. You will uphold our law. You will convict the unjust. You will rescue those in need. You will share your knowledge and build up your siblings in magic. Together you will add to and improve our understanding of, and use of, enchantments."

Another magician stepped forwards, reminding us of the lessons we had learned—healing broken bones, curing illnesses, creating beauty. Then they said, "Now, we invite the initiates to come forwards and receive their title from their teachers."

They called someone's name. A plump witch in a gorgeous, flowing white dress ascended the stage. I leaned in my chair, craning my neck to watch.

Her teacher, a short witch with curly gray hair, climbed the stairs on the other side of the stage to stand at her apprentice's side.

The witch in the black hat approached the two. "Madam Bellamy," she said, "do you find your student worthy of the title of witch?"

"Yes, I do."

The lead witch turned to the student.

"Miss Day, will you uphold the laws of the Council?"

"Yes, I will."

"Will you speak out against injustice, serve our Council,

and contribute to the community?"

"Yes, I will."

Her teacher smiled and drew closer to her student. "Then with this symbol, I declare you Madam Isabella Day."

All of a sudden, the girl's dress went from pearly white to a beautiful raven black, as if her teacher had poured ink all over the fabric.

The older witch beamed, turning Isabella to the crowd. "Madam Day, as a gesture of your zeal for your community, will you please show us the power of the gift you've been given?"

Madam Day took a deep, noisy breath, and then lifted her hands above her head. Beautiful, multicolored sparks appeared above her, twirling and fizzling and whirling to the floor. Everyone in the hall applauded; some whistled and whooped to cheer her on.

The teachers and students continued the ceremony, coming onto the stage one by one. After their clothes had been turned black, each certified apprentice proved their powers. Some leapt into the air and hovered for a few seconds. Some made moons or stars appear in the air. Some breathed fire.

Then, representing Queensborough, Robin took to the stage. Looking over their shoulder, they caught sight of me and grinned.

They looked beautiful. Like a moonbeam.

Their hair was white to match their outfit—a loose, lacy

blouse under a well-fitted vest, with a knotted cravat and a billowing skirt like the wing of a moth. They took their place beside the beaming Madam Ben Ammar.

The two repeated the vows, and after Madam Ben Ammar had enchanted Robin's gown, turning the magician's ensemble from that of a snow-white moth to a black butterfly, she pivoted her student towards the audience.

"Fellow magicians," said Madam Ben Ammar, "I would like to embarrass my student for a moment."

A wave of laughter spread through the crowd. Robin turned red.

"As I continue other work for our noble Council," said the witch, "I've decided to retire from my storefront. I hereby give Magistrate Robin Santos the deed to my shop. There is no one I'd rather have serving the good people of Queensborough than them." She handed Robin a piece of paper, and as the crowd erupted in applause, Robin threw their arms around their teacher.

Madam Ben Ammar smiled proudly. "Now then, Magistrate Santos, show them your power!"

Robin turned to the crowd, bowing amidst the continuing applause. When they lifted their head, their hair was long, black, and curly. They had grown tall, and their slim figure had gained curves. Their small nose was sharp and angular; their thin lips were full and dark red.

They'd turned into Madam Ben Ammar.

Robin grinned. Their former teacher laughed noisily and ruffled the thick, dark hair of her twin. With a turn of their heel, they turned back into themself and took a bow. The audience clapped and hollered in delight.

Then, I ascended the steps of the stage. I looked out at the audience, my heart pounding hard in my throat. When I turned my head stage left, I gasped.

Several magicians left their seats in the wings, walking across the stage to stand at Madam Ben Ammar's side. One by one, they arrived—Master Young, Madam Carvalho, Madam Albright, and Master Pierre. Nearly all my former teachers beamed at me. Madam Albright's lips were tightly pursed, but then again, her face always looked this way. Frankly, I was as surprised as she was that I'd finally qualified for my initiation.

Madam Ben Ammar crossed the stage and gently led me by the hand towards the others.

"It's only proper that all of your teachers be here to honor you," she said.

I looked from one smiling face to the next, tears dripping down my cheeks. But not all of them were there. I kept searching for Xavier's face among them—but of course, he was no longer considered equal to these esteemed witches and wizards. "I can't believe," I whispered, wanting to add more, wanting to say something thankful or intelligent. I was utterly lost for words.

Madam Ben Ammar cradled my hand in hers. "We are so proud of you, pet."

Master Pierre grinned so wide that his eyes squinted tight. "I knew you'd overcome your magic one of these days!"

"She had talent from the start," said Madam Carvalho, poking a startled Madam Albright on the arm. "Didn't I tell you, Althea?"

Master Young chuckled and waved his hand at the lead witch. "Let's not take away from Clara's moment, shall we?"

The witch in the black hat bowed her head. "Esteemed colleagues, do you find Clara Lucas worthy of the title of witch?"

"Yes, we do," they said in one voice—even Madam Albright.

Relief and joy were a brilliant, star-bright flood running through me.

The lead witch nodded to me. "Miss Lucas, will you uphold the laws of the Council?"

"Yes, I will." I stood on my toes, my heart fluttering as I searched the crowd for Papa's face, for Xavier's.

"Will you speak out against injustice, serve our Council, and contribute to the community?"

The fear and the joy and the excitement of the moment made the hall spin in my vision. I had worked so hard to fight injustice alongside the Council. Come what may, I would continue to do so. "Yes, I will."

I pivoted towards Madam Ben Ammar. In her gloved hand, she held up a golden, sun-shaped pin.

"With this symbol, I declare you Madam Clara Lucas." She pinned it against my dress, and in seconds, thread by thread, the fabric around the pin turned black as onyx, spilling from my chest to my feet. "Now—show us your power!"

I faced the crowd, craning my neck to find Xavier and Papa. I did not recognize anyone, but all the strangers smiled up at me. Then, someone bobbed up among the sea of faces—Papa sitting as tall as he could in his chair, waving a handkerchief at me with gusto. Warmth spread through my heart like a fire. To the left of my father sat the boy I loved, grinning in a way he only reserved for me. For just one moment, he wasn't shy or ashamed. He was proud of me. He loved me.

I clung to my knowledge of his and Papa's love as I lifted my hand to the ceiling.

Thank you, magic, I said to it. *Let's have some fun.*

The white arches and columns, from above me to the very end of the hall, turned a thousand colors as they were covered in leaves and blossoms of every kind. Garlands of heather flourished among the pews, bloomed between marble tiles, descended from above. Lavender and meadowsweet, tulips and roses, all the joy I could not contain.

Papa and Xavier leapt to their feet, applauding noisily. Barely a moment passed before Xavier's mother joined in the standing ovation, along with the rest of the hall, one by one. Even from afar, as I watched Xavier applaud, I could see his eyes gleaming like twinkling stars, bright and jubilant, full of energy and hope.

My magic glowed within me.

ACKNOWLEDGMENTS

This book has been through many drafts and many years and has stuck through it all. To everyone who has walked alongside me during this journey: thank you so much. Over the years, *Flowerheart* has had so many kind early readers who have cheered for me and have helped me hone the book to be what it is today. Truly, I won't be able to remember all of your names, but if you were an early reader, have geeked out with me over my silly doodles, or have expressed enthusiasm for this book, I thank you dearly. It is so encouraging to know that I'm not the only one who cares about this story.

To Jordan Hamessley, my agent, for your love of my wizard kids and your fearless email-answering and editing.

To Stephanie Guerdan, for your amazing editorial eye and for preserving the heart of this book no matter what. Clara and Xavier couldn't have been in better hands! My love to all those at HarperTeen who brought this book to life.

To my family, again. Thank you, Mom and Dad, for your support and for sending me meals while I was on deadline. Shout-out to my dogs, Cosette and Mr. Bingley, for the cuddles and serotonin boosts.

To my Llamasquad. Thank you for reading this book oodles of times and for letting me celebrate and whine throughout this publishing journey.

A special thanks to Lorelei, Allison, Elizabeth, Sarah, Cyla, Trisha, Lyndall, Mary, and Rachel, for reading my pages five billion times and giving me feedback no matter how last minute.

Thanks to Lucy, for your steadfast friendship, patience, movie nights, and love for my stories.

Ez, you are a gem, and I am so grateful to have you as a friend and a *Flowerheart* cheerleader.

Ive, the president of the *Flowerheart* fanclub. You are wonderful, and I am so excited to watch your book flourish!

Vika, thank you for your friendship and for teaching me about publishing and myself!

Thanks to Marcella, who read this book and squealed in my DMs in the best way and then spoiled me with amazing fanart.

To Emily, for your art and your jokes that leave me wheezing.

To Kathleen, for your kindness and your gentle heart.

To Becca, thank you for answering my strange,

out-of-nowhere medical questions while I was writing this. You are really great.

To Kalie, for your generosity and your love for this story. I am so excited to watch you soar.

To Taylor, for your cosplay, your playlists, and your beautiful enthusiasm.

To all my sweet high school buddies, especially to Jenni for our musical nights, Emma for being my tireless cheerleader, and Morgan, who pulled together my very first book launch.

Jake, thank you for fielding my existential crisis questions.

Thanks to all those at HPU who helped me on my mental health journey, and to my roommates for giving me a space where it was safe to learn and grow through my darkest days. *Flowerheart* holds the echoes of my journey with depression. I am so grateful to have the resources of therapy and medication. A special hug to the foreign language department for cups of tea and encouraging words.